THE
CHOCOLATE SHOP
ON
Amelia Island

SEVEN SISTERS
BOOK FIVE

HOPE
HOLLOWAY

Hope Holloway

Seven Sisters Book 5

The Chocolate Shop on Amelia Island

Copyright © 2024 Hope Holloway

The Seven Daughters Of Rex Wingate

Born to Charlotte Wingate

Madeline Wingate, age 49
Victoria "Tori" Wingate, age 45
Rose Wingate D'Angelo, age 43
Raina Wingate, age 43

Born to Susannah Wingate

Sadie Wingate age 35
Grace Wingate Jenkins, age 33
Chloe Wingate, age 29

Prologue

When Tristan Saint Pierre stormed into the Ocean Song resort's ballroom and made his heartfelt proclamation in the middle of her parents' anniversary party, Sadie Wingate wanted to believe him. She longed to fall into his arms, echo his words of love, and plan for an amazing future together.

But no matter how much she ached to trust the man she'd married on a blustery day in a Copenhagen wedding chapel, she...didn't. In fact, she doubted every word he said.

Yes, tonight's grand gesture thrilled her down to the bone. But would Tris *really* walk away from unimaginable wealth, an international brand that bore his name, and one of the most powerful families in Europe in exchange for a simple life of making chocolate on Amelia Island with her?

For Tristan, no act was too over the top. He'd proven over and over that no declaration was too bold, and no moment too dramatic when it came to showcasing his passions.

Sadie had found that trait—and everything else about Tristan—indescribably attractive. So much so that she'd gone along with the grandest of all gestures and eloped with him, marrying a man her family had never met.

Until tonight, when, in front of every member of Sadie's vast family, he begged her not to end their secret union even though his parents had offered her an enormous sum of money to do just that.

As the room vibrated with shock and all the people she loved stared at her in disbelief over the news, Sadie couldn't help but feel the itch of uncertainty.

Despite Tristan's eloquent speech, rich with promises to return after "disowning" his family and "restructuring" his life, Sadie's doubts intensified with each passing moment. The man she'd married, however unorthodox the ceremony, was controlled by the Saint Pierre family, her former employer. They would never let their golden boy leave Brussels and the chocolate empire they'd created in Europe.

At least, not without a fight.

But then Tris reached for her hand, that glimmer of love in his sky blue eyes and a hint of hope in his boyish smile.

"My jet goes wheels-up from the local airstrip in half an hour," he whispered into her ear, his distinct French- and Dutch-mixed accent as seductive as the rich chocolate truffles he effortlessly created. "Meet me there for a proper goodbye, Madame Saint Pierre."

As always, chills erupted all over her. As always, her own weakness for spontaneity and drama tipped the scales in his direction. And, as always, she knew she would follow the order and do exactly as he said.

Was that love?

It was with Tristan Saint Pierre.

She managed to catch her breath as he bid a quick farewell to the group without so much as a single introduction. Just his formal bow and a tip of his head to the company consigliore who'd accompanied him on this surprise mission, and he was gone.

"So...that was my husband," she finally said on a breathless laugh, holding up her hand to stave off what would surely be a barrage of questions. "I married him in a moment of alcohol-fueled madness..."

In truth, she'd barely had a sip that night, but she'd agreed to keep up the "drunken escapade" explanation that he'd given his family. She *had* been dizzy from Tristan's promise of forever, and might as well have been six drinks deep instead of stone-cold sober.

"And his family really didn't like that," she continued as they remained momentarily speechless. "It cost me my job and...and...I guess he's coming here."

Here. A small town in north Florida with no castles, no jets, no staff, and no...millions.

Would he do that *for her*?

They'd never discussed living here, but he knew she'd run to her family on Amelia Island when the powers that be at Chocolat de Saint Pierre terminated her marketing position the moment they'd learned of the marriage. With Tristan's father's threats to ruin her reputation and life if she didn't get the heck out of Dodge—well, Brussels—still ringing in her ears, she knew annulment papers would be forthcoming.

They came—tonight, as a matter of fact—but so did Tristan, insisting she refuse to sign the document that would end their secret marriage and leave her free, rich, and licking the wounds left from her latest impulsive act.

She didn't want to be rich, free, or *impulsive*. She wanted to be married to a man she loved, giddy that they'd pulled it off, and certain about the future.

She glanced down at the paper and the pen in her hand, trying to think of what to say to her family, all of them waiting not-so-patiently for an explanation.

"I hope you all love chocolate," she managed with a laugh. "And him."

"What about you?" her father demanded. "Do *you* love him?"

She wanted to scream, "Yes!" but some primal force of self-preservation kept her from confessing that. She mumbled a response, most of it lost in the next wave of questions fired by her sisters, mother, and extended family.

"What do you mean, he's your husband?"

"You got married and didn't tell us?"

"When did this happen?"

"Why did he leave?"

"Who is Tristan Saint Pierre?"

She sighed. They deserved an explanation—each and every one of them. But...

Meet me there for a proper goodbye, Madame Saint Pierre.

Closing her eyes to revel in the words one more time, Sadie knew she *had* to get that proper goodbye or she'd spend the next six weeks regretting the decision not to. Was that impulsive? Maybe, but she only had this chance.

As the questions continued, she looked around and locked gazes with her oldest sister, who walked toward her. Madeline had been her refuge when Sadie slinked into town two months ago, unwilling to talk to anyone or share the truth. She'd been then, and would be now—no questions asked.

Okay, there'd be a ton of questions. But now, Sadie didn't have to sidestep them with vague responses and a few downright lies. She took the hand Madeline offered, pulled her in, and hugged her.

"Whatever you decide," her sister said softly, "we all love you and we'll help you through anything."

"Good. Then would you take me somewhere?" Sadie breathed into Madeline's ear as they hugged. "Right now?"

Madeline's whole body stiffened and Sadie braced for an argument and logic and, of course, more questions.

"Please, please, *please*, Madeline."

Her sister drew back with a flicker of surprise in her dark eyes, but then her expression softened. "Go to the bathroom, slip out to the parking lot, and I'll cover for you and meet you there."

"God bless you," Sadie said, and never meant it more.

It took a bit of maneuvering, of assuring her family she'd answer all the questions, but she managed to break away and, five minutes later, climbed into Madeline's car, humming with anticipation.

"Oh, Sadie," Madeline said on a sigh as she slid behind the wheel far too slowly. "How could you get married and—"

Sadie reached for her hand. "He asked me to meet him at the municipal airport. It's just up the road, not three miles—"

"The *airport*?" Her voice rose, sharp with disbelief. "I thought you needed to get some air and pull yourself together. You are going to fly out of here without telling anyone?"

"No, *no*. I swear I won't. But if you think *you* have a lot of questions, imagine mine. I had no idea he was coming here at all, let alone planning to move here. His jet leaves in about twenty minutes. Please let me see him again so I can get some answers."

"Why didn't he just stay, meet everyone, and answer your questions and ours?"

She squeezed her eyes shut, hating that she didn't have an answer to that, only speculation. Maybe the family jet was due back in Brussels. Maybe he wanted to see if she would run after him. Maybe he knew she wouldn't like his answers to her questions.

Or maybe he was after the one thing she hadn't given him yet. She shifted in her seat at the thought.

"He's a bit of an enigma," she admitted. "But if I go, I have a chance of finding out more about his plans."

Madeline's brown eyes narrowed and she let out a noisy sigh before yanking on her seatbelt and stabbing the ignition button. "Fine. But do not expect me to speak to... anyone with him."

Sadie inhaled sharply at the thought of the security specialist who worked for the Saint Pierre family and had pressured her to sign the annulment seconds before Tristan had arrived. "I forgot you know Adam Logan, Madeline."

Even in the moonlight, she could see her sister pale and press her lips together in determined silence. No surprise—Madeline's history with the man was shrouded in more mystery than Sadie's elopement.

All Sadie knew was that Madeline had a romantic relationship with Adam twenty-five years ago, but it had ended when he disappeared without a trace.

Then, a few months ago, Madeline had found that trace...and it led to the Saint Pierre dynasty. Madeline had been looking through online information about the family—because Sadie had been cagey about why she'd quit her job—when she spotted Adam Logan, the Saint Pierres' security specialist.

Tristan once told Sadie that Adam was former FBI, and retired from law enforcement and, like many others in that field, consulted for wealthy families and big companies. Based on that information, Sadie had suggested that maybe he'd been undercover when he ghosted Madeline.

Madeline had known none of that about the guy she thought worked at a fabric company in New York, and never mentioned him again.

"I *knew* Adam, past tense," she said, the edge still in

her voice. "And you should remember, Sadie, that people are known by the company they keep."

"What are you saying?" Sadie asked. "That I shouldn't trust my husband because he's friendly with your ex, who works for him?"

"I didn't even know you *had* a husband until ten minutes ago," Madeline fired back. "When were you going to tell us?"

"I wasn't ever going to tell you," she confessed, getting another harsh look. "I thought I would sign the annulment and take the money or...or..."

"Or what?"

She swallowed. "Or that my prayers would be answered, Tristan would choose me over his family, and I would live happily ever after with the man of my dreams." She gave a wry laugh. "I think that's what happened tonight, but I'm still not quite sure, so please"— she jabbed her sister's arm—"hurry."

Madeline threw the car into Drive and flipped on the headlights to bathe the midnight darkness in high beams. "Look, I'll take you but you have to tell me everything. And I do mean *no more secrets*, Sadie."

Sadie nodded and let her head fall back with a grunt. "There's not that much to—"

"*Everything*, Sadie," Madeline ground out.

"Okay, okay." She closed her eyes, her mind bouncing around to find the right place to start.

The day she'd walked into his kitchen and met Tristan Saint Pierre for the first time? For her, it had been infatuation at first sight, if not love. But that was years ago and wasn't really the beginning.

No, their romance was launched eighteen months ago when she climbed on board the very jet that was currently sitting on the tarmac at the Amelia Island Municipal Airport. That day, they'd kicked off an international adventure that culminated in a wild and wonderful weekend wedding that was not fueled by booze, but by love—a love they knew no one in his family would ever accept.

"About a year and a half ago," she began, "I was assigned to assist Tristan Saint Pierre—who is the head chocolatier for Chocolat de Saint Pierre—in opening fifteen retail outlets all over Europe. He trained staff in the art of making the incredible chocolate, and I handled all marketing and branding, promoting each outlet locally. Every three to four weeks, we opened a new chocolate shop together in London, Paris, Madrid, Rome, Prague...everywhere."

"And Copenhagen," Madeline added. "Where you did more than sell chocolate."

"Where we secretly got married," Sadie acknowledged. "But two things happened during that time. Two things you don't know about me."

Madeline threw her a questioning look. "What?"

"One, I learned to make chocolate, and pretty darn well, I might add. I'm actually not a bad chocolatier."

"And the other?"

"I fell head over heels in love with Tristan." She sighed, realizing just how much she connected those two things. Love and chocolate. Tristan and travel. Secrets and...seduction.

"And you got drunk and married him in Copenhagen."

She winced. "It wasn't quite like that," she said, drawing out the words. "That's, um, a story he made up to appease his family because they are... Oh, I don't even have time to tell you how awful they are."

"You told me," Madeline reminded her. "You said his father is unfaithful and his mother turns a blind eye, and his brother is supposed to be CEO, but he's not qualified. Right?"

"That's the sanitized version of the facts," Sadie replied. "Gregoire is a power-happy serial cheater with more money than God, and his wife, Cecile, is a doormat in diamonds. Tristan's older brother is a people-pleaser who'd sell his soul for his father's approval, and his sister, is dumb as dirt and watered down the gene pool by marrying a moron and producing wretched children."

"Lovely in-laws you picked," Madeline said dryly.

"The feeling is mutual."

"What does that mean?"

She grunted, hating the truth. "They think I am a common, classless, lowly American who hitched her wagon to Tristan for money and status and ruined their plans for him to marry an heiress with even more money than they have."

She turned to look out to the blackness of the Atlantic Ocean on her right, but her mind was on the other side of that water, in Europe, remembering all the accusations Gregoire had flung at her and how halfheartedly Tristan had defended her.

That was why she left Brussels. Not because of Gregoire and Cecile...but because Tristan seemed to regret their decision to defy his family and elope.

Since then, they'd only spoken a few times, and he didn't show up when the Saint Pierres sent a small army of lawyers a few months ago. By then, Sadie had lost hope that the marriage was real and decided she'd made one big fat mistake.

She'd expected the annulment that day, but the paperwork hadn't been completed yet, so she'd signed a nondisclosure agreement and tucked herself deeper into her family on Amelia Island, quietly nursing her broken heart without telling anyone a thing.

With each day that passed and she didn't hear from Tristan, she was more certain she would sign the annulment when it arrived, take the money, and try to forget her wildest adventure to date.

"I don't know about his family," Madeline said gently when Sadie was quiet for too long. "But I thought he was pretty clear in his feelings and intentions."

Sadie clung to that. "Yes, he was. And that's what I dreamed might happen. I've ached for proof that he really wanted me and not..."

Madeline took her eyes from the road and looked hard at Sadie when she didn't finish the sentence. "Not what?"

"You know, just a good time," she said quickly, unwilling to share the fact that she, Sadie Wingate, a novice chocolatier, had invented an original recipe for arguably the best chocolate ever made. And she'd yet to share the final and most critical ingredient—the one that brought the whole taste together—with her husband because...

She didn't entirely trust him.

No, that was one secret too many. That and the fact that sometimes, on her darkest nights, she suspected it was that recipe that got Tristan into a wedding chapel in Copenhagen, and not her. He'd have done anything to have it...including marry her.

Her heart lifted when she saw the lights of the local airport that only serviced private planes. "Hurry," she pleaded.

"I am, but finish the story."

"I can't. I don't know the end. All I know is he showed up here, said he loved me, leased space for a chocolate shop, and claimed he's disowning his family. And then he told me to meet him at the airstrip."

Madeline turned into the entrance. "Sadie Wingate, if you get on a plane and leave—"

"I won't, Madeline." She punctuated the promise by putting her hand on her sister's arm. "I'm done running. I'm done looking for my next adventure. I swear on our family name that I am done."

"Then what are you going to do?" Madeline asked.

"I hope I'm going to live with Tristan and start our own chocolate shop and have babies and be happy. I'd like to do that here, near my family, which—as you prove every day—is the opposite of awful."

Madeline looked dubious. "You're a runner, Sadie. Always have been."

Sadie sighed. "I only run because sometimes I feel crushed under the weight of...Wingates."

"But now you need us."

"I do," she admitted. "Now, park near the front and let's go—"

"I'm not going in," Madeline said. "I don't want to exchange one word with Adam. You go and I'll wait. And you will come back, right, Sadie?"

"Of course I will." She leaned over and kissed Madeline's cheek. "I promise. And you taught me what a promise means, big sister. Wait here."

Madeline closed her eyes in resignation. "The last time I waited for Adam...he never showed."

"I'm not Adam," she said. "I'll be right back."

Tristan's face lit up when Sadie sailed through the glass doors, still handsome even in the milky yellow fluorescent lights of the aging terminal.

"You came." He seemed surprised as he bounded toward her.

She nearly fell into his arms, quivering as she hugged him. "Yes. And so did you. Why? What was that stunt you just pulled? You rented a shop here on Amelia Island?"

"On Wingate Way," he said proudly. "I had to stow away on the jet sent here for the annulment assignment.

Adam only discovered me once we were airborne and I convinced him not to turn around." He searched her face, looking as if he wanted to memorize every feature. "I couldn't let you sign that paper, Sadie."

She let out a noisy sigh of pure satisfaction. He did love her. He really did. Why did she ever doubt him?

"I might have signed it," she told him. "I hadn't heard from you in so long, I was beginning to think I...I imagined everything we've felt."

"You always doubt me, darling." He gave her another squeeze. "Let's call the shop Belgian Bliss. I'll bring Belgium, you bring...the bliss." He tapped her chin. "Whatever it is."

The secret ingredient missing from the recipe she'd created.

"Sadie," he whispered, pulling her closer. "You are my wife. And, soon, my business partner. You can tell me now."

"But why are you leaving?" she asked. "If you're ready to walk away from them, just walk. And stay. And we'll open the shop together."

An unreadable emotion flickered over his eyes, gone as quickly as it came. "I wish it were so easy," he said. "But I have to hire and train a replacement. No one in that entire company can make chocolate the way I can. Well, you're close."

Hardly, but she smiled at the compliment. "I'm just your apprentice."

"Who came up with a recipe I can't replicate," he reminded her. "As far as my family, I may loathe them all, but I plan to leave the proper way, with dignity and good feelings."

She rolled her eyes. "Your family is controlling and wealthy, Tristan, and you are the true talent at their company. Do you really think they won't do everything in their considerable power to keep you there?"

He gripped her waist and drew her in. "Check your phone."

"My phone?" she asked, confused by the request.

"Look."

She reached into her bag and brought out her cell, tapping the screen and sucking in a soft breath at the top notification. "Why did you send me that much money?"

"To give you the resources to turn the space into the chocolate shop of your dreams."

"Of *our* dreams," she corrected.

"That goes without saying, Sadie."

But she still wanted to hear him say it.

"No one knows how to build out a chocolate shop like you," he continued. "Make it sing, my love. Buy the equipment we ordered for every shop in Europe. Put your signature style on the retail and tasting areas. Get the place ready to roll. I'll be back in January. Maybe New Year's Eve. We can toast the coming year of *chocolat* and love."

For a moment, she couldn't comprehend what was happening. This was literally the definition of too good to be true.

"Tris." She sighed. "Are you serious?"

"Of course! We'll be a power couple. Do they have

those in this little town? Do they have a suitable place for us to live?"

Us. She smiled at the thought. "There's an apartment above the shop—" At his look, she snorted. "Right. You'll want a mansion. Well, my family owns Wingate Properties and my sister can find you, er, us a dream house." She shook her head. "Us. Still getting used to that."

He squeezed her again. "Why did you doubt me, sweet Sadie? Why?"

"Because...you're too good to be true." She had to verbalize it, just to hear his heartfelt denial.

But he didn't deny anything. He merely kissed her forehead. "Now that you have my word, my money, and my last name, why don't you give me the missing ingredient of the recipe and I'll start perfecting it while I'm back in Brussels?"

Why *didn't* she give it to him? Because his family, should they get their hands on it, would steal it, claim it, patent it, and make *more* millions, with no credit to her.

"When you come back," she said. "I'll tell you then, I promise."

"Tristan." They both spun to see Adam standing at the glass doors, the plane engine screaming behind him. "Wheels-up in five minutes."

Tristan nodded, then turned back to Sadie, true hurt in his eyes. "Until you stop doubting me, Sadie, we don't have a marriage."

She blinked at the words. "Tristan, I—"

He put two fingers on her lips. "We *don't*. I've done everything to prove I'm the man you want me to be. I've married you, I've defied my family, and now I'm moving here to work with you and live with you. What else do you want from me?"

"I just want...to be sure."

He let out a pained exhale. "I don't know how else to prove myself. Goodbye, Sadie." With that, he nodded, pivoted, and strode toward the tarmac doors.

She stared at him, squeezing the phone she still held in one hand. Looking down at it, she let that amount of money sink in. She could make that chocolate shop one of the most beautiful stores on Wingate Way and they would take Amelia Island by storm. They would live here, married, in love, maybe build their own international brand with...her recipe.

He was right. What else did he have to do to make it *their* recipe?

She smashed her finger on the screen and brought his name up for a text message.

One word. One ingredient. One single demonstration of her trust, and their new life would start. In fact, if she didn't tell him...*maybe he wouldn't come back in six weeks.*

That thought was all she needed to type the single ingredient and hit Send.

So much for *not* being impulsive.

He was at the bottom of the rolling stairs when he stopped and reached into his pocket. She swallowed hard as he pulled out his phone and read the text.

A few seconds passed, nearly a minute, as he stood in

the beam of the plane's lights, the breeze fluttering his flaxen hair.

Turn around, Tris. Blow me a kiss. Wave. Thumbs-up. Anything.

But he just jogged up to the door without even looking back to acknowledge that he now knew the one secret ingredient she'd been holding onto all this time.

Well, that was done. She'd told him. They'd start their lives together when he came back.

If he came back.

Chapter One

Sadie

Six Weeks Later

On the morning of New Year's Eve, Sadie walked up to the front door of Belgian Bliss and let out a happy sigh of satisfaction. She'd done it. She'd moved heaven and Earth and every contractor she could find in north Florida, worked through the holidays, and refused to give up.

With Tristan's money and her determination, she'd successfully transformed a slightly tired and outdated ice cream parlor into a destination chocolate shop on Wingate Way.

"He's going to love it," she whispered to herself as she approached the front of the two-story building, which she'd had painted a sunny yellow with blinding white trim, accentuating it all with a striped awning and a welcoming bright green front door.

On either side of the entrance, picture windows allowed passersby to admire some of the candies and see through the retail section all the way back into the chocolate kitchen. That way, everyone could watch Tristan work his magic from ground bean to gourmet bite.

She'd be making a lot of chocolate, too, but he'd be the lead chocolatier, and the real draw for customers.

She unlocked the door and stepped inside, inhaling the lingering scent of paint and freshly cut wood. But that would change soon enough.

Guests would be greeted by the warm and delicious aroma of cocoa and cream. A sound system would pipe in soft and soothing music encouraging them to linger, taste, and buy the bonbons and truffles that would fill the display case that ran the length of one side.

From the homey hardwood floor to the shiplap-covered walls lined with floating shelves for "grab and go" candy boxes, guests would be both enchanted and comfortable.

As they had in Europe, customers would sip coffee and taste candy at the marble-topped bistro tables. Then, they'd capture the experience in pictures against a white stacked stone feature wall designed specifically as a social media backdrop.

The only thing missing was the custom-made brass *Belgian Bliss* sign that would hang on the stone wall. She'd had the hooks installed last week, but the sign had only been delivered yesterday, and Sadie wanted it up before Tristan arrived.

She just wasn't sure when that would be. He had once said "maybe New Year's Eve" but they hadn't final-ized anything. They actually hadn't exchanged more than a few lines of text in the past week and not a single call since Christmas Day. He'd been distracted for weeks, busily handing over his duties to a new chocolatier.

In case he surprised her, she wanted to have the logo already hanging on the feature wall because there was nothing Tristan loved more than a bold declaration of quality and taste.

Humming, she made her way around the counter and pushed the swinging door into the kitchen where shiny new equipment had been installed last week. From the stainless prep tables to the long marble-top for smoothing and shaping candies, to the eight-burner cooktop, and all the way to a commercial-grade *melangeur* to refine the cocoa nibs, the kitchen was a chocolatier's dream.

Here, Sadie and Tristan would work side by side to create decadent delights and a whole new life together.

In the small office off the kitchen, she picked up the box that held the metal logo, which had to weigh forty pounds. Lifting the whole carton with a grunt, she headed back out, stopping dead in her tracks at the sound of someone knocking on the front door.

Tristan? She couldn't help hoping as she lugged the box toward the front and peeked out toward the street, her whole body bracing for the sight of...

Adam? Why was he here?

She almost dropped the heavy load, but somehow managed to hang on as she shouldered her way through the swinging door and into the store.

Easing the box to the floor, she called, "Just a sec!" but her throat was already thick with emotion.

Don't doubt, don't doubt, she chided herself. *He is*

probably on the next flight and sent Adam. But why would he send the Saint Pierres' computer security specialist if he'd separated from the family?

With a moan, she walked to the front door to open it, meeting the dark eyes of a man she knew only as another Saint Pierre employee—and Madeline's ex—although he'd always been friendly and professional.

"Adam," she said softly. "This is a surprise."

He looked down at her, reminding her that he was easily six-two, a few inches taller than Tristan, and the complete opposite in coloring. He had deep brown eyes and dark hair with a good sprinkling of gray, a cleft chin, and a clean-cut American look that somehow set him apart from the continental style of the Saint Pierre family members.

Quiet and deliberately in the background at all the company events, he'd managed to stay off the radar.

It was a trait she sometimes wished she could learn.

"Can I speak with you privately, Ms. Wingate?"

Ms. Wingate, not Mrs. Saint Pierre.

"Of course." She stepped back and silently invited him in, quiet as he took a quick look around.

"I was just about to hang the sign on the feature wall," she finally said when the silence lasted one awkward beat too long. "Would you like to help? It's heavy."

"Sure." He didn't sound sure, but she turned and walked to the box, flipping the top she'd sliced open yesterday.

"Look." She pushed the bubble wrap and revealed

the metal shaped into the words *Belgian Bliss*. "It's not Chocolat de—"

"He's not coming."

She stood stone still, staring at the gleaming brass, willing herself not to react. "Oh," she managed. "Not...yet?"

She hated how pathetic and hopeful that last word sounded. She hated how pathetic and hopeful she *felt* even more.

Come on, Sadie. You knew this could happen. You knew it probably would *happen. You knew all along.*

But she'd lived firmly in a state of denial.

"He's not coming...at all." He took a step closer. "I'm very sorry."

With a caustic snort, she finally looked up. "Are you? I'm sure you and Gregoire and Cecile and Ollie are just devastated that Tristan's little...*romp* has finally ended."

"He asked me to give you this." He held out an envelope, but she just stepped back.

"Whatever it is, I don't want it," she said in a strangled voice. "Just...go. Okay? Leave. Or..." She glanced at the envelope. "Do I have to sign an annulment?"

"It's not an annulment," he said. "I believe it's a personal letter to you from Tristan."

"Whatever." She fired the word like a bullet, wishing it could hit the man they were intended for, not this one, not his...messenger.

Silent, he put the envelope on the top of the display case, heaving another sigh.

"You don't have to sign anything," he added. "The

family had the records expunged by the Danish government and your marriage is...null and void."

The words scraped over her heart.

"So, no divorce? No annulment? No...marriage?"

"None at all. It's like it never happened," he said softly.

She reeled, but let out another dry laugh. "Honestly, is there anything their money *can't* buy?"

He looked at her, the first real emotion she'd ever seen on the man's face registering in his dark, hooded eyes.

"Me," he said simply.

She inched back, surprised at the word and the tone. "Haven't you taken an oath of fealty to the king and queen of Saint Pierre-land?"

A smile nearly tipped his lips at that. "I've terminated my employment with Chocolat de Saint Pierre, and I'm not returning."

"Over this?"

"This and a few other things that turned my stomach."

She felt her shoulders sink with the weight of what he was saying—and the truth of it. They could be a ruthless bunch.

"Well, good for you for seeing the light. I'm the fool who didn't."

"He used you," Adam said. "He was on the phone sharing your recipe before the wheels lifted that day he came here."

She took a step backward and felt for the nearest chair, sliding into it as she looked up at him. "Oh. That *is* why he came. That's why...the speech and the promises and..." She shook her head as it cleared and she looked around. "Why finance this if he didn't plan to come back?"

Adam just tipped his head, clearly uncomfortable with the answer.

"Guilt," she guessed. "He paid for that last ingredient by giving me my own shop."

"I believe he felt that was fair," Adam said. "But I haven't read the letter."

She stole a glance at the hated envelope. "Neither will I."

But even as she said the words, she knew they weren't true. She'd read the letter, probably a thousand times, with wine and plenty of tissues to dry her tears. And then she'd...

What *would* she do?

"I have business connections in Jacksonville, and some family there," Adam said. "You can call me." He reached into his pocket and pulled out a small leather case, removing a business card. "Here's my cell number and I am happy to help with whatever you need. I know a lot about the computer systems for a chocolate retail outlet."

She just stared at him, too gut-punched to respond when he put the card—no, two cards—on top of the envelope.

"I won't call you," she said. He was the last person—

well, the second to last—that she'd call. "I have plenty of family here myself."

Maybe none who knew how to program software for cocoa shipment management or retail business account-ing, but now, she didn't need to know any of that. This whole project was...finished.

He gave her an earnest look. "I know you have family here. In fact..." He shifted from one foot to the other, the first time she'd ever seen the man be anything but large and in charge. "I was, uh, hoping that you'd give one of those cards to Madeline."

She inhaled sharply, and almost laughed. "I doubt she'll call you, either. I mean, from what I know? You did the same thing to her that Tristan is doing to me."

"Not exactly. And I'd very much like the chance to explain what happened. After seeing her that night we were here, I...I realized that she..." His words faded out. "I would appreciate it if you'd ask her to call me."

She gave a noncommittal shrug, too buried by her immediate pain to get into Madeline's twenty-five-year-old heartache.

"I'll go, then," he said, backing away. "Please don't hesitate to—"

She held up a hand, not surprised it was trembling, to stop his meaningless niceties. She wanted him gone. She wanted every single thing that reminded her of Tristan Saint Pierre to disappear from the face of the Earth, including this entire shop.

"Just go," she managed to say. "Please go."

He nodded and turned, walking toward the door. Before he opened it, he looked back at her.

"You did a fantastic job here," he said. "And by every legal measure, you own the rights to that proprietary recipe he's using to make chocolate."

"I don't care if he's bathing in it," she said dryly.

"It's yours," he replied. "To use for profit. I hope you do."

With that, he pulled the door open and stepped out, leaving her shaking and shocked.

Silent, she stared at the door, then the windows, the tables, the display case, and her Instagram-worthy feature wall.

"Belgian Bliss this, you jerk!" She spat out the words, leaping from her seat as a fresh bolt of fury replaced her sadness.

"I hate him!" She gave the cardboard box a kick, the force of the metal on her sneaker toe jolting her whole body. "How dare he steal my ideas…"

Bending over, she used brute strength and fury to hoist the sign she had been about to hang. "And break my heart…"

Clinging to the cold brass, she powered through the swinging doors toward the kitchen. "And ruin my life…"

She trudged through the kitchen, straight to the back door, bracing the metal while she flipped the lock and used her hip to thrust it open.

"How dare he send his henchman…" She strode out the back toward the Dumpster she shared with her two sisters' businesses. "And pay off the Danish government and make our marriage...disappear!"

On the last word, she flung the sign in the Dumpster with a long groan when it clattered, metal-against-metal.

"You belong in the garbage, Tristan Saint Pierre!" she hollered. "Because you and your whole clan are trash!"

"Sadie!" The back door of her sister's flower shop popped open and Rose stepped out.

"What's going on?" That was Madeline, coming out of her dressmaking studio on the other side.

Sadie looked from one sister to the other; the tears welled and spilled, her body shaking, her heart shattering into a million broken pieces.

"It's over," she said brokenly as they both rushed toward her. "It's over. My marriage, my hopes, my dreams, everything is finished."

As she wept, they wrapped her in their arms and walked her toward Rose's flower shop, cooing and crooning and calming her down.

"Nothing is finished," Rose said, her natural optimism a little maddening right then. "You'll just start over."

Sadie looked at Madeline, bracing for a lecture about trust and men and the company you keep.

But her oldest sister just folded her into an embrace and patted her back, reminding Sadie that there was nothing quite like Wingate love. Suffocating at times, soothing at others.

"Yes, you'll start over here, Sadie," Madeline said.

"Right here, surrounded by the family that will support you forever and ever."

Could she do that?

Clinging to her sisters, they walked into Coming Up Roses and she prepared to tell them—and the rest of the Wingate women—everything. Just as Rose opened her back door, Sadie glanced to the chocolate shop she'd poured her heart and soul into for the past six weeks.

The chocolate shop that would never, *ever* be called Belgian Bliss.

Chapter Two

Susannah

"Rex? Rex?" Susannah shot up from bed as she realized the other side was empty. "Rex, where did you go?"

At the silence, she bounded out of bed, shoved her feet into slippers, and didn't even bother finding her robe. She simply rushed out to the living room and kitchen, darting back and forth in a low-grade panic around the large open area.

"Rex?"

She peered out the French doors and gauged the time to be barely sunrise, based on the peachy glow over the water. Where could he have gone at dawn on New Year's Day?

Work, of course. He'd been cleared by the doctor to put in a few hours a day with the start of the New Year. Which happened six hours ago, so Rex Wingate was no doubt at his desk downstairs already eyeing new listings and considering Wingate Properties' next acquisition.

She hurried to the stairs, down to the first-floor office and the family room they'd turned into a physical therapy center after his stroke. As she neared the bottom, she slowed her step, listening for the click of his keyboard or the rustle of paper.

But there was only silence.

Fighting the memory of the day she'd walked into that room and found him slumped on the floor after a stroke, she took a deep breath, came around the corner and...

Found an empty office.

"Rex?" She stepped into the family room and looked at the open sliding glass door that led to the beach. Was he out there? Why not go to the upstairs deck with coffee if he wanted to get up early and watch the sunrise?

She walked through the slider and stepped out, shivering at the chilly morning air. He shouldn't be out here alone! He shouldn't be...

...in the water.

But there he was, thigh deep in the Atlantic Ocean, wearing nothing but swim trunks and a T-shirt, his arms fully extended toward the sky, his face toward the rising sun.

"What in the world is he doing?" she muttered as she marched out, already quivering with fear and anger and disbelief. It was January first! That water couldn't be seventy-five degrees, maybe colder. The air was barely fifty. A solid wave—though the ocean was thankfully calm this morning—could knock him over.

And the beach was deserted at this hour.

"Rex!" she called at the top of her lungs but, of course, he didn't hear. Or didn't want to. "Rex!"

On the fourth and final shriek, twenty feet away from him, he turned and waved like a kid excited to get his mother's attention.

"Suze! Come on in! Cold therapy! It's the greatest!"

Had he lost his mind?

Before she could ask—and before the next wave hit his bare thighs—he walked out of the water toward her. On the way, he stooped over and scooped up a towel he'd left on the sand. He moved with remarkable grace for a stroke survivor, and wore a dazzling smile that was no longer lopsided.

But that didn't mean he was fully healed and able to take sunrise swims and navigate sand and shells under bare feet.

"Reginald Wingate the Third, what do you think you are doing?"

"Following doctor's orders," he said, drying his face and chest, and even bending over to pat his legs. Six months ago—maybe four—he wouldn't have attempted that move. "Justin told me about this health guy podcast and I woke up early and listened and decided not to waste another minute without a morning of cold therapy and sun in my eyes. Did you know it's the healthiest thing you can do?"

"So is sleeping in next to your wife."

He flipped the towel over his shoulders and grinned at her. "I feel like a new man, Suze."

She let out an exhale as churned-up adrenaline melted into her veins. "I liked the old one," she said, closing the space between them and putting her hands on his oh-so-icy cheeks. "I like him alive and well."

"Please. I couldn't be more alive. It's a new year, and a new me. You heard my resolutions when we went around the room with the family last night. Clean and healthy living. Had to give up my stogies and scotch, which wasn't that hard. And now I'm thinking I'll give that carnivore diet a try. Meat and eggs, baby." He patted his stomach and winked. "Strong and virile. I'm still a man, Suze."

A seventy-five-year-old man who refused to face his own mortality. She didn't want to discourage his quest for improved health, but she didn't want him to kill himself getting there, either.

"Carnivore?" She lifted her brows. "You'd give up your beloved before-bed cookies and tea?"

"I'd give up anything to have years and years with you..." He kissed her lightly on the lips. "And that crew we raised. Wasn't last night amazing? Goodness, I love our kids and grandkids. I wasn't expecting that impromptu party that turned into a life-planning session for Sadie. I think we've convinced her to stay and run that shop, don't you?"

Susannah exhaled, her worry over Rex making her forget all the emotions her dear, sweet Sadie had been through. "That poor girl," she whispered.

"She's not poor," Rex said. "She's lucky! She escaped what would surely have been a disaster of a marriage and she's home, like her six sisters. We're still having the party today, right? I know last night we ate most of what you planned to serve for the New Year's Day festivities."

"Well, we had to lift up our Sadie and that takes plenty of nourishment," she said on a laugh.

"And it took some champagne, but did you notice I didn't drink?"

"I did." She beamed up at him, remembering how much he'd helped Sadie last night. He'd showered her with motivation and love, the old Rex they all knew and needed so much. "Tori said she has tons of food because the café is closed. So our family celebration is on, if you can handle more socializing, Rex. We were up until one in the morning!"

"I feel great. People pay thousands to have special cold tubs installed for this therapy and we have the Atlantic Ocean in our backyard." He pointed his thumb over his shoulder. "Wanna give it a go?"

She glanced down at her flimsy nightgown, sand-covered Dearfoams, and bare legs. "I'll pass, especially dressed like this."

"Why *are* you dressed like that?" he asked.

"Because you were missing and I nearly had a heart attack when I couldn't find you."

He looked up to the sky. "What? No search-and-rescue helicopters yet?" As he laughed at his joke, he adroitly sidestepped a broken shell. "Whoa."

"Rex." She grabbed him, but he was firm on his feet. "Remember, you just gave up that cane before Christmas."

"And burned it in the fireplace." He angled his head,

tapering his dark eyes as water trickled from his silver hair to his black brow. "I'm okay, Suze. You have to trust me."

"I trust you," she said. "I just don't trust your legs with no cane and no shoes and no floor, just sand."

He sighed and jutted his chin toward the house. "Let's have coffee."

"You're not supposed to have caf—"

"Stop." He held up a hand and used a sterner voice. "Justin said a cup a day is fine. I'm free to walk about the world without a cane and I'm clear to go back to Wingate Properties when Raina is on maternity leave. If Dr. Hottypants says it is so, it is so."

Susannah chuckled at his use of their daughters' nick-name for his neurologist—who would most likely be family soon, at least based on the way he and Tori were glued together last night.

"I know he's given you a range of freedom and feels you are fully healed from your stroke," she said. "But that doesn't mean you should act like a teenager."

He responded by putting his arm around her and nestling his cold face and wet hair in her neck. "A teenager, huh?"

She laughed and let him kiss her, but then inched back to look into the depths of his dark eyes. "Rex, don't expect me to stop caring about you. I can't help it if I want to be sure you're safe and healthy."

"You don't have to stop caring about me." He snug-gled her into his side. "But you do have to stop fussing like I'm in a nursing home about to meet my maker."

"Don't even say that." She flattened her hand on his chest. The muscles underneath her palm were not nearly as developed as they'd been before the stroke and his chest hair was thin and gray. But the heart that beat in there belonged to her, and she couldn't help it if she wanted it—and him—to last for another twenty-five years. "I'm trying to be sure we're not flying in an ambulance on the way to the hospital again."

He groaned at the memory, which, for him, was foggy. But hers was crystal clear and it still scared her to think about that awful day.

"I get that, Suze, but you have to believe in me. And in the doctors, tests, and physical therapists. I'm fine."

"You're more than fine, Rex Wingate." She stood on her slippered toes and kissed his lips. "And I love you."

He ruffled her short hair. "Then let's go be...teenagers."

"Let's start with that one cup of coffee you're allowed to have." She smiled at him, her heart melting with love. "And get ready for the real teenagers who will be here in a few hours."

"Fine." He strode ahead, and threw her a look. "But I'll beat you to the coffee."

AFTER THEY'D DRESSED and poured two cups, Susannah followed Rex to the living room, settling in to take in the rest of the sunrise, ready to plan the afternoon with their family.

"So, you didn't share your New Year's resolutions last night, Suze." Rex took a sip and eyed her over the rim of his cup. "Do you have any?"

"Thou shalt not baby your husband?"

"Resolutions, not commandments, dear."

"Are they any different with you?" She tempered the tease with a smile.

He sighed. "I don't want to be the world's most demanding husband."

"You aren't." She leaned forward, setting her steaming mug on the coffee table to hold his gaze. "And I don't mean to be the most overprotective wife. But, Rex, you're twelve years my senior and I don't want to be a widow."

He grimaced. "I don't want you to be. Nor do I want you to be my nurse and babysitter."

"I'll try to ease up on that," she promised. "Does that count as my resolution?"

"You know what I think you need, Suze?"

"Oh, boy." She picked up the coffee for a fortifying sip. "Do I get a Rex Wingate motivational speech, too? You really worked magic on Sadie last night."

"Pffft." He flicked his hand. "She doesn't need motivation from me. She's going to do great with that shop, and once she settles down and quits her gallivanting, she'll meet a good man. You watch." He leaned closer. "But you?"

"You think I can meet a good man?" she joked.

"I think you need...a goal."

She swallowed, not sure she liked that advice. "My goal is to keep you alive."

His eyes shuttered. "A different goal. I can handle staying alive. You should find a dream or a project or a...something."

She considered that. "Well, I'd love to help Sadie run her new shop but..." She made a face.

"You're allergic to chocolate," Rex said with a nod. "You can't risk a blistering headache by tasting her product."

"I won't, but I am about to have two new grandbabies, and based on the way Raina looks? Thing One and Thing Two aren't waiting until their due date at the end of the month."

"How about Thing Just For Suze?"

She rolled her eyes. "You mean something to really get me out of your hair."

Chuckling, he shook his head. "That's not the only reason. You've put your whole heart into taking care of me, and helping Raina with the babies is more of the same. But you've always been an active and involved woman. You need to grab onto a new venture that gets you excited about life again, not just be everyone's nurse and assistant."

"I'm excited about life," she insisted. "All seven of our daughters live here now and I have you."

He lifted a brow as if he wasn't the "thing" he wanted her to have.

"I know when you sink your teeth into something, Suze, you're alive again. Like I am now." He grinned.

"And I'll be at Wingate Properties every day once those babies are born." At her look, he held up a hand. "Part-time, but still."

She let it go, and sipped her coffee, thinking.

"You're not wrong," she grudgingly admitted. "I miss being busy and part of this community, like before, when I was on every committee and fundraiser in town. But my priorities have shifted, Rex. When you had that stroke, everything changed for me, too. Family first and foremost, and that's that. I don't need to chair the Historical Society ball anymore."

"Well, I think a big part of my healing, if you will, is normalcy," he said. "Your constant nursing—which I know is motivated entirely by love—is a bit stifling and I'd like some freedom. I need some breathing space to make sure I can get back to being myself."

She cast her eyes down, hurt but completely under-standing. Rex was a fiercely masculine man—it was one of the things she'd always loved about him.

She nodded. "Okay."

"Is it?" he pressed, reaching for her hand. "I don't want you to be upset with me, honey. What you've done for me the past nine months is the greatest show of love a woman ever gave a man, and I'm beyond grateful."

She lifted a shoulder as if all that nursing was noth-ing. It wasn't—it had been achingly hard and sometimes impossible. But she'd done it happily because she loved him.

"In sickness and in health, remember?" She raised her mug for a toast.

"Till death do us part." He tapped her cup with his. "And may that death be many years from now." After they sipped, he looked into her eyes. "Susannah Wingate, I love you, and I know that I wouldn't be alive without you."

She looked at him, tears blurring her vision.

"Never forget that," he whispered, closing the space to kiss her lightly.

"I love you, too," she said. And she knew that if she meant that, she'd give him what he was asking for. She just wasn't sure how.

Chapter Three

Raina

After a long and delicious New Year's Day lunch at the beach house with family, Raina knew the time had come. She couldn't delay her dreaded task any longer, so she went in search of the two sisters who were also her soulmates and closest friends.

She certainly wasn't going to ask Sadie to witness the signing of a divorce decree, but these two? They were the right ladies for the job.

Tori brought humor and experience, while Raina's twin, Rose, could be counted on for optimism and sympathy. She'd need all of that as she penned the papers to end a sixteen-year marriage.

She found them both in the kitchen, helping to organize the leftovers and supervising the "cousins," as they called the teenagers of the next generation.

"You're not welcome here, Aunt Raina," Tori's daughter, Kenzie, quipped. "I heard Grannie Suze say you have to be off your feet and resting."

Raina rolled her eyes. "I'm sick of resting."

"Good," Tori said. "'Cause when those babies are born, you won't rest for eighteen years."

"If then," Rose chimed in. At the look from her oldest, Zach, she pointed playfully with a dishrag. "Unless you have the world's greatest son."

"You mean the one still working to pay off the repairs on Grandpa Rex's car?" Zach shook his head.

As the others teased him about his driving skills—now the subject of many family jokes—Raina leaned into Tori's shoulder and gave her a pleading look.

"I need a favor," she said under her breath.

"Anything, Preggers."

"Well, for starters, don't call me that." She eased her away from the others. "I need a witness."

Tori held up her hands and opened her mouth. "'Can I get a—'"

Raina put her fingers over her sister's lips to stop the bad Motown imitation. "It's serious." She glanced at Rose. "I actually need two."

Instantly, Rose scooted closer. "Anything, Raindrop. Why do you need witnesses?"

Tori flipped back a lock of strawberry-blond hair, leaning in. "For signing divorce papers?" she guessed on a whisper.

Raina nodded. "I could do it tomorrow at work and get Blake and Dani to sign, but the whole thing is just so... personal. And I fear there might be tears, so, can I steal you guys for a moment down in Dad's office? With Sadie's situation, I don't want to make a big thing of it."

"Of course." Rose turned to the kids and gave Zach a

playful snap with her dishtowel. "Kenzie's in charge," she said. "Do whatever she tells you."

"Except drive my car," Kenzie cracked, getting a dark look from her cousin.

As much as she'd prefer to hang out with the teenagers and her sisters, Raina headed toward the stairs that led to the first floor of the beach house. She had to get this over and done, as unpleasant and miserable a task as it was.

As the laughter faded into the background, Raina walked into her father's office, which felt brighter, lighter, and more lived in than it had for the past nine months. While he recovered, he hadn't been allowed to set foot in this room, the site of his stroke. In fact, the one time he did, he ended up scaring the heck out of them with a seizure.

Now, the keyboard was out, showing that he'd logged into his computer recently, and some papers were on his desk.

"Dad's back in the saddle, I see," Tori mused, glancing at the same things as she followed Raina. "That's the desk of a working man."

"Is he coming into the office very often?" Rose asked Raina.

"Occasionally, and it's always great when he's there to offer advice or give me some backstory on a particularly problematic client. He also has taken to mentoring Blake," she said, referring to their nephew, who was a high-achieving agent at the family real estate company. "Dad has become the chairman emeritus of Wingate Properties, and it's a great role for him."

"He's found a new purpose," Rose said as she sat down in the guest chair. "I think that's wonderful."

"If Suze will let him," Raina said as she lifted the tote bag she'd left behind the desk when she arrived today, planning to ask her sisters for this favor. "She told me he's begging for more space and less nursing."

"She said he wants her to work or get involved in the community," Tori added. "But she only wants to be with family, and she can't help Sadie because of her allergy."

Rose's brows lifted over blue eyes. "You know Kitty Worthington is begging for someone to run the spring fling or the Easter parade. There's the Fernandina Food Festival in a few weeks and a million other events. Suze used to love volunteering on those committees."

Tori shook her head and looked at Raina. "She thinks she's going to, uh, co-parent with you."

"I know," Raina said. "I'll want help, but I want to raise these kids by myself. I know, I know, it takes a village and all, but I want this job on my shoulders."

"I get that," Tori said. "Suze shines at hostessing and coordinating events. Who needs an event planner?"

"She needs a few weddings and all we seem to give her are..." Raina lifted the fat envelope. "Divorces."

"A wedding, huh?" Rose gave a sly smile to Tori. "Dr. Hottypants sure is happy to have you and the kids back on Amelia Island. When's he gonna pop the question?"

Tori shrugged, but there was plenty of warmth in her hazel eyes. "We're taking it slow. He's still living on his boat, and somehow the kids and I have fully moved into the house he bought."

"So by taking it slow, you mean you're living together," Raina teased.

"We're not," she said quickly. "I don't want to with two teenagers. And we just got back here permanently two weeks ago. I have to get the kids settled in school, get the café running like I had it last summer, and deal with this new normal after the change in the custody arrangement."

"Speaking of." Raina reached into the envelope from the Law Offices of Riley, Vitagliano, and Cumberland, pulled out a packet of legal papers and dropped them with a thud on the desk. "Let's get this ugliness over and done."

"It's not ugly," Rose insisted, leaning forward. "It's the start of a new life, just like we've been telling Sadie for twenty-four hours."

"Not to downplay what our sister is going through, but Sadie was married on a whim and for the wrong reasons. I'm ending this after sixteen years of what I thought was a happy marriage. But my husband cheated on me, fell in love with another woman, and knocked me up with twins on his way out. No matter how you cut it..." Raina's throat tightened with a sob that surprised her more than anything. "Wow, sorry. I haven't let him get to me in a long time."

"This isn't an easy task," Tori said, reaching her hand across the desk to take Raina's. "Divorce is awful, no matter how you cut it, whim or sixteen years. It's bad."

"But you both have found new lives," Rose said. "Raina, you're having two healthy babies after three miscarriages, living in your dream beach house, and Dad just said Wingate Properties had a stellar year, thanks to you. And look at Tori, in love with Justin, navigating single motherhood, and running the Riverfront Café better than anyone's ever done in the past."

Raina let out a long sigh. "Yes, you were the right two sisters for this job."

"Of course we are," Rose said. "And I'm serious. I see blue skies and two babies ahead for you. And...maybe love."

"Pffft. Trust me, I'm not on Hinge or Binge or whatever it's called trying to find Husband Number Two. My love is reserved for Thing One and Thing Two." She rubbed her big baby bump.

"You don't have to look on apps," Tori said. "Love can find you when you least expect it." She gave a droll laugh. "Like when you spill coffee all over Dad's doctor."

"That's right, Rain. Love could be anywhere for you."

"Uh, let's undo the last love I had before you two start finding me the next one." Raina fluttered the papers in front of her as if they were more important than hypothetical love. But that wasn't the real reason she closed that conversation.

The fact was, these two knew her better than anyone. One misspoken word, one sigh of longing, and they'd know what she'd spent nearly two months keeping a secret.

"Okay, there are fourteen places to sign, so—"

"What about Chase?"

Raina shot her head up at Rose's question, her heart flipping. So much for a secret.

"What about him? He's in Europe. I haven't seen him for months. I haven't heard anything about the hotel he owns, and he has no reason to come back here and..." Her voice faded out as her two sisters exchanged a look she did not like at all.

"Stop it, you two. I'm weeks from giving birth and not thinking about men."

"Then why do you turn three shades of red every time his name is casually mentioned?" Tori asked.

"Pregnancy hormones."

Rose pointed at her. "You do seem to light up when someone talks about his boutique hotel."

"Because he saved us when we needed a place to host a family party," she insisted, aching for the subject to change.

"I could have sworn I saw your little toes curl when Suze asked if you'd heard from him lately," Tori teased.

"I wouldn't know, since I haven't seen my feet in ages." She patted her belly again. "And that toe-curling might have been arthritis, since I'm forty-three and *not interested in a man*."

But humor and deflection didn't work. She could tell by the looks on their faces that they knew. Of course they knew.

Maybe they didn't know how bad it was.

The fact was, Raina missed Chase Madison every single day since he'd left and hadn't gone to sleep one night without thinking about him. Her feelings for a man she barely knew and never saw—a man who'd run off to Italy the very second there was a glimmer of chemistry between them—were her guilty pleasure and not going to be shared with anyone, ever.

Ever since the night Chase's grandmother died and Raina had discovered him up on her balcony fighting tears and grief, she'd nursed this little crush like it was a pet mushroom growing in the dark. A poisonous mushroom.

For one thing, she wasn't even divorced yet. So maybe...

No, he wasn't coming back. He owned properties all over the world and the one he had on Amelia Island, the boutique hotel, Ocean Song, could run without him on the premises. She might never see Chase Madison again, and that was fine.

Yeah, keep telling yourself that, Raina.

"Can we get me divorced, please?" She spread the decree on the desk. "That's the only problem I can fix right now."

Because her feelings for Chase? That was an unfixable problem that she hoped would go away with time and a couple of babies.

She stared at the words at the top of the first page: *Dissolution of Marriage.* Talk about problems she couldn't fix. Talk about facing your failures. Talk about...

"Oh, these pregnancy hormones," she joked, swiping at a tear.

"Raindrop!" Rose was up and around the desk in an

instant, bending over to hug her. "Don't cry." She crouched down to get eye-to-eye. "You're the winner, Raina. You have the babies."

"He doesn't want anything to do with them," she said, the words hurting every single time they came out of her mouth.

"Count your blessings," Tori replied, leaning on one hand to get closer. "You are avoiding a lifetime of renegotiating custody agreements. That last one worked in my favor, but it's been brutal with Trey and difficult for the kids. You won't have that problem."

"No, I won't," she agreed, flipping to page ten, because she'd practically memorized every word. "Says so right here—the phrase is 'termination of parental rights.'" She grunted. "Horrible bunch of words, aren't they?"

"You wouldn't want him to have those rights," Rose insisted. "He's making your life easier, and you know it."

"Until my kids demand to know why their father didn't want them. And you know that he'll have a kid with Lisa Godfrey before these two are a year old."

"What about his mother?" Tori asked. "I seem to recall she was, uh, strong-willed."

Raina looked at her, thinking about the hard-hearted woman who believed Jack Wallace belonged on a pedestal and Raina wasn't fit to polish the brass plate on the front of it. "I'm sure Valerie is overjoyed we're divorcing and that Jack won't even tell her there are babies."

Rose gasped. "That's cruel."

"Well, I'd never keep her away from the babies, but

I'm more worried about all the questions they're going to have when they get older."

"You'll know how to answer them," Rose assured her. "Because you'll have flawless maternal intuition."

Raina smiled at her, placing a hand on her twin sister's cheek, always marveling at how much they looked alike, with completely opposite coloring. "Never change, Rosebud."

"I'm serious, that's not me being crazy hopeful." She stood and went back to her chair, grabbing a pen from a small cup on the corner of Dad's desk. "Let's sign this thing and start your new life."

Raina nodded and turned the document around, lifting one page to the first yellow sticky note. "I have to do all the signatures and you have to watch. At the end, you sign."

"No lawyer has to be here?"

"Not anymore, and not when there's nothing contested. We've worked out the financials, and I already have the final settlement in my account. We just send this to the courthouse, and I'm completely free. In fact, instead of moping about this tomorrow, I'm going to go to the bank and pay off my mortgage so I don't even have to carry that anymore."

"Are you sure you want to do that?" Tori asked.

"Why wouldn't I? It's huge and I didn't get a great rate. I planned this from the moment I bought the house."

"But if you don't have a mortgage," Tori said, "then you don't have an incentive to let Chase Madison stay in the room he rents from you when he's in town."

Raina stared at her, considering all the ways to answer. "It's probably better that way," she said, opting for honesty instead of a snide remark.

"Better for who?" Rose pressed.

She let out a sigh and looked down at the sea of legalese. "Because I don't want his rent money for a room he never uses. Let's just sign this so I can go home and cry in my...Pellegrino."

"About Chase or Jack Wallace?" Tori asked.

Raina took a pen and signed her name on the line with a flourish. "Jack Wallace is done," she said, flipping to the next sticky note. "He's a cheater..." Signed, then flipped. "And a liar..." Signed and flipped again. "And a scumbag..."

"We got fourteen of these?" Tori joked, leaning back and crossing her arms. "Wake me when we get to 'Satan's twin brother.'"

"That's next." Raina smiled as she turned the page. "But I'll need help with all fourteen."

"Okay," Rose agreed. "He's a...terrible real estate agent."

Raina scribbled her name. "Not terrible, but he wasn't in my league."

"And he's never liked this family."

"Never," Raina agreed, signing the next page.

"Dad didn't trust him, so you should have known."

"You're on a roll, Rosebud." The next signature was barely legible.

"And he was terrible at Charades!" Tori added. "I hated when I got stuck with him on my team."

Raina laughed and signed.

"How about the time he wouldn't wear matching pajamas and ruined the family Christmas picture?" Rose's voice lifted with years-old disgust. "I was so mad at him."

"We all were!" Raina signed the next line. "Keep 'em comin', girls."

"He made you move to Miami!"

Tori snapped her fingers. "He turned a fifteen-pound brisket into a cinder. Ruined that Fourth of July."

"And he made really bad firefighter jokes about my husband." Rose made a face. "Who is mean to Gabe, the world's greatest guy?"

"The world's *worst* guy," Raina answered her as she signed. "That's who."

"And he always spit on the cake when he blew out birthday candles, remember?" Tori grunted. "I hated that."

"Don't start me on how terrible he was at beach touch football," Rose added. "He darn near drowned missing a pass one year."

By the time Raina got to the last signature, she couldn't see through the tears of laughter. She scribbled her name, and watched her sisters do the same on the witness lines.

"I've never been happier to say goodbye," she told them.

"And we could go on all day about Jack Wallace," Tori assured her.

"No need." Raina tucked the papers back in the envelope and dropped them in her bag for her assistant, Dani, to expedite to the Dade County courthouse. "I'm not even sad anymore."

"But you are divorced," Tori said as they stood. "Ever onward, sister."

Rose put her arm around Raina as they walked to the door. "And you never know about Chase. He could show up at any time and insist you name one of your babies Charles, after him."

Raina groaned at the memory of his promise to his late grandmother, who'd gone to her grave thinking these babies were his. *Charles.* She'd insisted that Raina name one after Chase and his beloved grandfather, Carlo.

"Well, that's not happening," she assured them. "Plus, I haven't seen him for forty-two days."

The second the words were out, she regretted them.

Because, of course, Tori stopped and turned. "But who's counting, eh, Rain?"

Chapter Four

Madeline

M adeline had said her goodbyes to everyone but Sadie, who'd slipped away from the party and gone up to her room. As she climbed the stairs to the third-floor guest suite where Sadie had been living for the past few months, Madeline heard her sister sniffle. The sad sound made her grimace with sympathy.

Of course, she'd come up here to lick her wounds. No matter how much they supported her and swore she'd be a huge success in her new business, Madeline knew her little sister. She knew the vulnerable spot in Sadie's heart that she tried to cover with impulsive decisions and the search for her next adventure.

Madeline had been an awkward fourteen-year-old girl when her stepmother had come home from the hospital with Sadie. From day one, that newborn had become Madeline's personal baby doll. Madeline had affectionately called her "Sadie, Sadie, Tiny Lady," with greenish-gold eyes the color of aged copper and gold-tipped butterscotch curls that were as messy as she was.

As they got older, their bond only deepened. Madeline was the oldest of the four Charlotte Wingate offspring, and Sadie was the oldest of Susannah's three daughters. All were Rex's "giggle gaggle" of Wingates. Their bond was why Sadie had shown up at Madeline's door when she needed somewhere to hide last fall, and it was why she'd asked Madeline to take her to the airport that night in November.

At the top of the stairs, Madeline tapped on the open door. "Knock, knock."

"I'm here. Come on in."

Madeline stepped in and inhaled a sharp breath at the chaos—the unmade bed covered with several sweaters and tops, shoes strewn all over the floor, and the bathroom door open to reveal a countertop covered in cosmetics.

"I know, I know—this is not up to Madeline Wingate standards. Don't judge." Sadie walked out of the closet with an overflowing laundry basket. "This is all clean but I need to put it somewhere and I don't have a somewhere." She moaned and dropped it on the bed, running pink-tipped fingers through wavy strands that had escaped her ponytail and brushed her cheekbones. "This place is beautiful, but it's a guest room in my parents' house. Where should I go? What should I do?"

She sounded so forlorn that Madeline went right to her, ignoring the mess even though it made her stomach churn, and put her arm around Sadie. "There's a perfectly nice apartment above the chocolate shop you're going to open and run," she said.

"I've used it as storage because I thought Tristan..."

She let her voice fade out. "Oh, man. It hurts to be duped by a guy."

Madeline nodded. "And the universe, in its infinite weirdness, used the one who duped me to dupe you. There really is some kind of karmic justice there, but I don't know what it is."

Sadie winced. "Madeline! I'm so sorry!"

"That Adam duped me?"

"That I was so wrapped up in myself that I totally forgot he had a message for you."

"For me?" Madeline drew back, trying to not over-react to that.

She'd done a good job of not talking to Sadie about Adam in front of their family because none of them knew her history with him. Only Sadie had any inkling that, by strange circumstances, the man who'd preceded Tristan into the ballroom that night last November was someone Madeline knew. Someone who'd changed her life, for better or worse.

"I'm sorry, Madeline," she said again. "I absolutely forgot he gave me his card and asked you to call him."

Call him? Madeline hooted softly. "Not happening."

"I think he got that impression, although honestly? I barely remember what he said, I was in such a fog. Wait. I remember that he wanted to give you an explanation and an apology."

Madeline rolled her eyes, so used to despising the very memory of Adam Carpenter—or Logan, which was apparently his real name.

"He's staying here."

"What?" Madeline's voice rose, not sure she understood what Sadie meant. "Staying...on Amelia Island?"

"Well, in the area, I guess. He said he was so mad at the Saint Pierre family for what they did to me—and maybe others, he just made a sweeping statement about how dreadful they are—that he quit working for them. He has a business connection and family in Jacksonville. And he asked me to ask you to call him so he could apologize and explain." Sadie gave her a contrite look. "Those were his exact words, more or less."

Madeline almost laughed at her sister, who didn't know the difference between "exact" and "more or less" but she loved her anyway.

"Does that sound right?" Sadie asked.

"About Jacksonville, yes." Madeline dug into her memory banks from conversations years ago. "He was born and raised in that area, as I recall. That was one of the things we had in common when we met. Both from northeast Florida."

"How *did* you meet him?" Sadie asked, climbing onto the bed, looking like she had zero intention of folding one piece of laundry. "I mean, I know you were working for the embezzler, which makes sense, since his specialty in the FBI was white-collar crime, but how did you get involved with him, Madeline?"

Embezzler. Involved. White-collar crime. None of those words belonged in the same sentence with Madeline Wingate's name. But there they were.

"Just tell me anything you're comfortable sharing," Sadie said.

The truth was, she wasn't comfortable sharing any of it, but Sadie deserved to know. She'd been through enough with secret-keeping and half-truths. Plus, had Madeline ever told anyone the full story?

She sighed and picked up two matching socks from the laundry basket and automatically rolled them into a neat ball, thinking back to those days. Those magical, memorable, different-world days.

"I was twenty-four and working as a bridal dress-making apprentice at Chanel in New York City, directly under their top designer, Elana Mau, or the embezzler, as you like to call her."

"I call it as I see it," Sadie said with a laugh. "But I know you respected her and learned a lot from her."

"I did...until I found out she was helping herself to company cash," Madeline said with a flick of her brows and the snap of a wrinkled T-shirt. "Anyway, back then, before she was arrested, I had to run a lot of errands in the garment district for that job. One was to pick up fabric bolts from a high-end satin manufacturer, North-east Fabric. Adam worked the loom, as I think I told you."

"But how did you meet him?" Sadie asked, getting comfortable against the headboard and wrapping her arms around her legs like she was settling in for storytime. "Eye contact across a crowded warehouse? Through a sewing friend? Bumping into each other on the...fabric floor?"

"Yes." Madeline smiled and stood, mindlessly smoothing the T-shirt and folding it into a tidy square as she let herself be transported back to the late nineties and open some well-sealed memory boxes.

They'd been good years in the Big Apple, though—halcyon days spent gadding about the city in high-waisted jeans, baby T's, long hair tumbling down her back.

Twenty-four-year-old Madeline Wingate was on top of the world, full of attitude and self-assurance, and used to admiring gazes from the many male vendors she dealt with in the fashion business. After all, she was a lead apprentice for Elana Mau, the darling of the district.

But that day? That fateful day...

"I was late for an appointment," she said softly.

"*You?*" Sadie shot forward so fast, she nearly fell off the bed. "You've never been late a day in your life."

"Well, I was that day, and rushing around town in a pair of platform clogs Elana had brought back from Mexico for me."

Sadie reached into the basket and grabbed a pair of clean shorts. "A money-*laundering* trip." She waved the shorts playfully, proud of her pun, then tossed them to Madeline to be folded.

"Stop." Madeline snatched the shorts up mid-air with a laugh that faded as she remembered the horror of seeing her hero in handcuffs. "Anyway, the day it started, I was flying down the middle of the shop floor. One of my clogs catapulted off my foot, and I ate it in front of the entire loom line."

Sadie chortled. "The loom line!"

"My bolt of fabric went flying and this one operator

launched from his machine to catch it and keep it from hitting the filthy floor."

"A loom launcher!" Sadie gasped, falling back again on a laugh. "What did he say?"

"He handed me the satin and said..." She cleared her throat and stood straight, holding out a blouse as though it were a bolt of shantung, squaring her shoulders and lowering her voice. "'Please tell me this isn't for *your* wedding dress, gorgeous.'"

Sadie slammed both hands on the bed and threw her head back with a howl. "Oh, *why* do they make us swoon?"

Madeline laughed at the drama—and the truth. "Except now we both know that Adam 'the loom guy' Carpenter targeted me because I worked for Elana. He was really Adam Logan, a young FBI agent trying to gain access to her staff and arrest her for stealing millions."

"Yeah, but in those suspense-filled romance novels..." Sadie handed a pajama top to Madeline for the next fold. "The hot FBI agent always falls for the chick he's using as his mark."

"There was no falling on his part," Madeline said. "It took him all of ten minutes to get my phone number and nine of them were spent following me into the street."

One eyebrow shot up. "Go, Adam."

"Please. He was part of the Elana Mau sting operation, and now I know his mission was to cozy up to her apprentice. It wasn't as if he followed me out to the street and made me laugh until I gave him my number *because he liked me.*"

Sadie shook her head. "I bet he didn't mind the job at all."

Madeline looked at her sister, but in her mind's eye, she was seeing young Adam, with those insanely soulful brown eyes and that heart-twisting half-smile and the precious cleft in his chin. He was tall and lean with dark hair that flopped over his forehead and kissed his brow. And she'd been one smitten kitten.

"He had this habit," she said softly as she remembered how he'd say goodbye after a date. "He'd take two steps back, never taking his eyes off mine, then hold up his thumb and baby finger next to his head like this..." She imitated the gesture, like he was holding an invisible phone.

"Ah, yes," Sadie laughed. "The international sign for, 'Had a great time, babe, I'll call you the minute I can because I won't be able to think about anything else.'"

"Yes!" Madeline practically squealed. "Why is that so..." She grunted. "Endearing."

"And by endearing, you mean sexy," Sadie teased. "Plus, it's a sure sign he was totally into you."

"Was he? Or was it all an act?"

Sadie groaned. "Honey, you are asking the wrong girl about men who act interested. So, what happened with Adam after he got your number?"

"We went out...every night. He picked me up at work, always. He'd show up early and come up to the design studio and offer to wait if I had to go downstairs for a fitting. Meanwhile, he was probably rifling through

Elana's files with a secret camera. I thought he was wonderful and patient and terribly chivalrous."

"Maybe he was," Sadie said.

"You don't have to defend him," Madeline said, flipping the arms on a blouse that she would iron but Sadie would not. "I was nothing to that man. But he made me think I was. He held me and kissed me and said...things. He told me he wanted to meet my family and he saw a future and...and..."

"And?" Sadie demanded.

She looked up from the blouse. "And then, one night, he didn't show. He never came to my apartment and he didn't call and the next day, when I went into work, the place was teeming with police and Elana was in hand-cuffs and..." She blew out a breath, still stunned by how blind she'd been to all of this. "I never put two and two together and came up with 'undercover cop using me for access' until a few months ago. That's when I saw him on your laptop, Sadie, and *you* figured it out. I *still* couldn't see it."

"Oh, honey."

She waved off the sympathy and swallowed an ancient pain that she had long ago locked away and tried to forget, looking around for something else to fold.

"I think he still cares about you, based on his expression when he asked me to give you his number."

Madeline stared ahead, too lost in the past to dissect the present yet.

"I tried so hard to find him," she said softly. So, so hard. Desperately, frantically. "When I went to Northeast Fabric, they said he'd quit, and I sat in the rain at a bus stop and cried for an hour. Then, when I called his number, I got that recording..."

The number you have dialed is no longer in service. Please check your directory and try again.

She could still perfectly recall the cold electronic voice, probably because she'd called it a hundred times that week. She called until she couldn't call or cry or care anymore because her dreams had...disappeared.

Sadie fell flat on her pillow and draped an arm over her face, drama-queen style, unaware of the true depths of Madeline's loss.

"Men!" she exclaimed. "How can we ever trust them? I swear I will never, ever give my heart, head, body, or soul to another man."

"Don't say that." Madeline abandoned the clothes to sit next to her sister. "You have so much love in your heart, Sadie. You'll make someone very happy. You just have to find him."

She lifted her arm and peered through one eye at Madeline. "You're perfectly happy as a single woman."

Madeline swallowed any response until she could formulate one that would help Sadie and not send her sailing into the life of an unmarried and lonely woman. She had to be honest, but not raw.

After a moment, she put a hand on Sadie's arm. "I let him win," she whispered.

Sadie sat up, bracing on her elbows. "Adam?" she asked.

Madeline nodded. "He broke my heart and I refused

to give anyone else a chance to fix it. Don't do that, Sadie. Don't let Tristan be the one who makes you live your life alone simply to protect yourself from pain. You're too young and beautiful and spirited."

Sadie narrowed her gaze. "Are you not happy, Madeline?"

"I'm fine," she said, getting up quickly at a question she didn't like or expect. "I'm forty-nine and so meticulous you gasp if I have a dirty cup in my sink. There's no reason for you to live that way, that...alone way. You're thirty-five and can still find a partner for life."

"So could you," Sadie said, sitting up all the way, her pretty features set in a determined expression. "You don't have to be alone, Madeline! You're beautiful and talented and own a business and you're..."

"Forty-nine," she repeated. "Look up 'set in her ways' in the dictionary and you'll see me."

But Sadie wasn't listening. She was shaking her head, her eyes dancing with unsaid words as she clapped her hands. "Madeline!" she exclaimed. "Why don't you call him?"

"Adam?" Madeline choked. "Not a chance in heaven or hell."

"I'm serious."

"You're crazy."

"No, no, no, *no*! Hear me out." She scrambled to her knees, clasping her hands and practically quivering in a classic Sadie Wingate pleading pose. "You have to call him!"

"Why?"

"Because...it might be real."

Madeline angled her head, at an absolute loss for words. "Real?"

"There was something in his face, Madeline. The way he said your name, the way he wanted to apologize and explain."

"Sadie." She gave her sister a warning glare. "You didn't even remember to tell me he mentioned my name. And now you're getting worked up over something that isn't going to happen."

"You have unfinished business, Madeline Wingate," Sadie exclaimed. "You of all people can't live with that! It's like that cup in the sink or a drawer that needs to be closed. You're a dressmaker who cannot leave threads hanging loose, and you know it."

She had to laugh, because the description was apt. But not enough to make her...*call Adam*.

"Why not?" Sadie challenged even before Madeline launched into a litany of why-nots. "Don't you want to hear his apology or explanation? You are owed both."

"To what end?" Madeline asked. "He'll just lie and that will hurt more than the truth."

Sadie looked at her for a long time, then lifted another eyebrow, a smug look in her green-gold eyes.

"Then you let him win," she said, deftly throwing Madeline's words back at her.

"He won a long time ago," Madeline replied.

"But that was Round One and this is Round Two. And you, my darling sister, have the home-field advantage." Sadie popped off the bed. "I have his card right here. I put it in my purse with the letter I have yet to open."

"You really didn't open it yet?" Madeline couldn't believe that.

"I will, but I have been wallowing so hard in self-pity that I didn't want to read his pathetic excuses. But..." She pulled something out of her purse and shoved it in Madeline's hand, the edges cutting into her palm before she looked down to read the black embossed letters.

Adam C. Logan

Security Specialist

Oh, boy. She was shaking.

She stuffed the card into the back pocket of her jeans.

"Call him," Sadie insisted.

"No."

"Madeline! Go win Round Two!"

"Win what, Sadie? What's the prize?"

"Love." She breathed the word and it hit Madeline softly, like a whisper of silk dancing over bare shoulders.

Love.

The very thing Madeline celebrated every time she designed and sewed a wedding gown. And yet had never worn one herself.

She tamped down the thought and cleared her throat, effectively ending the conversation.

"Let's finish folding your clothes, then head down to Wingate Way to look at your apartment," she said. "We can order furniture and get you set up so you can live very happily there."

For a long, long time, Sadie just stared at her, the

wheels under that unruly head of hair turning and churning.

Madeline had to smile. "I'm not calling him, Sadie."

"But Madeline! You're not a twenty-four-year-old clog-wearing apprentice anymore!" Sadie insisted. "You are a grown woman, a great beauty, and a world-class bridal designer with your own salon and internationally recognized brand."

Madeline gave a soft laugh. "No wonder you're in marketing."

"Then *I* might call him," Sadie said.

"And say what?"

"I don't know, but he said I should call if I need anything and what I need is for the two of you to rekindle—"

"Stop." Madeline pointed at her. "Would you want me to call Tristan and get him back here?"

The color drained from her face. "You wouldn't."

"No, and neither will you."

"Okay, I won't."

"Good." She slid her fingertip in her back pocket and grazed the edge of his card, hoping she didn't spend too much time thinking about...what it would be like to really hear that explanation and apology.

And what it would be like to tell him...the truth.

Chapter Five

Sadie

Looking around the underwhelming two-bedroom apartment above the chocolate shop she'd called home for more than a week now, Sadie's heart dropped with a sadness that was so totally foreign to her, she couldn't name it. Was she depressed? Confused? Exhausted? No.

She was lost.

That was the best word she could use as she wandered through the rooms, pausing at the three floor-to-ceiling arched windows in the living room to look down at the red brick of Wingate Way.

Just like her whole life, here she was, nested in the middle of Wingate sisters, with Rose's business on one side, Madeline's on the other, and Wingate Properties across the street.

It was this very positioning—the middle daughter, with four older and two younger—that always made Sadie feel like there was a vise squeezing her.

She loved them all. How could she not? Being Wingates, they'd rallied to help her these past ten days.

They'd furnished the apartment, hauled her boxes up the stairs on move-in day, and tasted and raved about the few chocolate bars she'd managed to make. They'd quietly spread the word all over town that "Sadie's," the new chocolate shop, would be opening soon.

More than that, they showered her with endless encouragement, support, humor, and love.

Her niece, Kenzie, asked if she could work every day after school, and Raina had given her a stack of decent resumes to go through. Rose offered up Lizzie, her flower shop manager, to assist until Sadie hired some staff.

Historically, all that love and support smothered her. That was when she took off for air and space and other countries and other families.

Now, she couldn't do that. She had to go down there and somehow find the nerve to flip the sign to "Open" instead of "Opening Soon" and make this new endeavor a success.

But instead of entering her beautiful kitchen to turn on the stove, fire up the *melangeur*, and mix cocoa nibs with spices and love to create liquid magic, she was up here, drinking coffee, staring out the window...weirdly *lost*.

Only Madeline seemed to understand that Sadie was suffering from heartache, having been dumped by the love of her life and made a fool.

Although...who was the fool, really? She'd rebounded from her bad decisions with a freshly-remodeled store, no actual divorce, and a quietly closed door that would never open again.

She turned and gazed at Tristan's letter, laying open on the coffee table next to an empty glass of wine from last night's reading and weeping. It had become a ritual for her around midnight, the letter read so frequently that she had it memorized.

Every doubt she ever had about Tristan had proven to be true. Oh, he couched his apology in claims that he had felt love when he'd arranged for them to elope in Copenhagen, or the closest thing to it he'd ever known. He swore he hadn't married her for the recipe or to derail his family's ridiculous plans for what amounted to an arranged marriage to an heiress named Asha Devereaux.

He assured her that the money to build her own shop wasn't motivated by guilt, but a gift, owed to her for years of service to the Saint Pierre brand. And he ended with a promise to always remember their year-and-a-half adventure and to think of her...fondly.

Fondly.

She fought the urge to tear the letter into shreds and erase him from her mind, but then she'd be sorry later tonight, around midnight, when she needed a good pity party.

The sound of a buzzer yanked her from her thoughts. Someone was trying to get into the shop from the front door. Couldn't they read?

Opening Soon...she just didn't know when.

She stepped back to the windows and pushed the sheer curtain aside to look down to the front door, only able to see that her caller was a man. He cupped his hands to peer inside.

It was probably a delivery—she'd ordered a new double boiler that should arrive any day. She wanted to order decals for the front windows with the shop name... but she couldn't think of one.

The maven of marketing had drawn a blank when it came to naming her own store and all she had was Sadie's. Which didn't say chocolate or delicious or bliss or anything.

It said, "Girl who will probably give up and run off soon."

The man buzzed again, so she put the coffee cup next to the letter and made her way down the stairs to the kitchen. As she walked through it, she purposely ignored all the unused equipment and polished stainless surfaces just waiting for racks of candy molds to fill and chill.

She swung the door into the retail section, squinting at the man on the other side of the storefront window. He wasn't terribly tall, maybe five-ten, with medium-brown hair that didn't look like it had ever been too friendly with a comb, dressed in a beige T-shirt stretched over...not exactly a Dad-bod, but no gym rat, either.

She unlatched the door and inched it open with a questioning look up at a man who looked to be about forty, with blue-green eyes and a tentative smile.

"Do you have a delivery?" she asked, glancing behind him to see if there was a truck on the street.

"A special one." He lifted a pink bakery box, holding it by twine, which was old-school and so unexpected. "A welcome to town from a friendly rival."

"Rival..." She took the box, reading the script across

the top. "How the Cookie Crumbles. Oh, the cookie place."

He laughed. "I know that's what people call the store. Or Crumbles, which will probably get me sued by the cookie conglomerate with the same name." He offered a hand. "Scout Jacobson, reluctant baker."

She laughed softly, shaking his hand and stealing a glance at the words "Opening Soon" on the door. "Sadie Wingate, reluctant chocolatier."

That made his smile wider, warming his whole expression and adding a light to his eyes. "Worried to be the victim of a judgy public?"

"Something like that." Without giving it too much thought, she stepped back and invited him in. "Would you like to see and judge?"

"I've been seeing and judging as you built the place out. You have incredible taste." He stepped in and glanced around, his eyes shuttering. "Dang. I'm doomed."

"Doomed?" She laughed. "Because you love chocolate?"

"Because you're going to snag all the 'sweeters'—that's what my mother called people who graze-eat at every sugar shack in town. Tourists, mostly, who are my bread and butter. Although if they want that, they go to a real bakery. For cookies, it's me. And for chocolate?" He shook his head and looked around. "You are going to destroy me."

"I'm sure there's plenty of room for another dessert offering," she said, watching him as he roamed the seating area, crossing his arms as he took it in.

"My tables are so...wooden."

And if hers were made of wood instead of marble, she might have a little more of the guilt money left.

"How long have you been in business?" she asked.

"I'm fairly new to the game, but the cookie shop isn't." He peered past the empty display case to the kitchens. "Wow. You spent some cashola."

She wanted to chuckle at the ridiculous word and the stark reality of her overspending.

"Maybe a little too much," she admitted. "I started off with...high hopes." And empty lies, but she kept that to herself.

"Go big or go home, right?"

She smiled at the sentiment, which, like the rest of him, was just so *American*. She might not have noticed it years ago. But after living in Europe, and then the constant contact with someone as classically *Euro* as Tristan, her fellow citizens stood out to her.

"Well, I am home," she said. "So maybe I shouldn't have gone quite so big."

He pulled out a cane-backed chair and offered her a seat. "Want to try one of my cookies?"

"Sure." She sat and placed the box on the table, running her finger over the twine. "Nice touch."

"My mother's thing." He gave a shrug as he sat across from her. "She owned a bakery in Pittsburgh for forty-seven years, called, unimaginatively, Jacobson's."

Sadie lifted a brow.

"What are you calling this place?" he asked.

"I was going to go with the equally unimaginative

'Sadie's.' Got any better ideas?" She tugged at the string wrapped around the darling cookie logo and the words How the Cookie Crumbles with the two O's made to look like cookies. "Yours is cute."

"Again, not mine. That was all Gayla Jacobson, like everything about Crumbles."

She looked up to study him, intrigued by his guile-lessness, and the sweetness that emanated from him like the aroma from the box in front of her. "Is that why you're reluctant?"

"Hundred percent." He leaned back and crossed his arms. "I was a CPA up in the 'Burgh—that's what locals call Pittsburgh."

"Of course they do," she said with a smile.

"Yeah, and I was fine. Up to my eyeballs in spread-sheets and tax forms, but it was fine. A living. Anyway, then my dad died."

"Oh." She let her shoulders sink when she thought of how close they'd come to losing her father less than a year ago. "I'm so sorry."

He nodded his thanks. "When that happened, my mom wanted to move to Florida and get in the sunshine and start a little business just for cookies. No wedding cakes, no pies, no cupcakes. Just cookies and brownies, her specialty. And she wanted to showcase her relentless love of all things from the fifties, a decade she pronounced the 'golden era of mankind.'"

She fluttered the twine. "Like string on bakery boxes."

"And pure ingredients, doo-wop music, muscle cars, and poodle skirts."

She snapped her fingers, remembering that she'd been in How the Cookie Crumbles a while ago. "Yes! There's a whole vibe in that store with the juke box and black and white movie star pictures," she said, remembering going in there recently with Raina. "I loved it. Very original and, whoa. I had a memorable brownie."

He nodded. "The Dreamboat. Named for my father, Martin, according to Gayla. She loved nicknames, which is how I somehow became Scout. I was born Martin, also, but apparently I refused to take my Cub Scout uniform off and I became Scout. Made it to Eagle Scout, for the record." He added a shy grin as he lifted the box lid for her. "Let me reintroduce you to...The Dreamboat."

She couldn't help smiling, and that grin just grew when she eyed the dessert with its glistening crust and perfectly cooked edges and a scent that promised heaven in the first bite. "Your mother's finest?"

"Um, actually, she passed away a little over a year ago, and it was either take over a thriving business or let my mother's dream die." He lifted his brows. "And that's the real reason I'm the reluctant baker."

"Oh, both of your parents are gone. I'm so sorry. And props for going from CPA to cookies."

He chuckled, a low, rumbly sound that came from his chest and sounded as sweet as his brownie looked. "Well, to be fair, I was born, raised, lived and breathed in a bakery. Only child of two small business owners. I learned the back office through my dad and that's where I got a lot of my accounting skills, but I was also in the kitchen with my mother a lot. Then I came down here to close up her shop after she passed and..."

"You never left?"

He threw his hands up like he didn't really have a choice in the matter. "It wasn't that hard of a decision. I was charmed by Amelia Island. The pace is slow, the people are nice, the sun is out every day. I couldn't go back to spreadsheets in the 'Burgh. So..."

"So here you are."

"Forty and living my best life," he said.

"So not that reluctant after all?"

He braced an elbow on the table, remarkably comfortable in his own skin as he looked directly at her with eyes that seemed to shift color every moment.

"I was really scared at first, too," he confessed. "Like, who was I kidding? A CPA who had no family, friends, or contacts in the business, baking cookies like my little old Jewish mother did? I knew that's what she wanted but..."

She heard the sadness in his voice. No doubt he still missed his mother.

"But I had to do it. I had to bake even if I felt...lost."

She sat up at the word, chills blossoming at the echo of her own thoughts. "What got you in that kitchen?"

He thought about that for a minute, a bit of a gleam in his eyes, maybe the hint of a tear that would prove he had a soft heart in his soft body. "Dough."

"Ah, money is always a powerful force."

"No... the kind you bake with. I happen to love it, and

I knew I could make the best darn cookies and brownies this town had ever eaten."

"I feel that way about chocolate," she admitted, as much to herself as her unexpected guest.

"Then you get it," he said. "My mother had handed me the opportunity to change my life and I took it. Never looked back."

She nodded, connecting with every word. She could make the best darn chocolate this town had ever eaten and Tristan had handed her the opportunity to change her life.

Scout inched closer. "You can do it, Sadie, if the rumors are true."

"Rumors?" She felt a little blood drain. Did everyone in town know she'd eloped and been dumped?

"They say you trained in Belgium under some of the best chocolatiers in the world."

Relief rolled over her. Of course her sisters would put a positive spin on her story. "I did work for some master craftsmen." Master liars, too.

"Then I'm right and you're going to knock this out of the park. And I say that as a man who'll probably lose a little revenue when you open these doors."

"Then why are you encouraging me, Scout?"

"A rising tide lifts all boats," he said, sliding the pink box closer to her. "I think a little competition would be good for me. Make me up my game, you know?"

She smiled at the idioms that rolled off his tongue, remembering how those expressions used to frustrate

Tristan when the English didn't translate to something that made sense.

But for Scout? They almost seemed like a love language, maybe an homage to the woman who'd named her bakery How the Cookie Crumbles.

She reached in and plucked out the top brownie. "I can't wait any longer."

"Music to my ears," he said with a nod. "*Bon appétit.*" He butchered the French but, like everything else about him, the bad accent was utterly endearing.

She inhaled first, letting her eyes close as her brain identified key ingredients. He'd used a quality American-made chocolate—maybe Ghirardelli or Guittard—perfectly browned butter, a scrape of vanilla bean, a sprinkle of coffee, a hint of cinnamon, cardamom, and... "Bourbon?" she guessed.

He just smiled.

The first bite melted on her tongue like sweet torture, then it hit her tastebuds and shocked every pleasure point in her brain. The mouthfeel was smooth with just a touch of pull, the flavor rich and deep and layered as it tapped salt, sweet, bitter, and even a hint of sour to round it out.

As she swallowed, her whole body simply wanted...more.

"Wow," she managed, dabbing at the corners of her mouth with her fingertip to get every crumb. "If that's reluctant, I'd hate to taste the overly-enthused cookie maker. I might cry."

He looked like she'd handed him a thousand dollars. "You like?"

"Very, very much." She took another bite, finishing the small brownie and completely forgetting to analyze the ingredients because it was so incredible.

"I think it could win," he said softly.

She looked up from the box where she was already eyeing another brownie. "Win...what?"

"The Fernandina Food Festival Best Bite contest," he said, sounding a little shocked she didn't know exactly what he was talking about.

"Oh, there's a festival?"

"At the end of the month. You could probably still get registered, if you know someone who could pull strings, but then we'd be competing for the grand prize in the dessert category."

"Which is?"

"Bragging rights, a sign in the window, and a feature article in *Amelia Life,* the magazine that is on the coffee tables in every hotel, motel, Airbnb, and inn in the county. That prize is money in the bank."

She drew back, eyes wide. "Really."

He regarded her for a moment, then shook his head with his chuckle again. "And I think I just added to my competition. I mean, if you can even register for it this late."

"I, um, I know people."

"Wingates, yes. You have a billion sisters."

"Just six."

"But I'm pretty sure one of them is on the committee organizing this." He pushed back and slowly stood, looking down at her. "Well, I better let you get into that kitchen."

"Thank you," she said, also standing. "For the brownies and the...motivation."

"Anytime."

"One of these days," she said, "I'll bring you truffles that I can only hope are half as good as your brownies." She tapped her chin, letting her tongue taste the delicious flavors still lingering. "Bourbon, right?"

He held up both hands. "If I told you, my mother would roll over in her grave and drop a family curse on me."

She laughed. "Hey, no one respects a secret ingredient like I do. Seriously, Scout, thank you." She extended her hand for a shake, looking forward to one more endearing smile from this man who was as pure and sweet as the treats he baked.

"No problem. Your place is..." He glanced around. "Charming. Like the owner."

"Ah, sweet."

"And the chocolate is, too, I'm sure," he added quickly. "There's your name: Charmed by Chocolate."

She gasped. "Did you just make that up?"

"This very moment."

"Can I use it?" she asked, pressing her hands together. "It's so clever!"

He laughed. "Yes, it's all yours."

"I'll pay you back in truffles."

"Or by not entering the contest and beating the daylights out of me."

She tipped her head, appreciating the humility, but not willing to make that promise. "We'll see if I can even get entered," she said instead.

When he left, she locked the door and stared at the open bakery box, wondering if an angel had just visited her.

The Best Bite of the Fernandina Food Festival, huh? Well, it wasn't *Bon Appétit* magazine, but in a feature article, she could reveal the secret ingredient and make sure the chocolate world knew it was hers, maybe getting a little vengeance in the process.

Suddenly ready to roast, grind, temper, and pour for the first time in forever, Sadie grabbed another Dreamboat for inspiration, and headed straight into the kitchen.

There, she spent the rest of the morning lost again... but this time, she was lost in the art of making chocolate.

While the cocoa nibs ground in the *melangeur*, she called the decal vendor and ordered the window lettering for the storefront...*Charmed by Chocolate.*

Chapter Six

Susannah

A blind woman could sense the change in Rex when he walked through the doors of Wingate Properties. He straightened ever so slightly and lifted his chin with pride and determination. Then he stepped onto the marble floor of the reception area with the air of a man whose grandfather built the bank building and whose last name remained on the door.

"Mr. Wingate!" Ellen, the receptionist, leaped to her feet and came around the reception desk in the lobby, all but bowing to the man everyone in the building loved and respected.

"Place looks great, Ellen," he said, greeting her with a warm handshake and half-hug while Susannah looked around. Her gaze stopped at the sight of their grandson, Blake, up on a ladder, taking down the garlands and lights that had made the lobby so festive.

"Hey, grands," he called, giving a wave and using the sweet nickname he'd taken to after the familial connection to Rex had been revealed.

"Be careful up there," Susannah said, coming closer.

Blake's father might be the result of a one-night stand Rex had as a very young man, and no real genetic connection to Susannah, but she loved him like all of her other grandchildren—many of whom were technically grandchildren from his first wife.

That didn't matter to her one bit. Family was family, and Wingates were the greatest family of all.

"I'm fine," Blake assured her. "But Sergeant Scrooge said Christmas has to come down now."

"That's Aunt Sergeant Scrooge to you," Raina called, leaning over a railing at the top of the wide staircase that led to her second-floor office. "And I didn't know you were both coming today. What a treat!"

Susannah walked toward the steps. "I have to stop by the inn to help Isaiah with some year-end stuff, so I thought I'd come with Dad and say hello. How are you feeling?"

"Well enough to get down those stairs but way too large to try and get back up again. Come see me?"

"I'll be up in a minute, Raina," Rex said. "Blake, were you able to finalize that bike store listing on Ash? I'd love to see you sell your first commercial property."

"Even better." Blake scrambled down the ladder. "I have the whole place cleaned out and ready for a potential buyer who wants to tour tomorrow. Want to go look at it? It's not a long walk."

"I'd love to," Rex said, putting his hand on Susannah's shoulder. "I'll be back in a few minutes."

She opened her mouth to say, "Be careful," or, "Don't walk too fast in the heat," and, "Maybe you could drive," but shut it—and all the warnings—again.

"I'll be with Raina," she said instead.

She headed up the stairs, pausing at the top to scrutinize Raina, taking in the soft shadows under eyes that were normally bright and clear, the choice of very comfy and casual jersey clothes, and, of course, her nine-months-pregnant belly.

But there was something different about her today, something...*sad?*

"Are you okay?" she asked, holding out her arms.

"Next-level tired from carrying my wide-load, and I should take my laptop into the bathroom I spend so much time in there." But her hug was warm and long. "I'm glad you're here."

"You're not busy?"

"Not terribly. I'm just preparing a few client files to hand over to Dad, if I can ever get him away from Blake."

Susannah threw a glance over her shoulder, catching sight of Rex and Blake walking out the door together.

"Sounds like my husband is back where he belongs," she said on a sigh, sliding an arm around Raina and walking to the door of her office.

"Morning, Mrs. Dubya," Raina's assistant called from a bank of file cabinets, her bright smile and high energy palpable. "Can I get you coffee or water?"

"Hello, Danielle. I'm fine, thank you. Did you have a good holiday?"

They made small-talk about Rex returning to the

business, then Susannah continued into Raina's office, where she found her daughter already sprawled in one of the comfortable swivel chairs around the small conference table, currently covered in paperwork.

"Do you not want Dad to come into work, Suze?" she asked softly. "Because you sound a little down about it every day we get closer."

"Of course I want him to." Susannah took one of the other seats and let her gaze move around the space that had slowly been transformed from the deeply masculine owner's office to one that reflected Raina's younger and more feminine personality "As long as he doesn't drag that awful leather sofa back in here."

Raina smiled. "He said he likes the way it looks in here and, honestly, we both know this is my office and will remain my office. Once I figure out this whole motherhood thing, I expect the only additional furniture in here will be cribs and playpens."

"Are you ready for all that?" Susannah asked.

"Kids in the office? Yes. Figuring out the motherhood thing? I guess we'll know by how many calls for help you get in the middle of the night."

"I can stay with you..." Her voice faded out. "Well, one of your sisters can. I don't want to leave Rex overnight."

"I understand, although I think he'd be fine." She leaned in. "And maybe not feel so smothered."

Susannah rolled her eyes, but let the topic go to focus on Raina. "How do you feel, really?"

"Like I'm having two babies in less than three weeks."

She put a hand on her belly, which she joked about being huge, but considering she was carrying twins and officially in her ninth month? She wasn't that big. "The Things are restless."

"Hang on a sec." Suze reached into her purse when her cell buzzed. "That could be Rex."

"He just walked out the door."

"Just want to be sure he didn't tumble down Wingate Way."

"Susannah!" Raina chided with a laugh.

"It's Isaiah." She read her phone. "He wants to see us both. Rex and me. Asked if that was possible."

"Oh, goodness," Raina said. "I wonder if something's wrong at the inn."

"It must be serious if he wants Rex there." Susannah felt a frown pull, already concerned.

"It's probably something that has to do with the building," Raina said with the authority of the person who managed all of the Wingate-owned properties. "My guess? It's that giant live oak in the back. It's caused leaks in the attic and one of the gutters had to be replaced. We should cut that tree down."

"Maybe," Susannah said, barely hearing Raina as she reread the text. "But I think he's going to quit the job as manager of the inn."

"Quit? He loves that job."

"True, but..." Susannah stifled a moan. "He said a few things at our family gatherings over the holidays about change and God's timing and...I don't know. He seemed tense, too."

"It could be anything."

"No," Susannah said. "I mean, he came here to give Grace a ring that belonged to her late husband and now he's running an inn. He might want to do something else with his life."

"Whatever it is, it won't be far from Grace and Nikki Lou. But businesses have turnover, Suze. That's life. Will it be that much of a problem for you?"

Oh, it could be, she thought.

"Rex will want me to jump back in and run the place," she said. "He'll say it's a miracle, since we were just talking about how I should sink my teeth into a new project. He'll pronounce this perfect and I'll be running that dang inn again."

"You can always find someone to manage guests on-site like you did when Doreen was alive."

She blew out a breath. "When Doreen was alive, Dad was healthy and I was...in a different state of mind. I love the inn, don't get me wrong, but Isaiah has spoiled me. Without a full-time manager who can fix roof problems at a moment's notice? It's a lot of work. But your father will think it's a great solution."

"A solution for *him*," Raina said with an understanding nod. "I won't let him do that, Suze. I promise I'll be in your corner and I get tons of resumes here. I'll find you a good innkeeper and manager."

"Thank you," Susannah replied, her brain still on what Isaiah's leaving would mean to her. "I loved remodeling that inn, and I wouldn't mind doing a little of that again. It could use some work. But on-site? Taking care of guests day-to-day? No, thank you."

"Well, tell Dad that when he suggests you work there and if he doesn't agree? I have your back."

Susannah reached over and put a hand on Raina's arm. "You're an angel, Rain. But when you have two crying babies who both want to be fed at the same time? You won't have the time, energy, or interest to solve everyone else's problems."

"Isaiah might have a different issue altogether," Raina said. "Starting with the fact that Wingate House isn't exactly the most profitable of our family-owned businesses."

"I knew reservations were down a bit. Is it a problem?"

Raina shrugged. "It could be. This town is inn-heavy, you know? It seems another B&B is opening up every month, and competition is fierce."

"Not to mention your friend Chase opening up Ocean Song this month."

"My friend?" It was easy to see the flush on Raina's cheeks in the sunshine. "He's merely a guy I bought a house from who then rented a room. He's been gone since his grandmother passed away."

"In Italy, right?" Susannah asked, eyeing Raina for more clues about the man she always dismissed far too quickly when his name came up.

"I don't know, but we put all that work into the third-floor suite at Wingate House," Raina continued. "Grace and Nikki are moving back into their apartment above the bookstore this week, so we can start reserving that suite, which might help."

Dismissed and changed the subject—every time.

"And maybe there's something else we could do to generate revenue there." Raina picked up one of the papers on her desk as if the answer might be right there...and the subject of Chase Madison would be permanently dropped.

But Susannah wasn't going to be put off that easily.

"Do you ever hear from him?" she asked.

Raina looked up and gave her a blank stare, but Susannah had been her mother for too many years, and she could see the tinge of fear in her blue eyes.

"Oh, boy." Raina suddenly pushed the chair back. "Time for my fourth trip to the bathroom this hour."

With that, she was up and out and Chase was off the table.

Which only confirmed Susannah's suspicions that Raina missed the man who had been renting a room from her and putting a flush on her cheeks since before the holidays.

But she heard Rex's voice downstairs and knew she had more pressing problems—such as convincing her husband she was not the right person to run their inn.

"HARD TO BELIEVE a place that looks like this isn't wildly profitable," Susannah said as she and Rex walked toward what had to be one of the most beautiful Victorian buildings in a town rich with historical homes.

"It has been hitting a few bumps," Rex agreed, proving that he was still on top of the nuances of his business. "And it could use a little bit of work."

Susannah noticed, not for the first time, that some of the pavers were chipped and the patio might benefit from a coat of fresh paint on the white trim. "Raina said there's an issue with the live oak."

"There's always an issue with that tree," Rex said. "Roots under the house, branches in the attic. Once, when I was a kid, my dad tried to cut it down, but there was a storm that night and three windows mysteriously broke, so he decided Grannie Coraline was mad and let it go."

Susannah frowned at him. "He thought...Coraline's ghost broke the windows?"

He laughed. "Not seriously, but he erred on the side of caution with that ghost. And everyone called it Coraline's Tree."

"Why is that?" she asked, digging through her deep knowledge of Wingate House and the family history, but coming up with nothing.

"Depends on which story you listen to," Rex said. "One theory is she planted it herself when this house was built, which makes sense. Another is that my grandfather, Reginald the First, put her ashes around the bottom of it."

"Not true," Susannah said. "I've seen her grave in St. Peter's Cemetery along with all the other Wingates."

He shrugged. "Family folklore. Oh, and my father used the tree to sneak out of the house in the middle of the night during Prohibition to smuggle moonshine. Once, she caught him and made him sit in the tree for twenty-four hours as punishment."

Laughing, she nestled closer to him. "Well, we have present-day problems to deal with now. I'm worried about why Isaiah wants to see us both."

"Maybe he has an idea to increase reservations," Rex said as he opened the iron gate with the iconic W wrought in the metal. "I'm always optimistic."

"And I love that about you," she said.

They weren't halfway up the walk when the front door opened and Isaiah came out to the wrap-around porch and greeted them with a huge smile. He still wore an apron from making and serving breakfast, and looked equal parts happy and nervous to see them.

"Thank you for coming here," he said, jogging down the two steps and reaching out his hands to invite them closer. "I would have gone to the beach house, but I...I wanted to be absolutely certain we'd be alone."

Oh, dear. He was most definitely quitting.

Susannah hugged him first, always marveling at the size and strength of a man who somehow carried himself with shocking humility.

"Hello, Isaiah. Is everything okay?" She simply couldn't wait any longer.

"We'll know soon enough," he said quietly, the answer doing nothing to calm her nerves.

He and Rex shook hands and man-hugged, talking pleasantries as they all walked up the stairs and into the inn.

"Oh, goodness, you made poached peaches for breakfast," Susannah exclaimed, taking a whiff of Isaiah's glorious cooking.

"Over waffles," he said. "The guests seemed to like them."

Rex glanced around and she saw Isaiah straighten with pride. He kept the inn spotless, made food that people raved about, and had ended the constant turnover with the housekeeping staff.

On top of that, guests loved his understated warmth, the fact that he could and would fix anything that didn't work properly, and all of the vendors had nothing but rave reviews of him.

None of that, apparently, was getting more reservations on the books.

"Are there many guests checked in now?" Rex asked as Isaiah led them into the large living area off the entryway.

"We had a decent bump over the holidays," Isaiah said, "but we only have four rooms booked now and not a ton of reservations for the rest of the month and in February. Maybe it'll pick up in the summer."

Rex nodded and sat down on the sofa, reaching for Susannah to sit next to him.

Isaiah stayed standing, tension drawing his dark brows together. "Oh, can I get you coffee, tea? Some poached peaches?" he offered.

"Nothing at all," Susannah assured him.

"I'm fine," Rex said. "Please sit, Isaiah."

"Of course." He settled on the edge of a wing-backed chair, looking huge in the delicate furniture, almost wringing his hands with nerves.

"What's on your mind, son?" Rex asked, no doubt picking up on Isaiah's tension.

Isaiah looked from one to the other, his midnight eyes intense and maybe a little nervous. Here comes the resignation, Susannah thought.

She'd never known this man to be anything but calm, no doubt due to the fact that he was deeply grounded in faith and made every decision with great consideration and prayer.

Something told her this moment had come after an abundance of both. Of course, he wouldn't quit without thinking long and hard about the people it would affect.

"Isaiah?" she prompted. "You know you're practically family. Please."

"Family, yes. And you called me 'son.'" He beamed from one to the other. "Then I'll just say it but the fact is, I have good news and bad news and I'm trying to decide which to tell you first."

"Good news," Susannah exclaimed the very moment Rex said, "Bad news."

They laughed, although Isaiah shifted on his seat and closed his eyes for a millisecond, his hands clasped. Was he praying? It wouldn't be out of character, that was for sure.

"Then let me start with a statement of fact," he said.

"When I came to Amelia Island, it was with the sole purpose of returning the wedding ring that your son-in-law, Nick, left with me the morning he was killed in Afghanistan."

They both nodded, and without thinking, held hands.

"Have I thanked you enough for that?" Rex asked.

"You have, sir."

Rex shook his head, as if he didn't believe he had. "Your gesture was not only thoughtful and heroic, but you really helped Grace heal. Something about having Nick's ring back seems to have set her on such a good course, even after the fire at the bookstore."

Susannah searched the face of the man who sat across from her. Isaiah Kincaid was a forty-year-old, bald, baritone-voiced gospel singer who might have been the last person she'd imagine with shy, unassuming Grace.

But he could not be more perfect for her. He loved like he cooked Southern soul food—with his whole heart and a bone-deep desire to please the God he so openly loved and worshipped.

"I think it was more than the ring that helped Grace," Susannah said softly. "It was *you*, my friend. You've been a rock for her and little Nikki Lou."

His eyes glinted at the mention of Grace's little girl. "That child is special and I sure don't mean because of being on the spectrum. There is such goodness in her, exactly like her mother. And with the new school, we've got so much more understanding of her situation."

We? Susannah's smile widened. "You certainly do.

And you've been a godsend during the rebuilding of the bookstore, Isaiah."

"I'm honored to hear you say that, ma'am." He paused for a moment, then leaned in. "I know God *did* send me, because I've never been more sure of anything than I am of how much I love your daughter."

Susannah sucked in a sharp breath. Not because the admission surprised her—Isaiah showed his love every day. But it was how genuine he was that took her breath away.

Was *that* where this was going? Despite the sunshine pouring through the bay window, chills rose over her body, and she saw the same goosebumps on Rex's arm.

"And that's why I'm sitting here," Isaiah continued. "I know it might be old-fashioned, but that's who I am. I'd like to humbly ask you for Grace's hand in marriage."

For a moment, none of them spoke. Isaiah's dark eyes darted from one to the other as he waited for their response, but Susannah and Rex took a few seconds to look at each other and communicate their joy silently.

That's why he was nervous, Susannah thought with a jolt of joy *and* relief.

"Young man," Rex said, leaning in. "You have our blessing and our love. We could not be more pleased."

"Yes!" Susannah added, clapping with enthusiasm.

Isaiah dropped his head back, raised both hands and pointed to the sky. "Thank you, Lord!"

"Surely you knew we would approve," Rex said with a chuckle.

"A man never knows," he said. "I came to give her a

ring that belonged to her husband, but God's plan was so much bigger than that. It always is."

"Oh." Susannah pressed her clasped hands to her chest. "You are simply a gem, Isaiah."

"Well, hold that thought, because you remember I said good news and bad news."

Susannah winced; she'd forgotten that part.

"Tell me the bad news," Rex said. "And if you think you're taking my daughter away from—"

He held up a hand. "No, no. She's not leaving Amelia Island, neither of us are."

"Oh, thank goodness," Susannah whispered.

"But I do want to make a change."

"What do you need?" Rex asked.

"For you to understand that no one could be more grateful about the role you gave me here at Wingate House and, of course, the privilege of living in the guest house in the back." He directed his words to Susannah, who could feel the metallic taste of disappointment in her mouth as she realized where this was going. "I've loved every minute at the inn."

"Oh, no," she murmured. "You *are* leaving."

"I'd like to help Grace run the bookstore full-time," he said. "She'll be moving back into the apartment upstairs and, once we are married in the eyes of God and the law—which I hope will be very soon—I'd like to live there with her. That means I couldn't be on-site at the inn, but the two of us have big plans for the store. She can have more time to work with Nikki Lou, since the program requires a lot of homeschooling, and, well, maybe we can have a child of our own together."

With each word, Susannah felt her eyes fill and when Isaiah saw that, he reached out his hand and his face melted in sympathy.

"I don't want to leave you high and dry at the inn, Miz Wingate."

"No, no. Isaiah. That's not why..." She dabbed under her eyes and gave a soft laugh of apology for the tears. "You are truly such a gift, such a blessing to her. Grace was broken, grieving, dealing with a challenging child and you..." Her voice cracked and Rex put his arm around her.

"What she's trying to say is we're not upset about the inn, but overjoyed that you found each other," Rex said. "We will figure out the inn."

Isaiah dipped his head. "Thank you," he whispered. "But I know it will be difficult for you to replace me at the inn, so I promise I won't leave you until you've got someone in place."

"Well, I know what you would say, Isaiah," she said with a teary smile. "When God closes a door, he opens a window, right?"

He chuckled. "Something like that, ma'am. But you need to know that I will love and honor and protect your daughter and Nikki Lou. Grace is truly the woman I've waited for my entire life."

They stood and hugged, and hugged some more.

"When will you pop the question, son?" Rex asked.

"Very soon. I'm not sure I can wait too long, but I want it to be perfect, and I want to include Nikki Lou, too, and ideally, all of the Wingates. After all, I'm asking to be husband and father to the world's greatest ladies and part of the best family I've ever known."

Susannah moaned and hugged him again, drying a fresh wave of tears. "And where do you want to get married?" she asked. "I can't wait to help plan another wedding."

"I think we'll keep it very small and intimate," he said. "Gracie and I have talked about getting married right here at the inn, with a ceremony on the lawn and a small party in these downstairs rooms. Very soon, I hope. Like..." He made a face. "Valentine's Day? Since we're not booked completely that week?"

"That would be lovely!" she exclaimed. "And doesn't leave us much time."

After they ended the conversation and walked back into the sunshine, she and Rex held hands and looked into each other's eyes.

"I couldn't be happier," he said.

"Of course! He's a rock-solid man who will love Grace and Nikki forever," Susannah agreed. "And, goodness, they both deserve that."

"And talk about two birds with one stone," he said excitedly. "Now we've got a solution for what you can do with your time. We'll hire someone on-site and you can manage the inn again."

She felt her whole body slump with disappointment. "I knew you'd say that."

He slowed his step, searching her face. "I thought you'd be thrilled."

"I'm not," she admitted. "But I want to make you happy."

"Suze." He slid his hands around her shoulders and drew her closer. "You're the one who needs to be happy."

Her heart melted. "And I don't want to breathe down your neck or baby you or whatever you think I'm doing."

"Well, you told Isaiah yourself—when God closes a door, He always opens a window. All you have to do is find it, Suze."

As they reached the gate, she turned and took a long look at the three-story inn, staring at the many gables, the blue clapboard and white trim, and the precious swing under a huge elm tree overlooking the river.

She imagined Grace as a bride and little Nikki Lou as a flower girl, with the family gathered round, and the inside decorated with—

"Oh, my goodness!" She gasped softly as an idea—a brilliant, perfectly formed, completely genius idea—appeared in her head.

"What is it?" Rex asked, following her gaze. "Does that elm have to come down, too?"

"No, no, but I have an idea, Rex."

"What is it?"

"I think...a window just opened itself," she whispered.

"Coraline's ghost?" Rex joked.

"No. God opened this one, and we're going to walk right through it."

As she shared her thoughts, she took one more look at the inn, and decided she'd solved all her problems and figured out a way to make Wingate House profitable again.

Now, she needed help from her girls.

Chapter Seven

Raina

T he Riverfront Café was closed when Raina arrived at five o'clock that evening, so she tapped on the glass to get her niece's attention.

"Oh! Raina's here!" Kenzie called out as she rushed to the front of the restaurant and unlocked the door. "You're first for Wingate Women Night." She gave a sassy toss of her long, mahogany-toned hair. "I'm one of those now."

"You've always been one of us, but..." Raina eyed her. "I know your mom's custody arrangements changed, but are you changing your last name?"

"Oh, how I wish. No, I'm still Mackenzie Hathaway, but in my heart, I'm a Wingate. Plus, Grace isn't coming, so I'll pretend to be the seventh sister."

"She's not?" Raina asked as she walked into the café, which was dimly lit as evening fell, but still soaked in the scent of coffee, baked goods, buttery sandwiches, and.... Raina stopped mid-step, forgetting Grace. Forgetting everything but what she could smell.

"Please tell me your mother had her turkey and black

bean chili as the special today. Please. And do not mock the note of desperation in my voice."

Kenzie cracked up. "She set aside a big bowl for you and Thing One and Thing Two." Kenzie reached out a hand and tapped Raina's belly. "You know I'm going to call my cousins that long after they're born."

Raina laughed and put an arm around Kenzie, who seemed to get more beautiful every day. "You're blossoming, Kenz. How are you fitting in at school?"

She lifted a shoulder. "I know we jumped in mid-year, and I'm supposed to be all moody and sullen because I left my friends, but..."

"You don't know how to be moody and sullen," Raina mused.

"I just love living here and, honestly, it's high school whether I'm in Boston or Amelia Island. It's warmer here and the kids are nice. I keep in touch with my friends up north and I'm making new ones here."

"Please teach your sensibilities to my children, Kenzie. What about Finn?"

Kenzie grimaced. "My little brother might be having a tougher time," she said. "Middle school is the actual seventh circle of hell. He and Justin are having male bonding time with Grandpa Rex tonight, so here I am, filling in for the missing Wingate."

"Oh, yeah. Why isn't Grace coming?" Raina asked as she followed Kenzie toward the kitchen and the aroma of chili.

"She's been banished," Tori announced as she met Raina halfway with a steaming bowl.

"For being too quiet, sweet, and perfect?" Raina asked, reaching for the chili with greedy hands.

"I don't know why, but Suze sent me a private text and told me that she wanted to talk to us about something without Grace here, and that's why I sent the invite personally and not on our 7 *Sis* group chat."

"Huh." Raina walked to the long table in the back where they frequently gathered as a family in off hours, taking the closest chair. "She was worried Isaiah was going to quit this morning. I hope nothing's wrong." She inhaled and moaned. "But nothing's wrong with this. God bless you, Victoria Wingate."

Raina ate, chatted with her sister and niece, and then, one by one, the others arrived. Madeline first, on the dot at five-thirty, of course, followed by Rose and Chloe, who showed up together.

Sadie was last, blowing in with that old light back in her eyes and a box of chocolates in hand.

"You look happy," Raina and Rose said in twin-like unison.

Shaking the curls that tumbled over her shoulders, Sadie sat across from Raina and put the chocolates in the middle of the table.

"I will be," she said, "if I get what I want tonight. And I come bearing a bribe."

Rose pushed back her sleeves like she wanted to dive into the sweet treats. "Consider me bribed. I've been getting whiffs of something incredible all day from your shop, Sadie."

As she reached for the box, Sadie held out her hand.

"Don't touch it unless you're on the Fernandina Food Festival committee," Sadie said.

"Not me, but—"

"I am," Chloe, the youngest of the Wingates, chimed in. "Roped into it by Susannah Wingate herself, who didn't want to join a single committee this year and needed me to fill her slot. What do you need?"

"To enter and be eligible to win the Best Bite contest and nab that feature in *Amelia Life* magazine." She grinned. "It's good PR and a nice stab in the back to He Who Shall Not Be Named."

"Woohoo!" Chloe said, fisting the air. "She's back!"

As they cheered the return of Sadie's good mood, she told them all about the chocolate she'd made that day, and then allowed them to sample it but Raina wasn't going to give up one bite of the chili for anything.

"So, Chloe, tell me you can pull the right strings," Sadie said.

"I can try," she said when she finished a truffle with another moan of pleasure. "The committee head is Kitty Worthington—"

"Meow," Tori cooed, making them laugh.

"And her husband, George, is the emcee," Rose added.

"All to say, it won't be easy," Chloe finally finished. "Especially since you're not even officially open yet."

"I can open this week, I think," Sadie said. "What's the cut-off?"

"A month ago," Tori told her. "And it's no small commitment. You have to put a tasting booth in front of the shop and give away almost as much as you sell, meet with judges, and reveal recipes. And, of course, you must bow deeply and with great reverence to the great and powerful Kitty."

While everyone laughed, Raina picked up her nearly empty bowl and looked at Tori. "Please tell me you're entering this."

"I'm going to have a tasting booth, but the competition in this contest is fierce," Tori said. "The savory section is always dominated by the high-end restaurants on Amelia Island, including the Ritz, which always makes a showing. But this chocolate?" She held up the half-bite in her hand. "Could definitely be in the running."

"Except How the Cookie Crumbles has won every year since that store opened," Madeline told them. "Even after the original owner died and her son took over."

"Oh, Scout!" Sadie exclaimed. "He's the person who told me about the contest."

"He's such a nice man," Rose crooned. "Not a disingenuous bone in his body."

"He really is," Madeline agreed. "His mother was such a character, too. It was sad when she died."

"I wonder why he's never married," Tori mused.

"Especially because he can make a brownie that could bring a woman to her knees," Sadie joked.

"Ah, The Dreamboat," Raina said on a laugh. "Of course, I'm intimately familiar with it."

"And he named my store!" Sadie added. "Are you ready?" Her eyes danced as she held out both hands, waiting a dramatic beat before announcing, "It shall be called Charmed by Chocolate!"

"Oh, I love it!" Rose exclaimed along with the others.

"And it needs to be part of the food festival," Sadie added, grabbing Chloe's arm. "Please make that happen, little sister."

Chloe waved her phone. "I just texted Kitty to ask if we can squeeze you onto the participating vendor list. We'll see what she says."

At the tap on the front door, Tori stood. "That's Suze. Let's find out why we're here and why Grace isn't."

A few seconds later, Susannah cruised in looking like she'd taken the same happy pill that Sadie had as she greeted them with hugs and kisses.

What is in the Amelia Island water these days, Raina wondered. Was she the only one who felt tired, worried, and stressed? Well, she *was* the only one almost nine months pregnant with twins...and single.

"All right, I have news," Susannah announced as she took a seat, brushing back some of her spunky blond hair, her blue eyes sparkling. "News we have to keep secret, but I doubt it will be for very long." She waited a beat for drama, then leaned in. "Isaiah has asked for our blessing to propose to Grace!"

Their cheer was probably loud enough to be heard on the wharf outside the restaurant as the sisters hooted in delight.

"This is so amazing!" Kenzie clapped. "I'm so happy for Aunt Grace!"

"No one deserves it more," Rose agreed, already misty-eyed.

They peppered Susannah with questions, who shared the details of how Isaiah asked for Grace's hand, bringing a few tears and much laughter.

"After all she's been through," Tori sighed. "Losing Nick and finding out Nikki Lou has autism."

"And the fire," Raina reminded them.

"And now she's found love with such a beautiful, kind man." Rose practically swooned.

"So we're planning a surprise engagement party?" Madeline asked. "Is that why we're here?"

Their mother exhaled and looked around again. "We can, but there's more. Isaiah wants to quit his job at the inn and work full-time with Grace at The Next Chapter."

The reaction rolled around the table, but Raina reached over to take Susannah's hand, knowing that was exactly what she'd expected. "And Dad thinks you're going to step in?" she guessed. "Do you want us all to talk him out of that?"

"You don't have to," she said. "I've talked him out of it with a better idea."

"Which is?"

"Something I need all of your help to accomplish. And I would have included Grace, but I simply can't spoil the surprise when Isaiah proposes."

They all quieted and gave her their undivided attention.

"Remember how you told me you had such a hard

time finding a venue when you planned our anniversary event?" Susannah asked. "Well, there's a plethora of inns and B&Bs on this island, but none of them are set up *exclusively* for weddings. I was thinking that, with very little effort, we could transform Wingate House into a stunning and unique small wedding venue."

"Oh, I like that," Raina said, easily imagining that kind of renovation.

"It doesn't have to be a formal space," she continued. "But we could set up buffets in the dining area, use the living room for socializing, and the library for dancing. Small weddings, with the ceremony outside by the river."

"It's brilliant," Rose replied without hesitation.

"And the guest rooms can all be reserved for the wedding party and close family," Raina said, already seeing the income potential without having to compete with other inns.

"Yes!" Susannah agreed. "We could use the third floor as the bridal suite and dressing room, and the kitchen is already set up for catering. And I thought we could turn the back cottage into a groom's dressing room when Isaiah moves out."

"This is *visionary*, Mom," Sadie exclaimed.

"I agree," Raina said. "And speaking as the official representative of Wingate Properties, it's a genius way to increase profits. But Suze..." She reached over to put a hand on her arm. "Are you up for a challenge like that?"

She tipped her head. "Not alone. But if I had, say... partners in catering—"

"Done!" Tori called out, sharing a high-five with Kenzie. "I love me some catering jobs."

"And a florist."

Rose just laughed. "I'd cry if you considered anyone else."

"And maybe a discount for brides who shopped with Madeline Wingate," Suze said.

"I'll do an exclusive Wingate House line." Madeline snapped her fingers, clearly loving the idea. "Only for our brides and their wedding parties. We'll name the styles after the rooms in the house, which are all Wingate women."

"Oh!" Susannah clapped. "I love that, Madeline! That leaves the cake."

"I can do weddings," Sadie offered quickly. "A truffle tower, a chocolate fountain, and personalized candies, which are always a hit with the brides."

"Unless you need a dog in the wedding, I'm not sure I can do more than cheer from the sidelines," Chloe said.

"I was hoping that with your extensive planning of your own wedding—"

"That never happened," Chloe said, rolling her eyes.

"But you learned so much and maybe, just maybe, you could be an on-site planning consultant on an as-needed basis."

Her eyes lit. "Mom, I would love that so much."

"But what about Grace?" Sadie asked.

"Other than being our first bride?" Susannah smiled. "I thought Isaiah could officiate if a couple is looking for that, and Grace could offer some of those fabulous favors and guest books. She might want a bigger role, but with Nikki's homeschooling and her own wedding, I'd leave involvement up to her. But overall, conceptually...do you guys like the idea?"

The reaction left no doubt about their feelings.

Raina leaned forward. "I feel a little like Dorothy in *The Wizard of Oz*, Suze. Nothing in that bag of tricks for me."

"That's how we want it, mother-to-be," Susannah said. "But I will need your help approving some changes. We'll need some new furnishings to reorient the first floor for receptions, and the property needs some work. New pavers, some improvements on the patio, and I think I do want to look into taking down the old live oak in the back. It's blocking the water view from some of the second-floor bedrooms."

"Whoa, careful," Madeline warned, waving a finger. "Coraline won't like that. Family folklore says her ashes are buried there."

"I've heard," Susannah said. "But Coraline is buried with the rest of the Wingates at St. Peter's. And there's no ghost in that inn, trust me."

Tori lifted a brow and leaned into Kenzie. "But we don't know for sure..." she said in an ominous tone, making Kenzie laugh.

"When can you start, Suze?" Raina asked. "I have a few weeks left to help you get the property stuff done."

"A few weeks?" Susannah pointed at her with a knowing brow. "If you're lucky."

Raina grunted and reached for her phone, already

sensing that this whole fun project would be off-limits to her because of the babies. And she wanted to help.

"Let me text Dani and ask her to look into a tree removal company," she said, squinting at her screen.

"Need some readers there, Mama?" Tori teased, plucking her glasses off her head and handing them to Raina.

"Shut it," Raina joked. "I just don't want to fat-finger a word."

"Aunt Raina, you can dictate your text," Kenzie said. "Just press that little microphone down at the bottom and speak into it."

"Really?" She put the phone down. "I'll do it later. What about the guests we already have booked, Suze? And do we stop taking reservations? I'm sure we have some into the spring or summer. Not a lot, but a few."

"I've done exchanges with other B&Bs in town before," she said. "I can move guests and offer to cover the costs for their inconvenience. And I will, because I want Grace's to be the first wedding there next month, and I want it to be perfect."

"And it shall be!" Tori raised a bottle of water, but Chloe interrupted the toast, holding up her phone.

"Got an answer from Kitty Worthington about the food festival."

"Whatever she wants," Sadie said.

Chloe tipped her head. "In keeping with our *Wizard of Oz* theme, she basically wants the witch's broomstick, better known as the following: you must be open two full weeks, which means by this weekend, and you must be 'sponsored' by another food retailer in your same space, not a family member."

"Meaning not me," Tori said.

Raina rolled her eyes. "That woman is drunk with power."

"And," Chloe added, "she wants to meet with you personally to discuss your small business strategy."

"Which means she wants to recruit you to volunteer for things," Madeline said. "Lots of things."

Sadie threw her hands up. "Fine. I'll meet, I'll open, and I'll recruit, and I'll volunteer. I'm not afraid of Catwoman."

A few of them shared knowing looks and raised brows, and Tori meowed again.

"She's the head of the Local Business Organization," Susannah explained. "She does wield a lot of power and can make or break a retailer when it comes to getting included in the big events and promos."

"Take Rose with you when you go to see her," Tori suggested. "Kitty basically eats out of Rose's hand."

Rose laughed and shook her head. "I don't know about that, but I seem to be able to handle old Helmet Head, which is what Zach calls her."

"So accurate," Tori murmured, patting a fake hairdo to mock Kitty's—one that really did resemble a steel helmet.

"Thanks, but I can handle her," Sadie assured them. "She can't be much scarier than Gregoire Saint Pierre."

Chloe flicked her brows, obviously knowing how formidable Kitty Worthington could be.

"Can you really open that soon?" Raina asked. Sadie had done very little to the location since she found out that Tristan wasn't coming, but she didn't want to press that point.

"I can do anything," Sadie proclaimed. "In fact, I can have a grand opening this weekend. On Saturday! Can you all be there?"

The response was a resounding yes, except for Raina, who nodded. She could be in the hospital having babies on Saturday. Or sleeping. Probably the latter.

"Then we'll fill the place with Wingates, bring your friends, and Chloe, get the festival committee there. I will...charm them with chocolate." She stood, raising the already sky-high energy in the room.

High for everyone but Raina, who rubbed her belly and starting dreaming about bed.

"You okay?" Rose whispered, leaning close.

"Yeah, just, you know. Exhausted. Terrified. So, so pregnant."

Rose laughed and put her arm around Raina's shoulders. "You're going to be the most amazing mother."

She hoped so, but right now? She didn't feel amazing at all.

THE LETHARGY still plagued Raina when she finally got home after spending a little extra time with Tori and Kenzie—who taught her how to dictate texts *and* how to call 911 without typing. They agreed she should know those things in case she went into labor all alone in the middle of the night.

The thought made her sad and scared, deepening a sense of foreboding that pressed when she walked into the darkened beach house. She flashed back to the times she'd come home and found her "roommate" cooking and listening to opera and being funny and smart and so darn attractive.

Yes, she missed Chase. She missed having someone to come home to and cook with and laugh with and...just be with.

"As if anyone would want to be with me now," she muttered as she kicked off her flats—heels were a thing of the past—and headed into the kitchen for a bottle of Pellegrino. Grabbing her handbag, she hauled herself up the stairs to her room.

But before walking into her favorite sanctuary, she turned left down the hall, to the larger of two other bedrooms. She tapped the wall switch and smiled as soft light poured over the nursery, which, unlike Raina, was completely ready for two new occupants.

Sadie had insisted on buying a world-class changing table, but really, they all had a hand in it, culminating in the baby shower Susannah had held for her over the holidays.

Side-by-side cribs were draped in yellow and teal comforters that Madeline had made, embroidered with tiny script that read "Thing One" and "Thing Two" as a nod to what Raina had called her babies from the beginning.

Rose had pressed dried flowers into a frame in the shape of BFF with *Twins...Born Forever Friends* hand-painted on the canvas. Stuffed puppies from Chloe lined the shelves, next to a gorgeous collection of baby books from Grace and Nikki.

Rex had given her a family heirloom rocking chair, and Susannah had it refinished, complete with the iconic Wingate W on the backrest.

Tori and Kenzie had chosen an electronic picture frame that would display baby and family photos, like an endless, growing, constantly changing photo album.

All of the gifts, all of the love, all of the support she could dream of having was evident in this room, where two little Wingates would live and grow and know the joys of a great family.

"Then why am I so lonely?" she whispered to the empty room.

No answer, but her phone vibrated from her bag. Fishing it out, Raina left the room and headed to hers, smiling at the text from Kenzie checking on her. They knew she was glum and hormonal, and she imagined the mother-daughter duo talking about her well-being all the way home. Then, dear Kenzie texting her.

She replied by hitting the microphone. "I'm fine sweet little niece of mine—period. Polish up your babysitting skills—period. I'm sure I'll need them—period. I love you—exclamation point."

She sent the text with a smile, proud of getting the punctuation right, and told herself to hold onto the love of her family. It had to be enough for—

The phone vibrated in her hand again, this time with a name that took her breath away.

Chase Madison: *How are you?*

For a long, long moment, she stood next to her bed and stared at the words. Her head felt a little light, like she was underwater.

She hadn't heard from him in weeks. He'd sent a text from Italy on Christmas Day, a brief hello, and said he'd taken care of his nonna's ashes and loved the Sicilian weather. That was it. Asked how she felt, and said Merry Christmas.

She tossed the phone on the bed with a huff. "How am I? That's a great question, Chase. I'm...*pregnant*." She looked down at her distended belly, blocking any view of her feet. "I'm the size of a small country. I'm carrying two humans who never, ever, ever stay still, and this is the easy part. I'm lonely. I'm sad. I'm scared."

And she was crying, she thought as she ripped off her top and tossed it into the hamper.

"Also, I'm wondering...is everything fun over? Will I ever have a great time again in my life or will I just be a mom who can't do anything because I'll have not one but two children who need my constant attention? No partner. No husband. Yes, yes, an awesome family, but..."

She choked on a sob, then went into the bathroom to wash her face and brush back her hair. She looked longingly at the tub but getting in and out of it was too challenging and...not safe. She took a shower instead.

"I can't even take a bath!" she whined as she returned to the bedroom in her comfy bathrobe. She might just sleep in it, she thought. It was the only thing she could bear to wear.

"I know, I know, it will all be okay, but..." She slid a look at the phone, thinking of his text.

How are you?

Dropping back on the bed, she closed her eyes.

"How am I, you ask?" she whispered into the dimly lit room. "Well, for starters, I miss you, okay? I feel stupid for saying it, I won't admit it to anyone, but I think about you all the time and, let's be honest, the ink is barely dry on my divorce decree and I got some serious baggage in my belly. But I wish I had kissed you that night. Because I may never know what that would feel like, but I wish I had..."

Turning her head, she looked at the cell, realizing the light on the screen was on. Was he texting again?

She grabbed the phone, but fumbled, and somehow managed to snag it before it hit the floor and—

"Oh my God. Oh my God!" She stared in horror as her words suddenly appeared in a massive blue box full of text. She must have somehow dictated her whole endless sob story! And, no! Did it...*send*?

"No!" she screamed as she realized the blue box meant...*yes*. It had flown through cyberspace and Chase had that text right now.

"No, no, no!" She stabbed at the screen in fury. "Unsend! Unsend! Please, God, unsend that text!"

But it was too late and even she knew there was no way to take back what she'd sent. Cringing and moaning, she thumbed up and read as far as *I'm lonely I'm sad I'm scared* with no punctuation like Kenzie had taught her, because she wasn't *dictating* she was *complaining to thin air*.

Except...it *sent*.

Heat rolled up her chest as she imagined him reading it, a lump lodging in her throat as a shameful sob, which finally released when she thumbed to the end of her punctuation-less diatribe.

I miss you okay I feel stupid for saying it I won't admit it to anyone but I think about you all the time and let's be honest the ink is barely dry on my divorce decree and I got some serious baggage in my belly but I wish I had kissed you that night because I may never know what that would feel like

She almost cried out, but she was too scared *that* would be sent to him, too. Instead, she put the phone on the bed—dictation off and face down—and got up. She flung open the French doors to her balcony, deeply inhaling the ocean air and hoping for a reprieve from her pain in this, her favorite place on Earth.

But instead of looking out to the silver moonlight dancing on the dark ocean waters, her gaze moved to the chaise. All she could do was think of the night she'd sat there with him, holding his hand and stroking his arm as he mourned the loss of his nonna.

I wish I had kissed you that night...

Because that night, that moment, it all became crystal clear.

Chase wasn't just a friend or a person who rented a room or a boutique hotel owner who'd helped her out of a jam for her family. He was a man. A man who was so deeply attractive to her, it kind of hurt to look at him and it hurt more not to kiss him.

And now he knew that!

She gripped the railing and groaned, letting out the rage of not being able to fix the problem, and the shame of what she'd admitted, and the frustration at her stupidity.

One of the Things gave her a solid kick in the gut, as if to say, "Yeah, Mom, that was dumb."

"So dumb," she murmured, turning because she heard the vibration on the bed.

And now she had to face the music and see how he'd responded. Swallowing hard, she walked back to the bed with about the same spirit as a man on his way to the gallows. She picked up the phone and looked at the screen, his name, and his response...a single laughing face emoji.

Okay, *okay*. Relief pressed on her heart.

He thought it was funny. He would tease her—if she ever saw him again—and the whole thing would simply be a hilarious memory that he'd let her sweep under the—

Another text buzzed from him. This time...one red heart.

What did *that* mean?

She stared at the phone, waiting and wondering. She stayed still and looked and looked and waited and waited, but that was all he sent. Ten minutes, half an hour, and then it was past eleven and he hadn't texted anything else.

Just one red heart.

Finally, she gave up and climbed under the covers, giving in to sleep. When she woke at two a.m. for her first trip to the bathroom, she grabbed the phone to check, but there was nothing but that one red heart.

Whatever it meant, she wasn't going to find out tonight. She may never know.

When she came back to bed in the dark and lonely room, she put the phone on the sheet next to her.

With a sigh, she placed her palm over the screen and wished that one red heart was the real one, *his* heart... beating next to her all night long.

Chapter Eight

Madeline

Setting aside the buttercream shantung fabric she'd been cutting, Madeline picked up her phone when it buzzed with a text from Sadie.

Sadie: *Come over NOW! Urgent, urgent, urgent!!*

"Oh, Sadie. Why is your entire life an emergency?"

But Madeline would never say no, so she texted back a thumbs-up, then headed downstairs. She slowed a bit as she passed the salon, which was quiet after a morning flurry of bridal shoppers.

"Cathie?" she called to her floor manager. "I'm running next door for a moment. You don't need me for any appointments, do you?"

Cathie King stepped out into the back hall, a bagged gown over her arm. "Someone just called to peek around with her mother, so I'm pulling a few dresses. Nothing custom. Take your time."

"Thanks, I'll be back in a few." A very few, she thought as she left through the back door and strolled to Charmed by Chocolate. Even the name brought a smile to her face, like the flower shop, Coming Up Roses, and

Grace's bookstore, The Next Chapter. Now they had Charmed by Chocolate and...Madeline Wingate Designs.

Oh, well. It was what she'd always wanted to name her salon and dressmaking business, not...Nights in White Satin or some cutesy thing. She wasn't *cute*. She was just Madeline Wingate, simple, structured, on time, and...not cute.

She pushed open the back door to the chocolate shop and saw her sister wearing loose denim overalls with a simple tank top underneath, her crazy curls falling from a giant clip, a smudge of chocolate on her face. Now that? *That* was the very definition of cute.

But no jealousy tweaked her heart, just amusement and maybe a little frustration because unless the place was on fire, it wasn't enough of a crisis to drag Madeline from her cutting table.

"What is the emergency?" Madeline asked, unable to fight a smile as Sadie danced toward her holding a Dixie cup.

"I did it!" she sang. "I replicated my secret recipe with three slightly different variations. You have to taste for me, because the old mouth buds are done for the day. So you, my dear, must taste chocolate. Is that so bad?"

Madeline laughed and shook her head, taking in the changes of the last few days. The kitchen had finally lost its spanking-new gleam and looked wonderfully in use, even if it was a typical Sadie Wingate mess. Pots, pans, utensils, towels, and a thousand ingredients were scattered over the stainless prep tables, everything dotted with cocoa bean shavings, but it all smelled so, so divine.

"I guess you could twist my arm to taste some chocolate," she said instead.

"I knew you would." Sadie tugged her by the sleeve to one of the tables where there were at least a dozen Dixie cups with varying levels of dark and milk chocolate in each. "Can you try three and rank them best to worst? I can't tell which mix is the winner."

"Sure, but I'm no expert," she admitted. "You lived at my house. You know I'm pretty happy with a bite of those Dove things with the cute saying in the wrapper."

Sadie cringed. "That's chocolate...ish. I'm not looking for a connoisseur. I need an average, ordinary person on the street with an opinion."

Madeline snorted softly. "Pretty sure you described me to a T."

Sadie made a face, sticking out her lower lip. "You are not average or ordinary."

Madeline tipped her head, not willing to argue how obvious it was. "Just give me the chocolate and let me get back to my shantung. I had a vision for a dress."

"And I have a vision for my chocolate." She lifted a cup and handed Madeline a small plastic tasting spoon. "Oh, the sign people said they can rush the decals and I'll at least have the Charmed by Chocolate name on the window by this weekend's party. Cool, huh?"

"Extremely. Should I just dig and drink?"

"Yeah, it's not cold or molded yet, but this is liquid from the nibs, as we say in the biz, and it's really the best way to really let it slide over your tongue to find the plea-sure points."

Madeline rolled her eyes, not sure her tongue *had* pleasure points.

"Should I be trying to taste anything special?" she asked.

"Just tell me—on a scale from one to ten—how it tastes. One is awful, ten is divine."

She glided the spoon through the liquid chocolate, already amazed at the consistency. She dragged the curve along the cup edge to avoid a drop on her silk blouse, then slipped it between her lips.

And had to physically fight the urge to moan. Guess her tongue had pleasure points after all.

"Sadie," she whispered once she could manage to talk without buckling. "That is...holy...*wow*." She let her eyes slip shut as every tastebud in her mouth came to life and danced with pure delight.

"On a scale of one to ten?" Sadie asked, biting her lip, up on her toes, hungry for feedback.

"Twelve? Twenty? I don't know how it could be any better."

She puffed out a breath. "Oh, good. Okay, let's try Cup Number Two."

"Not sure I can take it," Madeline joked, putting a hand to her chest. "It's a lot of flavor."

"Let me get you a water."

"Okay, but can I have another little scoop of this one?" she asked on a laugh.

"All you want, darlin'." Sadie rushed to the refrigerator while Madeline dipped the tasting spoon for Round Two. "And before you try the next cup, let's cleanse your palette and—oh, *no*."

Madeline looked up from the prep table to see Sadie's entire expression change as she looked out the glass window toward the street.

"What is he doing here?" Sadie whispered.

Following her gaze, Madeline squinted and froze mid-swallow of the most delicious chocolate she'd ever tasted. Somehow, she managed not to choke or gasp or react at the sight of Adam Logan. Instead, she let the cream slip through her mouth as she stared at him.

Why did he look as good as this chocolate tasted? *Why?*

He stood with his hands tucked into the pockets of a faded jean jacket, his salt-and-pepper hair disheveled by the breeze blowing off the river, his face still strong and handsome, but somehow less threatening with age.

"I can't believe you did this to me," Madeline whispered.

"Did... No! I didn't do anything!" Sadie insisted, slamming the fridge door closed and leaning against it, eyes closed. "In fact, I told him *not* to come."

"You talked to him?"

"I had to call him with one question about the software. There was no way I could have a grand opening party without ordering through a vendor site and...oh. It doesn't matter." She shook her head. "I left a message and asked him to call me back, but I was clear that he didn't need to come up here from Jacksonville."

Taking a deep breath and stealing another look, Madeline flipped the used plastic tasting spoon in a trash bin. "I'm out."

"No, please, stay and just talk—"

Madeline silenced her with a glare. "If you set this up with some wild idea that we—"

"I didn't!" She launched toward Madeline, reaching for her, all the light in her happy eyes replaced by sincerity. "I promise you, on our sisterhood, on our last name, on everything, that I didn't plan this. It's fate or kismet or—"

"Bad timing." Madeline wrested free of Sadie's desperate grip. "I don't want to talk to him Sadie, period, end of story. I'm leaving."

Sadie nodded and stepped back. "Okay, I understand. Truly, I do. And I'm sorry."

"It's fine," she muttered, but it was anything but fine.

With that, she stepped out the back door, still tasting the sweet chocolate, so good she was a little lightheaded. At least, she told herself it was the chocolate.

Somehow Madeline managed a brief chat with the customers and Cathie in the salon, and then rushed up the stairs to the safety of her studio, counting each of the seventeen stairs between the salon and the studio as she took them.

She needed something in her head besides the name...Adam.

Adam *Carpenter*, which was who he'd always be to her, the man she once loved and gave herself to in every possible way. The man who...who won. She'd never loved again, never given another man a chance, never really recovered.

And now he was next door.

Shoving thoughts of Adam out of her head, she dove straight into work, attacking the shantung on her cutting table with her sharpest shears and most determined hands.

But no matter how hard she tried to concentrate, all she could see was that dark shadow of a man separated from her by two windows, forty feet, twenty-five years... and one monstrous lie.

She believed Sadie, but she certainly would never be dumb enough to believe *him*. Why was he here? Would he want to see her? If so, she had to square her shoulders, lift her chin, and act like she barely remembered him.

Could she do that? Or would she crumble at their first exchange? Her fear, of course, was that she'd give him the satisfaction of knowing how deep a cut he'd made in her heart, and that she'd been an absolute naïve fool to believe he really cared that much about her.

"Rex Wingate didn't raise fools," she muttered.

She scooped up the fat bolt of cream fabric to replace it on the rack and choose another. She wasn't in the mood for this dress. Maybe she'd go back to the starlight charmeuse for something a little more playful and feminine.

But as she crossed the studio floor, her thoughts weren't on gowns.

Could she fake indifference and pretend that two and a half decades had erased any feelings and...what had happened? Yes, of course she could. When the time came, she—

"Madeline?" Cathie's voice, and hurried footsteps, floated out from the stairwell to her right. "There's a man here to see you. Mr. Adam Logan."

And the time was...now. No, no. *Not now!*

She slammed the bolt into place, already hearing heavy male footsteps on the first of her seventeen stairs.

Seventeen. That was all the time she had to come up with a way to stop this.

"Um, I'm really deep into a project, Cath." Reaching over her head to the top rack, she grabbed the charmeuse to slide it free, but the edge stuck. And the footsteps continued. "Just tell him..." She yanked harder, but the material didn't budge. "We'll have to schedule something else."

"He said it was urgent."

Oh, did he? *Now* it's urgent? After leaving her in the pouring rain at a bus stop on Thirty-fourth and Eighth, her hair soaked, her dress ruined, her pride demolished?

She jerked the bolt with so much force the entire metal rack swayed forward, nearly toppling on her head.

"Whoa!" He launched into the room just in time to brace the rack, easily righting it. "Careful, Maddie."

She froze, her hands in the air, all of her blood draining as she realized what almost happened...and that he'd saved her with fast feet and faster hands once again.

"Is this the one you need?" he asked after a beat, reaching up to the bolt of silk.

She just stared up at him, digging to her very core for that indifference and cool, but one look into his eyes and she nearly toppled like the fabric rack.

Oh, those eyes.

Still impossibly deep, still direct and soulful, still locked on her like no one else in the room—in the world—mattered to him.

She wanted to hate him, but just couldn't. He didn't know what he'd done to her, but that was his fault.

"Yes, thank you," she managed, stepping back to let him ease the bolt out.

He slid it free and turned to her, presenting it with precisely the same flourish he had that day in Northeast Fabrics. "Your material, ma'am."

Only then, he'd called her "gorgeous" and she'd flipped her long hair and limped on one clog to pick up the other, a picture of sass and confidence.

That girl...was gone.

She took the bolt from him and hated that their fingers brushed, because even that casual contact made her feel like she'd powered down a double shot of Sadie's chocolate.

She dug for the courage to meet his gaze with one as direct. "Hello, Adam."

"I saw you take off from the chocolate shop," he said simply.

She squeezed the bolt and strode across the wide-planked floor to the cutting table under the bank of windows. "I'm working on a dress that I promised a bride..." That was a lie and she didn't want to give him the satisfaction of her lying the way he had. She dropped the bolt with a thump, finishing with the truth. "And I'm never late for anything."

"I see," he said, a few steps behind her. "Well, I saw through the display window and it sure looked like an escape to me."

She didn't bother to defend herself any more, but flipped the bolt to spread the fabric.

While she did, he leaned a hip on the side of her cutting table, eyeing her for a moment, the strong sunlight streaming in over her. No doubt the light showed him that she was no longer the twenty-four-year-old hotshot design intern he once knew.

Feeling the pressure of his gaze, she glanced up at him, noting his own crow's feet and silver threads, but of course, on a man, he was...distinguished. For a woman, it was—

"Wow, you look great, Maddie."

She felt some heat on her cheeks but managed a nod to acknowledge the compliment.

"And sorry about barging in, but I had to see you."

"Had to?" She notched a brow, biting back all the comments that surfaced to go along with that question. Starting with why he'd never *had to* explain what happened twenty-five years ago but just let her...break.

"For one thing, I want to congratulate you on your

success in building this business." He gave a quick, sweeping gesture to the studio. "I remember that having a place like this was your dream."

He *remembered* that?

Liar. That's what Adam Carpenter-now-Logan was—a big, tall, still-really-handsome *liar*.

She gave him a tight smile that probably didn't reach her eyes. She almost challenged the statement, almost tossed her sharpest, "Is that so?" into his face, but something inside held back. Because one serious conversation, and she'd say too much.

She softened the smile and angled her head. "That's sweet of you to remember," she said in her warmest voice. "It's like a dream come true every day when I come up here to work."

Not the only dream she'd ever had, but...

"And you," she said coolly, turning the bolt to free up a few yards. "Not the wholesale fabric distributor you hoped to be."

He chuckled easily, as if standing in her studio and chatting about old times was the most natural thing in the world.

"I, uh, left the fabric business."

She gave a quick laugh and got a bone-deep kick from how natural it sounded. She *could* do it. She could act casual and indifferent, even joke about that lie he'd told her. All of them, even the most personal and intimate ones.

"Maddie," he said softly.

Intimate ones like when he called her that. She

almost responded with, "No one calls me that anymore and lives," but it wasn't true. She'd broken everyone in the family of the habit, except Dad. He refused to go along with her request that she only be called "Madeline."

No one ever asked why. But the reason was right in front of her, the man who made "Maddie" sound like music.

"Adam," she countered. "I guess it's Logan. Not Carpenter?"

He angled his head in concession. "It was never Carpenter. But you know that now, don't you?"

"I do." She billowed the fabric down the table, then flicked her hand to get him to step out of the way.

"I'm sure you weren't surprised," he said, inching left, but not far enough away to suit her.

She lifted up her shears and managed not to point them at his chest. "Nothing surprises me."

"So you knew?" he asked. "The next day, when Elana was arrested? You knew? Or did you go back to the fabric shop and find out that way?"

Went back, got kicked in the gut, called his disconnected number from a payphone, and stood in the downpour crying like a fool when she heard the recording. And then...that week. That dark, miserable, agonizing week that changed everything.

But she certainly wasn't going to tell him that *or* lie. "I can't imagine what difference that makes now, all these years later," she said.

"It makes a big difference."

"Why?"

He looked surprised by the question. "I didn't want to hurt you."

No, she thought, letting out a noisy sigh.

He wasn't going to do this to her. He wasn't going to invade her studio and life, toss off an apology, and call it a day. *No.* Not after what he did to her.

She put down the shears and turned, crossing her arms to mirror his posture and look right up into his eyes. "Adam, there's no need to discuss ancient history. I barely remember the day or that whole time in my life. You were there, then you weren't. My boss was my hero, then she wasn't. I lived in New York, then I didn't." She shrugged. "History and life. Now, if you don't mind..." She gestured to the table. "I'm extremely protective of my time and space, so..."

He searched her face, barely blinking, as though he were memorizing every feature.

"Of course," he said. "Then we'll continue this over dinner."

"Excuse me?" She almost sputtered, but recovered. "I don't—"

"Eat? Date? Have anything to say to me?"

She stared at him, trying to come up with a quip but he had the maddening ability to make her feel like he could see right through to her soul and assume she would say yes to whatever he proposed. Like...dinner.

As if that would happen in this lifetime.

"C'mon, Maddie. We have a lot to catch up on and I want to...I really want to make it up to you."

She bit back a caustic laugh. As if one dinner could make up for what he'd done when he disappeared.

"I don't think that's a good idea," she said slowly.

"Why not?"

"Because...I...don't think that's a good idea."

He laughed softly. "I heard you the first time, and still don't agree. It's a great idea, unless you're married or engaged or living with someone or...you can never forgive me."

She never would forgive him and maybe, just maybe, he needed to know that. But not now. Maybe not ever. All she did was shake her head.

"Good. I'm taking that as none of the above," he said. "Please let me take you out to dinner, deliver the heartfelt apology you think you don't want but richly deserve, and I'll tell you the whole truth about what really happened that summer in New York."

And maybe she'd do the same. Could that free her somehow? Maybe it would.

"I'll be back on Friday." He pulled out his cell and tapped it to life. "What's your number?"

She stood like a complete idiot, dumbfounded.

"Or you can just type it in." He handed her the phone, which felt heavy and oversized in her damp palm. "Right there. You can enter it. And don't give me a fake, because I can find you."

Swallowing, she looked down and somehow managed to remember her cellphone number. And then, like a woman possessed—by *him*—she typed it.

"Perfect. Friday night. It's a date."

No, it wasn't, but she didn't want to argue. She wanted to think and remember and plan exactly what she would say to him.

He backed away, holding her gaze, tearing down years and walls and every ounce of her willpower to say no. He lifted his thumb and baby finger next to his head, once again making that universal gesture for...

Brace for impact, baby.

With one more heart-stopping smile, he turned and walked into the hallway and down the seventeen stairs, his footfalls on each far lighter than the hammering of her heart.

When the door closed behind him, she collapsed on the velvet bridal sofa, dropped her head back, and closed her eyes, letting things that should never see the light of day climb out of their locked boxes.

Okay, okay. Dinner on Friday. Well, maybe it was time he carried some of those things around, too.

Chapter Nine

Sadie

S adie looked up—*way* up—at an older woman who had to be five-foot-ten in socks. Although Kitty Worthington looked like she wouldn't be caught dead without shoes on. Even today, at her Fernandina Beach home, she wore a crisp navy dress with a scarf that made her look like an old-school stewardess, gold-rimmed glasses, and sensible pumps. And that stiff cloud of silver hair truly earned her Zach's nickname of Helmet Head.

Pushing her nephew's jokes out of her mind, Sadie delivered her brightest smile as the door opened, raising a box of truffles as a peace offering before the woman even invited her in.

"Mrs. Worthington?" Sadie asked. "I come to charm you with chocolate."

Behind the glasses, eyes rolled. "I can't be bought." But she took the box nonetheless and opened the door wider. "I hear you're the rule-breaking, gallivanting Wingate."

Sadie laughed. "I'm the one that has lived in Europe

for the past five years, and several other places before that, which is why you might not remember me."

"There are so many of you, who can remember?" She gestured her into the small two-story home, toward a dining room as though couches and chairs might be too cozy for this meeting.

She sat down at the head of the table without inviting Sadie to do the same. "You can't just blow into town and be part of our greatest events, you know. You have to pay dues."

"I'm willing to pay whatever fees are associated with the event." She pulled out a chair and smiled again. "As a brand-new small business owner on Amelia Island, it's very important for me to be part of the Fernandina Food Festival."

A deep inhale caused Kitty's nostrils to flare. "The operative words, Sadie, are *brand new*. You haven't proven yourself worthy of promotional programs that the Fernandina Beach Local Business Organization has worked tirelessly to bring to our most committed local businesses."

"I realize I'm new, but my family—"

"Oh, I knew you'd throw your family name around," she scoffed. "Wingate this, Wingate that. Being named Wingate doesn't give you the right to barge in and take the place of more deserving food services."

"Would my participation displace another business?" she asked. "I wouldn't want to do that."

"Only as far as the Best Bite contest. There can only be four finalists in each category, so if you are a finalist, then someone else who's been around a lot longer loses the chance of a lifetime."

It was a big win, but hardly one of a lifetime. Still, she wanted it. "Shouldn't the *best* bite win, regardless of how long they've been in the community? Anything else would be a disservice to tourists and locals, don't you think?"

She sniffed and finally lifted the lid of the candy box, examining the row of dusted truffles. "I heard you studied in Belgium."

"I did," Sadie said, scooting her chair forward. "Under a great chocolatier." Who also happened to be the worst human alive, she added mentally. "I think you'll taste the quality."

She pushed the box away without taking one, looking over the rims of her glasses with an accusing glare. "Where were you when your father was in the hospital? I heard you couldn't be bothered to come home."

Sadie blinked, drawing back in surprise. "I was traveling on an extended assignment in Europe," she said. "I did come home for my sister's wedding but..." Her voice faded when Kitty's brow shot north.

"But she bailed and ran through town in a wedding dress like some kind of movie heroine." She snorted. "Shame you're not all as dependable as Rose."

Sadie sat straighter. "We are all cut from the same cloth, Mrs. Worthington, and you know that my family has done as much, if not more, for this community than any other. I intend to uphold that tradition."

Possibly chastised, she looked down, eyeing the chocolate again.

"Please," Sadie said. "Have one."

She didn't, but crossed her arms. "You must be open for a full two weeks before the festival, and even that is not enough time to show you'll be a viable business."

"The grand opening is on Saturday," she announced. "I very much hope you and Mr. Worthington, and all of your friends, committees, and relatives will be there, too. Free chocolate for everyone."

She didn't get so much as a smile in return, just a threatening glint in the older woman's eyes as she regarded Sadie for a few heartbeats too many.

"Did you have any other questions?" Sadie asked.

"Yes." She leaned back. "Why did you come back here?"

"To be with my family," she said without missing a beat.

"And why was your store filed with the LBO in November under the name of Belgian Bliss?"

A slow heat rolled up her chest. "I changed the name to Charmed by Chocolate. I think it fits the Wingate Way vibe better, don't you?"

Her brows flickered. "And who is Tristan Saint Pierre?"

Sadie managed not to react, except for the splash of ice in her veins. "My former employer in Belgium."

"He was listed as the owner when you filed the paperwork. Where is he?"

Dang it! She'd totally forgotten she'd filled out that

form weeks ago. "He's in Brussels," she said. "He's opted not to be part of this operation and I'm the sole proprietor now, leasing the building directly from Wingate Properties in my own name."

Because Raina, bless her heart, had changed the paperwork for Sadie, wanting to be sure it was done before she went on maternity leave.

"Well, how do I know you're good for the rent? How do I know you're legitimate? At least he was a renowned chocolatier." At Sadie's look, she flicked her hand. "Yes, I googled the name, because we don't let just anyone blow into our town."

Sadie almost laughed. Just anyone? Her last name was on the street sign, for heaven's sake.

"Kitty," she said softly. "You taste that truffle and tell me if you've let 'just anyone' blow into town."

"I don't—"

"Please."

With a sigh that sounded as though she'd been asked to sample arsenic, the woman plucked one dusted ball from the top row with two fingers. Sadie had made mini-truffles, small enough to pop in the mouth, but Kitty simply nibbled on the edge.

Her lids fluttered, then widened. She took a second bite. And then she popped that sucker all the way in and let out a mew that was worthy of her first name.

Sadie sat back and couldn't resist a smug smile. "It's good, right?"

As Kitty swallowed, she shook her head. "You're going to steal the prize."

"I'm not going to steal anything," she replied. "I'm going to bring the best chocolate imaginable to the guests, tourists, and residents of Amelia Island."

She stared at the box like she wanted to inhale them all.

"Gayla would cry."

Gayla? She frowned, knowing she'd heard the distinct name before but not quite placing it. "Gayla...oh, Gayla Jacobson!" she said, remembering Scout using the name to refer to his late mother. "I met her son."

"He's my son now," she said softly.

"Excuse me?"

"Gayla was my best friend and Scout..." She shook her head. "He works so hard and he deserves everything, including the Best Bite contest, which their cookie place wins every year."

"And that's why you don't want me in the festival?" Sadie asked. "He came to my shop and welcomed me. In fact, he's the one who told me about the contest. He joked about the competition, but I don't believe he'd want to keep me out of the event."

She closed her eyes. "You can join, assuming you meet all the other criteria, and that includes a fully functioning booth on the sidewalk with free samples and—"

"Of course!"

"*And*," she continued with a fierce look. "Scout sponsors you personally. If he doesn't, then I can't let you in."

Whoa, small-town politics was...shady. But Sadie just nodded, and stood. "I'll talk to him. And, please, enjoy the rest of the truffles."

"I'll save one for George," she said, closing the box.

Sadie doubted that, but smiled and said goodbye, rushing out before Kitty could add one more stipulation or requirement.

How the Cookie Crumbles was hopping for mid-week, with three people in line to order, several patrons sipping coffee and eating cookies, and two women behind the counter busily boxing Scout's beautiful creations. Sadie carried truffles tucked in a small bag, but this time, she worried that her bribe might not do the trick. If Scout tasted and feared the competition, she might have made a huge error.

But since the old bat wanted him to sponsor her, she had no choice but to try.

She looked around as she walked toward the display case, smiling, because there was no way you could come into this shop and not smile. Yes, his tables were wood and not marble, but the floor was black and white check-ered, the walls were covered with photos of James Dean and Doris Day, and an authentic Wurlitzer jukebox was playing "Rock Around the Clock." The entire place had a festive, nostalgic vibe that she—and a whole lot of other people—totally loved.

As she stood in line and read the menu board, she couldn't help but think about sweet, soft, completely kind Scout Jacobson and his mother, who'd given every cookie offering the most precious name straight out of the fifties.

In addition to The Dreamboat—clearly the store's most popular dessert—there was The Beatnik with white chocolate and macadamia nuts; The Square, a traditional brownie, no doubt without the secret bourbon; The Rag Top, a crumb-covered cake candy; and an all-dark chocolate cookie called Made in the Shade.

"Sadie?"

She turned at sound of her name, seeing Scout step through a door from the back kitchen, his brown hair mussed, his apron splattered with ingredients, his smile bright enough to light the room.

"Hey, Scout." She stepped out of line to get closer, meeting him halfway.

"Wow, hi. It's really great to see you," he said with a surprised laugh.

"I bear gifts." She held up the plain white bag and decided the very best course of action was to be direct and honest. "And a massive favor to ask. Do you have a moment?"

"Yeah, of course." He wiped his hand on his apron, a tiny bit flustered, but still had that beautiful light in his eyes when he looked at her. "Come in the kitchen? I'd love to show it to you."

"Yes, please." She followed him back, getting a few looks from his staff behind the counter.

"It's crazy back here, but that won't be news to you," he said, ushering her into a kitchen that was about the size of hers but absolutely slammed. A man and a woman in aprons, hairnets, and gloves worked side by side at a long prep table, rolling dough and shaping cookies.

Four double-deck Blodgett bakery ovens glowed with racks full of cookies and brownies, all facing a fridge wall and massive pantry. The kitchen aroma was nothing short of glorious, and everything was pristine, from the fan hoods to the floor tiles.

Scout introduced her to the crew, announcing her as the owner of Charmed by Chocolate on Wingate Way, and showed her around with that appealing mix of pride and humility that he carried off so well.

"Come in my office?" he asked, opening the door to a small, windowless space that was as neat and organized as the kitchen.

Instantly, her gaze went to the photograph on the wall, a woman and a man with a small boy, standing in front of a bakery with the sign "Jacobson's" easy to read in the background.

"Oh, these must be your parents."

"Yep, that's Marty and Gayla, gone but never forgotten."

She walked closer to get a better look, instantly seeing the resemblance to his father. "So you're a junior?" she guessed.

"You remember my name is Martin," he said, a little surprised. "Yep. Only child, only son, only hope."

She laughed. "I'm sure they're smiling down from heaven at how you've carried on their legacy. This is an adorable shop, Scout. Oh, and..." She put the bag on his desk. "A peace offering."

"Peace?" He lifted a brow. "I had no idea we were at war."

"Not at all," she assured him. "But a certain Kitty Worthington has put a very strict parameter around my participation in the Fernandina Food Festival and Best Bite contest."

He looked skyward. "She fancies herself my surrogate mother, even though, at forty, I don't think I need one."

"We all need one," she said gently. "And she doesn't want me in the festival competing with you for the Best Bite."

He peeked in the bag. "Neither do I."

"Oh. Really?"

At her tone, he looked up. "I can't stop you, Sadie, and I wouldn't."

"Well, you actually *can* stop me. Queen Kitty has proclaimed that if I want to participate, I need a sponsor and that sponsor has to be you."

He inched back, thick brows rising. "*Has* to be?"

"I think she makes up rules as she goes."

"So true," he agreed. "She must think you're going to win the Best Bite."

She was, but only answered with a shrug.

"Or she..." His voice trailed off.

"Or she what?" Sadie pressed when he didn't finish.

He gave a self-conscious laugh. "She can be what my mother used to call a *mensch*, and I mean that in the nicest way."

If *mensch* meant "bully on a power trip," yes. But Sadie just smiled. "She said she was your mother's best friend."

He tipped his head. "They were good friends from the time my mother arrived on Amelia Island. Gayla had a way with her, a power few people have, and could really keep ol' Kitty in her place."

"One of my sisters has that secret talent," Sadie said. "But I don't. Anyway, would you consider sponsoring me to enter?"

He let out a fake put-upon sigh and pulled one of the two guest chairs for her, then took the other. "I guess I better taste your wares first."

"Please do." She gestured toward the bag.

With a teasing look, he kept his gaze on her as he reached in, pulling out a simple white box.

"I don't have logo boxes yet," she said.

"And no bakery twine," he added with a wink, making her laugh.

"I will not steal or borrow any of Gayla Jacobson's clever ideas, I promise."

He opened the box and took a good thirty seconds to admire her work, silent but smiling. Before taking a truffle, he offered one to her.

"I think it's bad luck to eat chocolate alone," he said.

"Really?"

"No, I just made that up, but it seemed like a nice thing to do."

She imagined that everything he did was "a nice thing," and as she reached for her own candy, she had a flash of Tristan in her mind. They'd shared a lot of chocolate tastings in eighteen months—hundreds, no doubt. And yet this seemed so different.

Probably because no man could be more different from chiseled, sophisticated, cunning Tristan Saint Pierre than soft, rumpled, *nice* Scout Jacobson.

"Cheers," he joked, making a mock toast with his chocolate.

"Cheers to you."

He ate it the proper way, one whole bite of the small candy, closing his eyes as he chewed like a vintner tasting his best cabernet. Then he swallowed, but still didn't open his eyes.

She finished her bite and waited, surprisingly nervous to get his reaction.

"I'm going to lose for the first time," he finally said.

"No!" she said. "I mean, you don't know that."

He let out a hearty chuckle. "You are going to destroy that contest. I honestly have never tasted anything like that in my life. You're gifted!"

She smiled as a little shiver of appreciation rolled through her. "Thank you, Scout."

"Can I have another?" he asked.

"They're all yours."

He nodded his thanks, and took a second, this time giving a moan of delight. Then he looked at her, shaking his head.

Did that mean no?

"I'd be out of my mind to sponsor you," he said.

Her smile faded and her jaw loosened at the words. "Oh..."

"But..." He regarded her with a look she couldn't quite read, a little bit of awe, a little bit of curiosity. "I wonder..." he said, still studying her. "Has any man ever said no to you, Sadie?"

She snorted. "So much it would make your head spin."

"It is spinning," he murmured, then smiled, reaching over to give her hand a friendly tap. "The world needs to taste this chocolate, my friend."

"Oh," she repeated, falling back in the chair, weirdly honored to be his friend. "Thank you."

"Dang," he muttered, plucking one more chocolate. "Not only am I going to lose, but..." He gave his stomach a pat. "I'm also going to gain."

She laughed, not quite sure what to make of this man who was unlike any she'd ever met. He was just so...*nice*. The word didn't really have much zing to it, no sex appeal or allure, but that's what he was. Nice. And she only realized at that moment how long it had been since she'd engaged with a nice man.

"So is that a yes?" she asked. "You'll sponsor me?"

He shuttered his eyes and sighed in resignation. "On one condition."

"Which is?"

He dabbed at his lips as if he thought he might have chocolate dust, or maybe was just a little nervous. "I get to come to your grand opening."

"Of course! I would be sad if you didn't."

He smiled and stood. "Then I'll sponsor you. But if you must know the truth? I never would have said no, not in a million years."

"Oh, thank you!" She gave a clap. "I'm so grateful,

Scout, really. Please, enjoy the rest of the truffles, and thank you."

When she left, she practically danced down Wingate Way to her shop, as happy as she could remember being since her world fell apart. Was that because of the food festival...or that very nice man who'd just agreed to sponsor her?

Chapter Ten

Susannah

Susannah awoke two days after the decision to transform the inn, her whole body damp with cold sweat, upset from a dream where someone was screaming and something was falling and everything was dark and terrifying.

Turning, she whimpered with relief when she saw her husband sound asleep next to her. "Oh, thank goodness," she muttered. "You haven't gone for cold therapy yet."

"Ten more minutes," he replied without opening his eyes. "Go back to sleep."

"I can't. I had an awful dream."

"What about?" he asked, wrapping a strong arm around her.

"I don't know." She squinted into the pre-dawn light, trying to conjure up details, but none came. "Something scary, someone screaming."

"I told you not to eat sugar before bed. That cookie was no good. Meat is the answer."

She would have laughed at his new carnivore kick,

but the edges of the dream haunted her. She closed her eyes and forced the images to the surface.

"There were...flowers," she whispered. "Faded roses, pale pink with curlicue stems, but then there were roots, like...the tree!" She clutched him tighter. "We have a meeting with the tree removal guy today. Should we cancel? Maybe Coraline is sending me a message."

"The message was more protein, less sugar. I think I'm ready to go out to the water now."

"Rex, I'm serious!"

"About a ghost?" He gave her a side-eye.

"And the tree. It's Wingate history in that tree."

"You've done more to preserve my family's history than any other person who ever had the name." He added a grateful hug. "That tree's been nothing but a headache for years. And transforming Wingate House into a wedding venue is one of the best ideas you've ever had."

She bit her lip, unsettled from the dream. "I just get the sense she wants me to know...something. I don't know what."

"She's part of a long line of real estate experts, so what she wants you to know is that tree isn't doing us any favors. Not only does it block the views, but one decent-sized storm with the wrong bolt of lightning, and it could destroy Wingate House. She's also telling you that weddings are a hot commodity up here and we're going to be booked for years and she appreciates a good boost in family income as much as the next Wingate."

Susannah sighed. "I hope she's not furious."

"Come on, Suze. Don't let something as silly as a ghost keep you from this magnificent idea."

She looked at him. "You sure it's a great idea?"

"So much that Raina and I can't believe we didn't think of it ourselves," he told her. "We had a chance to sit down and run some numbers and we're convinced it's the best way to build revenue on that property. And, hey, if it's a huge failure, then we'll go back to running an inn."

"It can't be a failure," she said, catching his always-infectious enthusiasm. "We'll perfect everything with Wingate weddings first and iron out all the kinks."

"Weddings? Plural?" He sat up a little, his interest piqued. "The only one I know about is Grace, and Isaiah hasn't even asked her yet."

"He told me he had news to share, so maybe he's picked a proposal date." She tapped his chin. "Want to come with me to the inn today? I could use your professional and personal opinion on that tree and some of the changes I'm thinking about."

"If you let me drive."

She narrowed her eyes. "You haven't been behind the wheel of a car since your stroke."

"Justin said I'm clear."

"But, Rex, what if—"

"What if the sky should fall, Suze? I'm fine. I don't have a single physical reason for not driving except you stopping me." He hugged her tighter. "Don't make me beg, woman. You'll lose."

She laughed, so deeply happy to have her man back. "Of course you can drive," she said, just as easy and casually as if he'd asked for a cup of coffee. Which she limited to one a day. She felt her shoulders sink as her whole body softened toward him. "And I'm sorry for keeping you on a short leash."

"Wholly forgiven," he said. "But can you get back to the plural weddings? You think Tori and Justin will be next?"

"I do," Susannah said on a happy sigh. "As soon as Tori gets settled in, I think they'll make this official. And I know they're not that serious yet, but Chloe and Travis seem very happy now that she has the rescue business up and running."

Rex groaned. "And maybe this time she won't run away."

"You know she did the right thing that day," Susannah said. "But if she does settle down with Travis, I doubt she'll want a big wedding after that last one. And that leaves three of my girls unattached."

Rex flicked a brow. "Raina has her hands full, Sadie just got out of...whatever you call that. And Madeline?" He gave a sad smile. "My Maddie is never going to find love."

"Oh, Rex, don't give up on her."

"She's happy," he said. "Found her place in the world and is doing just fine. Not every woman needs a man, you know." Rex locked his hands behind his head, staring up and thinking.

Susannah took a moment and just looked at him, awash with unexpected pleasure.

"What?" he asked, sliding a sideways look at her.

"I treasure these moments," she whispered. "Talking about our girls and their lives. Being married. It just makes me happy to be your wife."

He gave that Rex look that was a mix of amused and bewildered and like he was not sure what to say. Then he freed one hand and pulled her in. "Then kiss me and make me happy to be your husband."

She lifted a brow. "We might be late for the tree removal meeting."

"Then Coraline will be thrilled." He drew her in for a long kiss and she let his tender and oh-so-familiar touch wipe away the dark dream and replace it with nothing but joy to be married to Rex Wingate.

THE TRUCK PARKED in front of Wingate House bore the logo of Crosswater Cutting Company, making Susannah wonder if they really *were* late for the meeting.

As Rex parked, he peered toward the house. "There he is, walking to the back with Isaiah. Come on, we'll meet them by the tree."

Together, they walked hand-in-hand down the side of the house, coming around to the large enclosed backyard that included a small pool, three sun decks, a summer kitchen, and the one-bedroom cottage where Isaiah had been living.

But the whole yard was dominated by the shadow of an ancient oak tree that seemed to have grown exponentially since Susannah was last back here.

"Hello, Miz Wingate, Mr. Wingate." Isaiah nodded to both of them, gesturing for them to join them. "This is Al Dunlap, who owns Crosswater Cutting."

They exchanged greetings and introductions, and Isaiah tipped his head toward the house. "I better finish up breakfast for our guests. When you get a minute, Miz Wingate? I want to run something by you."

She nodded and turned her attention back to Al and the tree.

"She's a beauty," Al said, studying the thick trunk and knotted roots. "But I bet she can cause trouble."

"What kind of trouble?" Susannah asked.

"A tree this big? Unless it's in the middle of a field with a hundred feet clear in all directions, she'll be nothing but misery. But that's pretty common for a live oak that's passed the century mark."

"Do you think that's the tree's age?" Susannah asked, her heart dropping. Was it right to remove a hundred-year-old tree?

"We can't know until we cut her down and count the rings, but based on her girth? She's been around a long, long time." Al walked around the base of the tree, which was a good ten feet from the house, then peered up into the gnarled branches, checking out every inch of the tree. "If you cut her, you'll need approval from the Arboriculture Society, but I can help you get that because she could be an imminent danger to people or property."

"What would happen if we cut her down so she was only as tall as the first story?" Rex asked.

"Besides ruining your backyard by being the ugliest

tree in the neighborhood? You'd likely shock the life out of her and she might not survive. Oh, look at this." Al got down on his hands and knees and started poking at some of the exposed roots that were at least eight inches in diameter. "You've got root rot."

"What exactly does that mean?" Susannah asked.

"It means that if a hurricane comes through here, you'll lose the second and third floors of this pretty house."

Rex gave her a look. "Exactly as I suspected."

"Could we move it somewhere?"

Al looked skeptical. "If you want to spend upwards of thirty grand, yeah."

Susannah grunted at the price, which would wipe out any profit from her new venture.

"Y'all think about it for a minute. I'm going to get some measuring tools from my truck."

Susannah nodded. "You want to go inside, Rex?"

"No, no. I want to sit right on that deck and look at the tree, because you and I both know it's coming down."

"Oh." She pressed her fingers to her lips. "And that upsets you?"

"Not really," he said, walking toward the deck. "Things change and life moves on. It's a new stage for the house, like a person."

She sighed and gestured toward the back door. "I'm going to chat with Isaiah for a moment." With one more look at the tree and a weirdly heavy heart, she walked into the back of the inn, down the hall past some currently unoccupied guest rooms, and around the corner to the kitchen just as Isaiah came out with two plates of gorgeous pastries and fruit.

"Oh, one sec, Miz Wingate."

"Take your time, Isaiah." She glanced at the back stairs behind him. "You know, I wanted to peek at the tree from upstairs. Which rooms are empty?"

"The Coraline suite hasn't booked in a while," he said. "You can go right in."

"Thank you." She headed up the stairs, around the landing, and all the way to the top. The whole inn even smelled better than when Doreen was here, she decided. Isaiah had brought new life to the place. With a new purpose—intimate weddings—this grand old lady of Wingate Way could have her best days ahead.

Maybe it *was* time to get rid of that tree, she thought. If Rex was okay with the idea, then she should be, too.

At the top of the stairs, she looked left and right, then straight ahead to the double doors of the inn's most impressive—and most expensive—suite, not counting the apartment on the third floor.

Out of habit, she tapped on the door and, for a split second, she thought she heard a noise. A thud on the floor, maybe.

Surprised, she backed up. Who could be in there?

She knocked again, harder, and called, "Hello?"

When no one answered, she opened the door, inching into the room that was truly one of the most beautiful in the inn. With the huge king bed, an ornate marble fireplace, a well-appointed ensuite and a walk-in closet, it should be one of their most popular rooms. But it was expensive, and frequently sat empty.

She stood at the foot of the bed and looked up to the canopy gathered in a crown, then sucked in a soft breath as her gaze landed on the wallpaper above the woodwork.

Were those...faded roses with curlicue stems?

It felt like her blood froze. She tossed her shoulder bag on the bed and walked closer, squinting at the wallpaper that she herself had selected when she renovated the inn.

But she'd picked it because she'd seen a picture of Coraline with curtains of a very similar pattern, and she wanted this to be a nod to Rex's grandmother.

She'd totally forgotten that—except, obviously, her subconscious hadn't. Those were definitely the faded roses in the dark, dark place of her dream.

With a shiver, she backed away from the wall and walked to the window, pushing the drape aside to see...a thick branch pressed against this window and the one to the right, one story higher, a tiny opening to the attic. The river view was indeed completely blocked, and the room wasn't cheerful with sunlight because of the tree.

It really *was* hurting the value of the property.

She looked around, thinking of the woman who'd once lived and slept and, sadly, died in this room. She'd caught the influenza that had gone through town, allegedly from tending to the sick.

So Coraline Wingate couldn't have been a terrible woman, even if she made her oldest son sit in that tree for twenty-four hours as a punishment for breaking Prohibition laws. She had to have had happy moments in here, as a mother and a wife.

At the thought, she turned to the double closet doors across a small alcove. She knew the history of that closet —it led to another door that connected to the Madeline suite. Back when Coraline slept here, the rooms didn't have the names of Wingate women—who hadn't even been born yet—but Susannah had christened them years ago when she did the major renovation.

But in the early 1900s, Coraline slept here alone, and Reginald, Rex's namesake and grandfather, slept in the suite connected through the closet. When one or the other wished to share a bed for the night, they used the adjoining closet to go to each other, the staff none the wiser.

She smiled at the quaint custom, opening the doors to look into the closet, which was long and dark and... reminded her of that dream again.

"Miz Wingate?"

She startled at the sound of Isaiah's voice, slipping out of the closet to meet him in the hall. "I'm in here," she said. "And, yikes, that tree is a view blocker."

"I know. It's hard enough to book the Coraline, but Yelp reviews complain about the ruined view, so people often ask for a different room."

And that's why it made no money; so the tree would have to go even if they didn't reimagine the purpose of the Inn. Accepting that, she shook off the creepy feeling she got in the room.

"You said you wanted to talk to me today?" she asked.

He gestured to a velvet-covered window settee in the hall, silently inviting her to sit. "I wanted to run an idea by you."

"Of course." She perched on the edge of the cushion, making room for him. "What do you need?"

"It's about Saturday's party," he said. "The one for the opening of the chocolate shop."

"Yes? You can make it, right? It's in the afternoon, so you should be free."

"I can and I'd like to..." He took a slow breath. "I really want to ask Grace to marry me with the entire family present."

"Oh, lovely!"

"You think so? I thought that might be a good day, but I don't want to steal Sadie's thunder. I wanted your opinion, ma'am, on whether or not that's an appropriate time for me to get down on one knee."

"I think it's a perfect time for you to do that," she assured him. "Sadie won't mind. In fact, if I know her, she'll do a special chocolate fountain or something very festive."

He whole face lit up. "Oh, I think Grace and Nikki would like that."

How sweet that he always included little Nikki Lou. "Are you going to—"

She heard a soft thud, then a sudden loud rumble, and a mechanical screech from outside.

"Are they cutting it down already?" Susannah stood, rushing toward the Coraline to see, but came to a complete stop two steps into the room.

Her jaw loosened as she stared at the bed. The *empty* bed. Where was her purse? She patted her shoulder, looked around and...gasped.

Her bag was on the floor, upside down with all the contents spilled.

"How did that happen?" she whispered as a fresh explosion of goosebumps erupted on her arms and neck, making the hair stand on end.

Isaiah walked past her, not noticing the bag as he flipped the drapes and looked down.

"I don't think they're cutting it," he said. "Looks like Al just took a low branch off."

But she couldn't move. All she could do was stare at the purse, the bed, the wallpaper, and the closet door she'd left open.

"Oh, what happened here?" Isaiah said, rounding the bed to see the mess on the floor.

The ghost of Coraline happened.

But she swallowed the words, and murmured an excuse as she crouched down to stuff her pen, lipstick, wallet, and phone back into her bag. When she stood, her legs were trembling.

"I'm going to make sure that branch is all they cut today," she said, realizing she was making her voice louder than usual so...Coraline heard.

Which was *insane*.

Isaiah nodded and glanced around, then looked at the open closet door. "I'll make sure everything is straightened up in here."

She gave him a look, longing to tell him that her purse

had been in the middle of the bed while they talked in the hall, but she couldn't. She simply couldn't.

"Okay," she managed. "I'll be downstairs."

She rushed down and darted out the back door to find Rex and Al deep in conversation.

"Let's leave the tree," she exclaimed, praying they didn't ask for an explanation.

"Not a chance of that," Rex said.

Al turned the cut side of a thick branch toward her, showing a nearly hollowed-out center. "It's been eaten and rotting. You really have no choice but to get rid of this thing."

"But...but..."

Rex put an arm around her. "He told me that they'll cut a slice of the healthiest section of the main trunk and we can have a table or something made from it. It will still be part of the family, just in a different form."

She stole a quick glance at the window above her and hoped that would be good enough for Coraline.

Chapter Eleven

Raina

"The Riverfront Café lunch rush is officially over," Tori said, dropping into the empty chair across from Raina and next to Rose. "I've had FOMO watching you two talking and laughing over here for the past forty-five minutes."

"Don't fear missing out, Tori, only one of us is laughing," Raina said with a pretend dirty look at her twin. "I'm still licking my wounds."

"No word from him, huh?" Tori asked. "No more emojis?"

Raina shook her head. "He should just text a capital L for Loser, which is what you would call a woman who'd make that mistake."

"Not a loser," Tori said on an exhale. "Just a woman with...a big, bad crush and no understanding of how text dictation works."

They'd dragged the truth out of her the day after the Great Text Debacle, which didn't take a whole lot of work. Raina had been desperate for advice, and, of course, turned to these two.

They'd urged her to follow up with another text. Tori said she should joke about it and Rose insisted she should own up to her feelings. But Raina decided to do nothing.

Until she knew exactly how to fix a problem, she liked to consider all options. Currently, her favorite was "pretend it didn't happen."

"I'm paralyzed," she confessed. "Hoping it will all go away and that I'll never see him again or, when I do, enough time will have passed that the whole thing will have been forgotten."

Tori reached for her phone. "Can I read it again?"

"If that will amuse you some more over what an idiot I am."

"You're not an idiot, Raina," Rose assured her. "Kenzie forgot to tell you that you have to tap the microphone twice to turn it off. There was no way you could know you were dictating all that."

"I just think it's...interesting," Tori said, skimming the evil text.

"That I admitted my longings?"

"Longings?" Tori lifted a brow at the word. "Don't text that to him. Or anyone."

"Well, I hate to call them feelings, because that carries more weight," Raina said. "It was a momentary madness brought on by exhaustion, stress, and hauling around two fully formed humans in my uterus. So, I had a...longing."

"What I think is interesting is the heart," Tori said, putting the phone down. "The laughing face says he probably figured out what you did and thought it was hilarious."

"Which it kind of was," Raina agreed.

"But the heart..."

"Says he feels the same way," Rose said.

"You mean he *longs* the same way," Tori joked.

"It was him letting me off the hook," Raina told them. "It was a 'that's okay, you made a mistake, kid' kind of heart. It was a friend heart. A guy who rents a room at my house heart. An 'of course you like me but I won't act on that because you're pregnant and the ink hasn't dried on your divorce decree yet' kind of heart."

Tori and Rose looked at each other, both of them obviously using everything they had to keep from laughing. They failed miserably.

"The heart doesn't *mean* anything," Raina insisted when their laughter subsided. "It was a conversation closer and...whatever."

"I think it was exactly the opposite." Tori tapped the phone with her nail, looking from one sister to the other. "I think he was saying, 'Hey, now that this is out in the open, even by mistake, I feel the same way.'"

The same way? Raina swallowed hard. If he felt like she felt, then—

Her phone lit with a text from Dani, saving Raina from this conversation. "I don't think he feels anything," she said, picking up the phone to read it. "I think he's...*at my office?*"

"What?" Rose and Tori exclaimed in unison.

Raina stared at the words swimming in front of her eyes.

"Dani says, 'Hey, you have a surprise visitor. Chase Madison just dropped by. Will you be back soon?'" She looked up, right into Tori's "I told you so" smirk, then over to Rose's "I was hoping for this" little grin.

"No," Raina said, tapping the screen. "I won't be back—"

Tori yanked the phone away just as Rose put a not-so-gentle hand on Raina's arm.

"No, you guys," Raina whined, but didn't care. "I can't face him. Not yet, not this soon after I poured my heart out and he knows I thought about kissing him."

"Of course you can," Tori shot back. "He's in the States and he wants to see you. Maybe he wants to give you a chance to laugh about it."

"Or he wants to tell you he felt the same way that night," Rose said. "He's sweet like that. Remember he got the single Ocean Song rose every day for his grandmother? I always liked him."

Raina felt her shoulders drop in defeat. "Let me put it this way—I don't *want* to face him. Not only am I next-level embarrassed by the text, I'm...big and pregnant and...this thing happened." She pointed to a lovely little pimple that had arisen that morning.

"That means you're having a girl, you know," Rose whispered.

"Good, then he can't force me to name it Charles."

"Charlie Wingate." Rose practically cooed the name. "I still love that. Charlotte, after our mother."

"So what are you going to do?" Tori asked.

"Sit here until he gives up waiting for me." She wrested the phone back from Tori. "I'll ask Dani to tell him I'm in a meeting for...a month."

"Raina." Tori glowered at her. "You know you want to see him. And obviously he wants to see you. Talk about it, laugh about it, go back to being friends and clear the air."

Raina huffed out a breath, knowing she was right. "I guess."

"He's a good man," Rose said for what had to be the twentieth time. "Anyone who loves his grandmother that much is a good man."

"He is," Raina agreed with a smile. "Nonna was probably the reason I fell—" She caught herself. *In love.* Was she going to say in love? No. Unthinkable. "—so hard for him," she finished, which was almost as bad.

But Tori and Rose just smiled at her.

"You're not going to get shock and awe from us," Tori said. "I fell for Hottypants about two seconds after I met him, and I'm still falling."

"And Gabe had me when I was fifteen," Rose said. "Well, not literally, but you know what I mean."

Raina smiled at that, a wave of affection for her sisters rolling over her.

"What are you going to tell Dani?" Rose asked.

"You do it for me," she said, nudging the phone to the middle of the table. "Tell her..."

Tori picked up the phone and typed, then turned the screen to Raina. "Is this okay?"

I'm at the café and will be back in a few minutes.

No, Raina thought. Nothing about this was okay. It was scary and exciting and nerve-wracking and felt like she was a teenager again. "Yeah."

Tori tapped the phone. "Sent. Now, let me get a chocolate croissant and you can take it."

"Why?"

"It was his favorite when he lived here," she said, pushing up. "He used to come in for them all the time."

"I'm not taking him a croissant."

"Oh, I think you should," Rose said, her voice rich with implication as she read her own phone.

"Why?" Raina asked.

"Because Lizzie just texted me that one of our favorite customers is back in town and he stopped in for a single Ocean Song rose. Now, that can't be for his grandmother, can it?"

Raina stared at her, jaw loose as her whole body reacted with some chills and tension and a fluttering in her stomach that was not, for once, a kick from Thing One or Two. "He did?"

"Oh, boy," Tori teased. "Someone is...longing."

"Stop it," Raina said, but, try as she might, she couldn't wipe the smile away. An Ocean Song rose, huh? "Go get the croissant, Tori. And wish me luck."

∼

With the white to-go bag clutched in a damp palm, Raina headed up Wingate Way mentally practicing what she'd say to Chase when she saw him.

But no words really formed. Should she start with an apology for the crazy text? A hug? High-five or a sly smile?

Just a hello, she told herself. It didn't have to be more complicated than that. Although...that text had made things complicated and she had to face—

"Please tell me there's a chocolate croissant in that bag."

She slowed her step and managed not to whip around—not that whipping around was in her wheelhouse these days.

Instead, she stopped, and gave in to the smile that formed at the sound of Chase's voice. Then she turned to the side to see him sitting on a park bench in front of the new chocolate shop, holding a tissue-wrapped rose.

"There might be," she teased, putting her hand up to shield her eyes from the sun and really get a good look at him. Oh, man. The way he looked made things even more complicated. "If that rose is for me."

He stood and walked toward her, the rose extended. "I wanted to bring one from the garden in Palermo, but it wouldn't survive the trip." He dipped his head and, for one crazy second, she thought he was going to kiss her.

But he merely smiled. "Hello, Raina."

She lifted the bag to meet the rose. "Hello, Chase."

Neither said a word, but each took the offered gift, then gave one another a very natural, very warm hug. He felt taller, stronger, and even better than she remembered. And surely she felt...bigger and more pregnant.

They parted and both laughed softly, the moment somehow both awkward and wonderful and not too terribly complicated after all.

"How do you feel?" he asked. "How are the Things?"

She tapped her belly. "I feel...restless and ready. And I think they're bigger than last time you were here."

"You look great."

"Thanks. And you...well, what a surprise."

"Yep, your roommate's back."

She tsked. "I told you not to give me that rent anymore. I paid off the mortgage and own the house outright. I'll return the rent you paid."

He gave her a look like she'd lost her mind. "And I told you I never knew when I'd need a place to stay on this island, and now I need one."

"You...do?" She drew back, nearly swaying a little.

He laughed at the reaction. "Weren't expecting that, were you?"

"No, I...no. What I'm expecting are...these two." She rubbed her hand over the rise. "I'm weeks, if I'm lucky, from giving birth."

"I know. I'm so relieved I made it back before the big day."

She searched his face. Was he just pretending to be dense? No one this close to labor and delivery wanted a houseguest. It didn't matter how much rent they paid or how well they cooked or how spectacular they looked in a blue button-down shirt and khakis.

For the record, pretty spectacular.

She shrugged, trying to stay casual. "Well, D-Day is soon, so..."

Chuckling, he put a light hand on her shoulder and glanced to the sun-washed bench where he'd been sitting. "Come on, Raina. Let's talk. I have a friendly proposal for you."

She let out the softest sigh and walked to the bench with him, lowering herself carefully with another laugh.

"Nothing I do is exactly graceful these days," she said. "Walking, sitting, lying down." She bit her lip. "And don't start on how I can't *gracefully* send a text."

There. It was out. And his smile widened and his eyes glinted in the bright light.

"I guess it depends on how you define graceful," he said.

"The usual way—with style and ease and no wrong-fully dictated soliloquys meant for the privacy of my bedroom."

He chuckled. "I disagree. I could picture you there, and hear your voice."

The little bit of blood that wasn't swooshing around her babies shot straight to her face. "Chase, you're not making this any easier."

Quiet, he opened the bag, took out the extra napkins that Tori had packed and slid out the croissant. "Split with me?"

He didn't wait for an answer, but pulled the flakey crust apart and nestled half in a napkin, then handed it to her.

"I'd like to stay with you," he said simply.

Taking the buttery offering, she regarded him, sensing they were too good of friends to dance around things. "Wouldn't you be more comfortable at Ocean Song or...Nonna's house?"

He lifted a shoulder that was still as broad and strong as she remembered. "I want to put the house on the market—hoping you know a good real estate agent, by the way—and Ocean Song is booked."

"You're the owner of the hotel and I know for a fact they keep an emergency room."

"Actually, no. It's booked. I'd have to sleep on a sofa in my office. You don't want that, do you?"

"Then you can live in Nonna's house and leave during showings. Yes, we can list through Wingate, but I'm not taking any listings personally."

He gave his chest a light fist tap. "You're killin' me, Rain."

"Chase, I...I am not going to say you can't live there. We have an agreement and it was supposed to go a few more months. You are paying for the room and don't seem to be interested in ending that deal. But I'm honestly not the best company these days. I just sleep and...wait."

"Alone."

"Yes, *alone.*"

"Are your sisters or parents or even your niece spending the night with you?" he asked, true concern in his voice. She'd forgotten that subtext of tenderness he'd always shown, and the genuine care about her well-being and the babies'.

"No one is spending the night with me," she said. "And that's fine. I'm a big girl, and about to be a single mother."

"Well, I promised my nonna—"

"Who's in heaven and probably hasn't forgiven me for the Big Lie we told before she passed. And..." She gave him a playful dirty look. "You can't invoke her name every time you want something from me."

"I don't want anything from you, Raina," he said. "I just can't stand thinking about you alone when you're this close to giving birth."

She started to respond, but nothing came out. Which was good, because her brain had disengaged and if she put her feelings into words, there'd be no turning back.

Feelings like...gratitude and hope and tenderness and...and, oh God, was that *longing* again? Or something even harder to admit?

"And I want to be there," he finished. "As backup or a helping hand or..." He lifted a brow. "A friend. We're friends, right?"

"Of course we are, but why? Nonna's gone, Chase. These aren't your babies, so they're not your responsibility, and neither am I."

For a second, just a split millisecond that came and went in a blink, she saw disappointment in his eyes, but then it was gone, replaced with humor.

"She could still be watching," he teased, looking up at

the sky. "Pretty sure she is. Italy was replete with signs from her."

She took a bite of the croissant, brushed some crumbs off her belly that would have hit her lap if she *had* a lap, and dabbed her lips with the edge of the napkin. "Tell me."

"Well..." He took his own bite, thinking. "When I got there, all the Ocean Song roses were dead. They'd had a blight of some sort and I wasn't sure what I could do. I'm not the gardener my grandfather was. I was certain I'd have to take them all out and start over, and I was clueless."

"What happened?"

He swallowed the next bite and grinned. "I took her ashes out to the Tyrrhenian Sea, right where she made me sprinkle Carlo. And a storm came up, and a lot of wind, and it was a little messier than I expected. Anyway, I got home and still had half the container full of ashes."

"You put them on the roses?" she guessed.

"Yes! And in a week, green leaves were growing. By the end of December, there were blooms. The entire bed was alive and well."

"That's so sweet. You should have poured her favorite limoncello on the soil for good measure."

"I poured it down my throat," he said dryly. "And...then..."

She waited for him to finish. When he didn't, she leaned a bit closer. "And then?"

"Then I got that text."

"Oh, Chase, it was—"

He held up a hand. "It was what precisely I needed."

What he needed? "For what?"

"To know I had to rush back here before Thing One and Thing Two were born without me here to witness it."

She shook her head. "Chase, when I accidentally dictated that text, I was exhausted and hormonal. But let's get one thing perfectly clear—we may be friends, but you are *not* going to witness the birth of my children."

"I didn't mean literally," he said with a smile. "And, yes, you may have been exhausted and hormonal but what I heard was a woman—a woman I care about— admitting that she felt alone in the face of a daunting and terrifying life change."

She stared at him and all of those emotions—all that *longing*—came bubbling up and threatened to make her do something stupid, like lean closer and take that kiss she never got.

Common sense, thank God, prevailed. "A Wingate is never alone," she said.

"I get that. But I want to be there for you. Living downstairs, able to help you, make you amazing and comforting food, to give you foot rubs and play opera for the babies and help you enjoy these last few weeks and days like, well, like a happy vacation. I want to do that for you, and for your children, Raina. No strings—not a single one—attached."

"Chase, I—"

"You did so much for me."

"I fibbed to your grandmother."

"You got me through my grief." He put his hand over

hers. "Even when you were thousands of miles away, you...helped. Just knowing you helped."

Her heart melted as she looked at him and sighed. She didn't know what she was feeling or why, but somehow the weight on her shoulders—and her heart—eased and lifted. It all seemed so *doable* with him. So possible. And so right.

Why was she holding him at arm's length when he wasn't asking for anything but a chance to give her help?

"I could use some pasta Norma," she whispered, her whole body lighter as she breathed the words and his lips tipped up in a smile. "And the foot rubs. And the company. And..." She swallowed hard, tamping down her fears for the sake of honesty. "And..." She turned her hand over and threaded her fingers through his. "And a friend like you."

He smiled and, as always, the whole world seemed sunnier because Chase Madison was in it. Why fight it?

Because it could all come back to haunt her when she was facing life alone again, but she was willing to take that risk. What he was offering was exactly what she needed. Complicated, but needed.

Chapter Twelve

Madeline

A t the sound of her doorbell on Friday evening, Madeline snapped the clip to hold back her hair and inched away from the full-length mirror, her gaze lifting from the black slacks and gray sweater to land on her horrified face.

That couldn't be *Adam*...could it?

She said she'd meet him at the restaurant, and never gave him her home address. Could he be at the front door half an hour before they were supposed to meet?

"I wouldn't put anything past him," she murmured, sliding on leather flats and walking down the stairs of her townhouse. It couldn't be him, she told herself, and if it was anyone else?

She glanced at the kitchen clock on her way to the front door.

They'd have to skedaddle, because she was due at Cassano's in twenty-six minutes and that meant she had about twelve of them to get out the door and walk there.

Preparing to send away whoever it was, she peeked

out the side glass and grunted in frustration, opening the door with a sigh.

"Sadie. What are you doing here?"

Her sister lifted one brow, gave Madeline a cursory up and down, and sailed inside. "I knew it. I *knew* it."

Madeline turned, following her. "You knew what?"

"That you'd dress like a nun on her day off."

"How I dress isn't your concern and I'm late—"

"Well, you're going to be even later, so deal. You've got to change."

"I don't want to change."

"And that, my darling sister, is at the root of all your problems."

"*My* problems? You're the—"

Sadie cut her off by leaning closer, squinting right in Madeline's face. "Do you even have mascara on? And..." She turned her by the chin, looking at the back of Madeline's head. "A *barrette*? With those gorgeous dark chocolate waves?"

Madeline rolled her eyes. "You're not writing a marketing brochure, Sadie. I always pull my hair back, nor do I wear a lot of makeup."

"Understatement alert." She gestured toward the stairs. "Come on. Up you go. You have to have something better in your closet and if you don't, we'll go to your studio and find a dress."

"A dress?" Madeline stood frozen. "I sell *wedding* dresses there."

"And some evening wear. I'd rather see you show up in a pink bridesmaid gown than..." She plucked at the gray sweater. "Seriously, Madeline? You're an icon of fashion with a fabulous sense of style. Why are you dressed like this for a date?"

Digging for composure and resisting the urge to steal a glance at the clock, Madeline refused to move. "It's not a date."

"Really? Tell him that. He's been at the shop all afternoon kindly loading my inventory management software while I made batches of chocolate for tomorrow's event."

"So?"

"So I definitely heard the words, 'I've got a date with Maddie'—*Maddie*—come out of his mouth. I knew you weren't ready for that, so consider this a save."

"I don't need a save."

"You want to show up dressed for choir practice when he's in Armani and taking you to one of the nicest restaurants in town?" Sadie challenged.

She didn't care how she was dressed for him.

"Look, the man strong-armed me into having dinner at some old-school, expensive restaurant so he can give me that long-overdue apology and, I'm sure, spin some tale about what happened twenty-five years ago and then...I don't know. I'll finish a salad, plead a headache, and come home. Not a *date*."

Sadie started up the stairs, waving Madeline along.

"I've changed my mind about him," she announced. "No, to be fair, I've finally *made up* my mind about him, because I basically never knew the man before. He's really a good guy."

"Don't tell me," Madeline said. "He talked trash about the family you hate so now you think he's a god."

"He doesn't talk trash," Sadie replied. "But he did tell me he doesn't trust Tristan, or any of them, so the best thing Tristan ever did for me was leave. Plus, he spent hours working magic on my computer and register—why is technology so complicated?—and saved me money and time and trouble. Come on. Let's dress you."

"I am dressed," Madeline muttered as she reluctantly followed, hating that she could never, ever, *ever* say no to Sadie. "So the guy clicks a few keys and now I'm supposed to dress up to have dinner with him?"

"He's got real feelings for you."

Madeline almost tripped on a stair. "Oh, please. He's spoken to me for five minutes in over two decades."

"I can tell by the way he says your name. '*Maddie*.' It just rolls off his tongue like *buttah*."

"You're out of your mind."

"No, but Gregoire is. Can you believe he had Asha Devereaux the heiress waiting at the Saint Pierre compound in Brussels when Tristan got back? He still wants that marriage to happen."

"Oh, so *that* is the reason I'm supposed to be thrilled and overdressed to have dinner with Adam? Because he loathes the same people you hate?" Madeline demanded as she reached the top of the stairs.

"It tells me his character." She gave Madeline a gentle nudge toward the bedroom. "Come on, *Maddie*."

His *character* was to abandon her when she needed him the most. Madeline grunted and took a few steps, steamrolled by Sadie as she'd been so many times in her life.

"And why does he get to call you 'Maddie' and no one else?" Sadie asked. "You told us all we had to call you Madeline or else. It took me six months to get used to it."

"Dad calls me that."

"I think you hate the name because it's what Adam calls you," Sadie mused, already swinging her way into the room.

"*Called* me. Past tense. He doesn't call me anything now, except..." She checked her watch. "Late."

"He'll wait, trust me." She stepped inside the closet, turning with a whimper. "Color-coded and alphabetized, of course."

"It's not..." She didn't bother to argue about her neat closet with a woman who considered the back of every chair a place to hang clothes. "And what would you have me wear with Adam in his Armani suit?"

"Something stunning and suitable for a romantic dinner date and comfortable for a little make-out sesh in the living room."

Madeline choked. "As if."

"As if what? You'd make out, or risk rumpling the throw that's perfectly placed on the back of your sofa?" Sadie chuckled.

"They are both out of character." Madeline leaned against the doorway. "Like everything else in my life, my closet and my home is organized, structured, tidy, and..." Madeline lifted one of the shoes from rack, a brown Stuart Weitzman pump, closed-toed and..."Boring."

Her sister turned to her. "You're not boring, Madeline. A man who hasn't had a substantive conversation with you in twenty-five years is chomping at the bit for your evening together. He's not expecting to be bored by you."

"I wasn't boring...then," she admitted, dropping the shoe that *young* Madeline would have ridiculed mercilessly. "But I am now."

"I don't agree," Sadie said, pulling out—then discarding—a favorite sand-toned sheath. "You're confusing classic with boring. You're elegant, restrained, understated, and so darn together it hurts. Don't you see how attractive that is?"

It was safe, not attractive, and that was just fine with Madeline.

Quiet, she watched as Sadie flipped through her dresses, finally pulling out a backless black silk cocktail dress with a gasp. "Holy cow, this is gorgeous! Is this Alexander McQueen?"

Madeline snagged it out of Sadie's hands. "It's Madeline Wingate. I made it on spec for the store but...ended up keeping it."

"I can't believe it didn't fly off the shelf."

Truth was, it was never for sale. There was something about the cut, the fabric, the absolute soul of that dress that made Madeline keep it for the sheer pleasure of owning it, not actually wearing it.

"Then we have our winner." Sadie flicked the hanger Madeline held.

"No. No, Sadie. I'm not wearing that tonight."

"Why not? Just give me one good reason and I'll back off."

She'd *never* back off. "If I wear that dress..." She couldn't even imagine what could happen if she wore that dress. Magic, she supposed. "He'll...he'll think I...care."

"Don't you care?"

"Not about him."

Sadie leaned in. "Then don't give him the power of showing up in your slacks and sweater. Make him writhe in regret. Make him sorry he let you go. Make him wish he'd kept you and married you and had you on his arm today as his life partner and the moth—"

"Stop, stop!" She closed her eyes with a sigh, the truth of her life bubbling up. She almost said it. She almost told Sadie the saddest thing in her life.

But she'd save that for Adam.

"I know you're not going to give up until I change," she finally said, reaching for another dress, not as much of a statement, but...what had Sadie said? Elegant, restrained, and understated? The deep violet sweater dress fit the bill. "I'll wear this."

"With heels." Sadie grabbed a pair of black slingback sandals.

"They're open-toed, and it's January."

"It's Florida." She shoved them in Madeline's hand and slipped by her. "Change, Maddie."

When the door closed, Madeline stood stone still staring at the dress and heels, Sadie's parting order ringing in her ears.

Change, Maddie.

Change? She already had.

Half a lifetime ago when she'd stood in the pouring rain at a bus stop and realized she'd been...left. And in the agonizing days that followed, alone and wrecked. She put herself back together again but she was never Maddie, the carefree, passionate, courageous apprentice designer.

But that's who Adam knew. That's who Adam was expecting. That's who...deep inside, she wanted to be again. Just one more time.

Tonight.

Because it would be the one and only time she ever sat alone with him again, across a table, sharing...the truth.

She dropped the violet dress and shoes on the floor. Stepping out of her slacks and sweater, she turned back to the hangers and pulled out the black silk. With slightly shaking hands, she took off her bra, since she couldn't wear one with this backless style, and shuddered when the cool fabric touched her bare skin.

She slid into the sandals, stepped to the full-length mirror and, very slowly, reached up and unclipped her hair. With a shake of her hands and a finger comb, she draped it over her shoulders.

Dark chocolate waves indeed.

"Did you change?" Sadie called from the other side of the door after a minute.

Completely. Madeline opened the door and stepped back for inspection.

"Oh." Sadie put her fingers to her lips and stared.

"Please don't sit me down and put makeup on me," Madeline said.

"You don't need it," Sadie whispered.

"Thank you." She took one more look at her watch and nearly cried. "If I leave now and walk fast, I'll only be a few minutes late and that, my dear sister, is as much as I'll push my envelope."

Sadie gave her another hug. "Give the guy a chance, Madeline."

"I'll give him more than a chance."

"Now we're talkin'!"

She'd give him...a punch in the gut that she hoped would hurt him as much as it had hurt her.

With that, she grabbed her bag, a wrap to cover her back, and headed downstairs.

When she stepped out into the night air, she stood still for a moment. Taking a breath, she walked very, very slowly toward Centre Street and was eleven and a half minutes late for a meeting she'd waited twenty-five years...and seven months and about three days...to experience.

"Maddie." Adam got up from a bench in the restaurant entryway the moment she walked in, tugging at the sleeves of his sports jacket—yes, Armani—over an open-collared linen shirt and dress pants.

"Hello, Adam."

"I wasn't sure you were coming," he said softly.

She opened her mouth to apologize for being late, but stopped herself. Tonight, she wouldn't be sorry for anything.

"I told you I'd be here," she said instead.

"Mr. Logan?" The *maître d'* approached them, holding two leatherbound menus, reminding Madeline that everything about Cassano's was like a restaurant from decades gone by. Was that why he chose it? "Your table is ready."

"Thank you." He put the lightest touch on Madeline's back, making her grateful for the wrap.

They didn't talk as they threaded white-cloth-covered tables, stopping at a booth in the back lit by one candle and a dimmed sconce on the wall.

"Is this suitable?" the man asked Adam, who looked at Madeline for her approval.

If by suitable, he meant intimate, romantic, and secluded, then yes. She gave an infinitesimal nod and slid into the booth, half expecting Adam to sit next to her like he used to.

Thank goodness, he took the bench across from her after she sat.

As the waiter handed them menus, Adam leaned in. "Do you still like Bordeaux, Maddie?"

A memory jolted her—a night in New York, a restaurant like this, a bottle of Lafite. She hadn't had it since, and rarely drank, but tonight? She could probably use a few sips.

"Yes," she said. "That's perfect."

He looked up to the waiter, ordered the wine, and waited until they were alone and had both placed their napkins on their laps. Then, he braced his elbows on the table, leaned his chin on his knuckles, and slayed her with a direct look.

"Before one more word is exchanged," he said, "I owe you a heartfelt, genuine, and very candid apology."

She stared back at him, taking a few heartbeats to just drink in the sight of him a full two and a half decades since their last encounter. Time had given him plenty of silver at his temples, a few creases around his eyes, and a small scar on his jaw she didn't remember. Handsome, yes, but older and not as chiseled.

It was sad she hadn't had the chance to see that change happen gradually over the years, but that was his decision, not hers.

"You do owe me that," she agreed. "But the time to deliver it was years ago."

He closed his eyes and nodded. "I couldn't," he said simply. "It would have cost me my job and my entire future."

"What kind of job requires you to lie to people you trust and..." She almost said love. And why shouldn't she? He'd told her he loved her. Many times, in fact. "And disappear without so much as a forwarding address in case they need to reach you?"

"An undercover job for the Department of Justice," he said simply. "Your life could have been in danger until we had everyone involved under arrest."

"And after that?" she pressed. "You couldn't have called?"

He looked down. "I was already reassigned and living in another state."

"But we were...together," she said, old feelings bubbling up. "Regardless of what you were doing and why, we *slept* together. We loved each other."

He took an unsteady breath and swallowed. "I shouldn't have let that happen, but my feelings for you were real. Way too real and I actually got in trouble for—"

"You did?" she fired back. "What do you think happened to me?"

He searched her face, and with each passing second, her heart slammed harder and the truth—the dark and painful truth—rose closer to the surface.

"I wasn't allowed to contact you, Maddie. There were legal issues and...and...undercover means just that. I couldn't let you know until I'd testified and by then..."

"I'd left New York," she supplied. "But you knew I was from Amelia Island. You knew where I went after the dust settled at Chanel."

"I did," he acknowledged. "But I decided you didn't deserve the life of being married to an undercover agent. The work is nothing but secrets and lies and fake relationships—"

"Was ours fake?" she demanded.

"No. Only in the fact that you didn't know who I was or what I was doing, but my feelings were real." He shook his head. "I couldn't give you what you wanted."

"Shouldn't I have had a chance to decide that?"

He looked down as the waiter returned and spent a few minutes uncorking and offering Adam a taste of wine. Through it all, Madeline relived the pain of his disappearance, the aching loneliness, the...loss.

And then the months and years, the questions and heartache, the walls of self-protection she'd erected so that kind of mistake never happened again.

When they were alone with freshly poured wine, he lifted the glass.

"Don't you dare toast," she ground out, narrowing her eyes.

His brows flickered in response. "I'm apologizing."

"You can't."

"I can try."

"There are no words that will ever make me forgive you, Adam."

He drew back, confusion and hurt in his eyes. "I know I hurt you—"

"You have no idea," she said.

"I think I do."

She leaned closer, her heart slamming hard against her ribs, because it was *now*. Finally, after all these years, it was now.

"All you needed to do was have one conversation with me," she said. "One moment. One call. One single phone call. But you abandoned me."

He heaved a sigh, casting his gaze down. "I'm very, very—"

"And I was pregnant."

With a gasp, he looked up and stared at her, his jaw looser with each passing second. "What?" He blinked, looking as if he were literally sinking into himself as he backed into the leather booth.

Relief rolled over her like icy water that was both deeply painful and wonderfully cleansing. Finally. Her secret was out.

"I was ten weeks pregnant and going to tell you that night."

"Maddie," he barely breathed her name. "What...happened?"

She closed her eyes, knowing that she couldn't ever communicate the magnitude of it, the pain or the heartache, so she kept it simple.

"I tried to find you. I stalked Northeast Fabrics, I haunted your apartment, I called and cried and..." Her voice cracked and she took a moment to compose herself. "Five days after you left, I started bleeding and..."

"You lost the baby," he guessed on a whisper.

She nodded, swaying a little when he put both hands to his face, covering it, lowering it, the reaction so visceral she almost reached over the table to offer comfort.

"Maddie. I...had no idea."

"No one on the face of the Earth knows," she said softly. "Not my family, no one."

He finally looked at her again, anguish in his eyes. "I'm so—"

She cut him off with a raised hand, her heart still pounding, her whole body quaking.

"Don't," she said. "Don't try to apologize. You didn't

just lie. You didn't just use me and leave me. I'm not so fragile that I couldn't take a man losing interest and ghosting me, or whatever we called it back then." She pointed at him. "I blame you for that miscarriage. Your coldness, your cruelty, your decision to not even give me a chance to say goodbye."

He looked at her, his eyes filling, but she didn't care.

"Because of that, I never loved again. I never trusted again. I never let my guard down so I didn't have to experience that kind of pain. So, keep your apologies, Adam. I am not going to forgive you."

He stared at her. "Maddie, I...I...I'm at a loss." He grimaced as though it all hit him again. "You're right. An apology is just...lame."

Silent, she stared at the deep red liquid in the glass in front of her.

"But I have to try," he said. "I have to try and make it up to you and—I know, I know, impossible—but please believe me that I would never have left like that if I'd have known. And that's no excuse," he added quickly. "I don't know how to make it up to you or...or..."

She looked up at him. "I don't think you can, and I'd rather you didn't try."

He leaned closer, inching his hand across the table. "Then can we—"

She held up her hand to stop any suggestion of what to do, and when she brought it down, she purposely placed her fingers on his arm.

"No, Adam," she said gently. "We can't do anything. And that, I'm afraid, includes having dinner, drinking wine, and making small-talk. I appreciate the effort, I really do. But I can't."

"Do you want to...just take a walk and talk?"

"I want to go home," she whispered as she realized just how much she wanted that. "You've delivered your apology, I've shared my truth. There's nothing left for us. I'm..." She almost said "sorry" but she wasn't. Not at all.

"Maddie—"

"I wish this could be a date, Adam." She reached for her wrap and bag. "I wish we could have dinner and laugh about old times and offer and accept forgiveness, and carry on. But when I look at you, I see my greatest disappointment, my biggest sadness, my most miserable months. That's all I see. That's all I'll ever see."

"I don't know what to say."

"Say nothing, to anyone, including any member of my family. You, the great keeper of secrets, will not tell a soul that this happened. Thank you for making the effort and for your apology."

"I understand. I don't...like it. But I understand."

"Good night." She stood, walked through the restaurant, making it all the way home before a single tear fell.

But then, they poured out until she had none left.

Chapter Thirteen

Sadie

"I brought flowers!" Rose called as she came in the back door of Charmed by Chocolate. "A bouquet for every table."

Sadie looked up from her last batch of blueberry ganache bonbons, not even able to see her sister behind the tall stands of roses in every imaginable color. "Oh, perfect!"

"I used the tall vases for weddings because people sitting across from each other can see under, and they'll make everything so festive. Grace and Isaiah are out there with folding chairs from the bookstore, and Tori's got all the extra cups and fancy tasting plates, since you'll probably need them."

"Thank you so much." Sadie finished the tray and scooped it up to fill the last section of the display case. "Follow me to the front."

"The front?" Rose said as they walked through the swinging door. "You need a better name for this area."

"In the business, it's just the front of store, or retail area. Some call it a tasting room. I call it..."

Rose put the first glorious bouquet on one of the marble tables.

"Beautiful, now," Sadie finished. "Thank you for these flowers. I really hope people show."

"I do, too," Rose said, making a slightly worried face that was entirely out of character for her usual optimistic self.

"Why? What's wrong? You think my grand opening is going to be a bust?"

"No, no, not for a moment."

"Then what's the problem?"

Just then, Isaiah came in, carrying folding chairs under his strong arms, followed by Grace and Nikki Lou.

"I can't have any chocolate!" Little Nikki announced, prancing close to Sadie.

"I have very special strawberries for you and Grannie Suze, Missy," Sadie said, bending over to give her little niece a hug. "I know you two are special that way."

"Grannie Suze gets a headache," Nikki Lou told her. "But I get wild!"

Sadie threw her head back and laughed. "Maybe that's my problem."

"But I promised Isaiah I'd be so good today." She stood on her tiptoes to whisper in Sadie's ear. "He said it's a secret special day!"

"Really?" She looked at Rose, who just made a "you never know" face, but didn't say anything as Grace joined them.

"You're always good," Rose assured the little girl,

then turned to Grace. "Were we right?" she asked under her breath.

Grace nodded and glanced at Sadie. "It'll be okay, though. It can't take all day."

"What can't?" Sadie asked. "This event? It goes on to the afternoon. Do you have somewhere else you have to be?"

"No, no," Grace said quickly. "We'll be here all day for whatever you need."

"Then what is it?" She looked from one sister to the other. "'Cause I'm picking up a vibe here."

"The vibe you're picking up is an unexpected event on the beach," Rose said. "Not town-sanctioned, but the high school is sponsoring a 'clean and craft' day that is getting lots of locals to spend the day at the beach. Doesn't help that it's glorious and seventy degrees, but they can't stay there all day."

"Well, there are plenty of tourists in town, right? It's January."

Grace made a face. "It's also the annual car show at the Ritz-Carlton, which is earlier than normal this year, so just about anyone visiting Amelia Island this week is down there."

"Well, that's only about twenty minutes away," Sadie said, but even as she did, she knew that event kept people way south of town for the entire day and into the evening.

"And the farmers market," Isaiah added as he flipped a few chairs open and lined them up under the feature wall. "But God provides, Sadie."

"Plus all the Wingates will be here," Rose added. "So it will feel crowded."

Sadie tamped down disappointment. "Well, it's not like I had a choice to pick a less busy weekend. It was do or die to make my official opening deadline for Kitty."

"Aunt Sadie, look." Nikki Lou tugged at her arm and pointed to the door. "There's a person for chocolate."

She glanced out to see Scout trying to open the door with hands holding a large box. What did he bring her?

"Come on, Nik," Isaiah said. "Let's get the next batch of chairs."

As they left, Sadie unlocked the door and beamed at Scout. "Welcome! You are my first official customer," she said. "And you're supposed to come hungry and empty-handed."

"I have a grand opening gift," he said. "And I hope you like it."

"Scout! You're so kind." She ushered him in and he greeted Rose and Grace as he put the rather sizeable cardboard box on one of the tables.

"I know you just came up with the name for the store a few days ago," he said.

"Thanks to you." She turned to her sisters, beckoning them closer. "Charmed by Chocolate was this guy's idea. And I did manage to get a decal," she added, pointing to the gold foil letters she'd carefully pressed on the window a few hours ago.

"I saw that, and I figured you didn't have logo bags." He reached into the box and pulled out a small white shopping bag, the perfect size to hold a box of chocolate. "Candy boxes take a while but my bag vendor was running a special and he turns things around in a day, so..." He held the handle on his finger and let it swing, the words *Charmed by Chocolate* matching the script on her window. "Happy new store, Sadie."

For a moment, she was nearly speechless, looking from the perfectly centered letters in exactly the right golden color to his blue-green eyes that seemed to twinkle with the joy that only came from giving the perfect gift.

"Oh, my goodness, Scout." She slipped her finger next to his to take the bag he offered. "This is...wow. Beyond necessary and so nice. Thank you!"

"Look at that!" Rose cooed, reaching in to get another bag. "And two sizes. Scout Jacobson, it's wonderful people like you that make Amelia Island so special."

He chuckled and flushed ever so slightly. "I figure it's good for business when people are walking around town with your name on their bags."

"It is," Sadie agreed. "And I...I'm a little over-whelmed," she admitted with a hand to her chest. "I don't know how to thank you."

"No need," he said. "Just being neighborly."

Grace reached out her hand to him. "How very kind you are, Scout. And for a competitor, too."

"There's room for both of us on this island," he assured them, then glanced around. "Place looks great."

"Thank you," Sadie said. "I've just heard we have some stiff event competition."

He winced. "Yeah, I think town traffic might be slow

today, but would you like to put some flyers in my store? I get the sweaters, you know."

"I'd love to," Sadie said, stepping away to grab a few for him, still not quite sure how to show her gratitude for his kindness.

Grace and Rose chatted with him until Sadie came back from the office with a stack of flyers.

He promised her he'd give them out and left after a little more small-talk, many thanks, and his hope that she had a banner day.

"Wow," Grace said when the door closed behind him, picking up another bag. "I've always thought he was a nice man, but this is...something else."

"Yeah, I'm not sure what," Sadie said.

"I am." Rose lifted a knowing brow. "He likes you, Sadie."

"He's a great guy," she replied, plucking through the bags that she loved so much.

"No, I mean, he *likes* you."

Sadie rolled her eyes and took a stack to put by the register. "Take off those rose-colored glasses, woman who only sees good in all of humanity and wants everyone happily married like she is." She tucked the bags under the counter. "He's just a very nice man, which, I have to say, I was starting to think didn't exist anymore, but color me jaded."

"I think she's right," Grace said. "And, honestly, I'd say he's one of the most eligible bachelors on Amelia Island."

Sadie straightened and pinned her gaze on Grace.

"Then why didn't *you* date him?"

She shrugged. "Other than the fact that I was a grieving widow and single mother, I think Someone"—she pointed upwards—"had a different plan for me. I was waiting for Isaiah."

"Well, I'm waiting for the sting of the last bad relationship I was in to subside." Sadie walked back to the box, looking in to see he must have ordered hundreds of bags for her. "Although, this was the act of a saint."

"A saint who looks at you the way Isaiah looks at Grace," Rose said.

Sadie just laughed. "He likes my chocolate." Probably wants the secret ingredient, she added mentally.

Would she ever trust another man, she mused as she headed to the back to bring the last bonbons out. Or had Tristan ruined her the way...the way Adam ruined Madeline?

Speaking of... She checked her phone but didn't see a text yet.

"Has anyone heard from Madeline?" she asked as she came back out to see Grace and Rose were still setting up flowers.

"She texted that she's going to be late, if you can believe that," Rose said.

"Late? Madeline?" Sadie nearly dropped the tray of chocolate. "And no one went to check to see if she's sick?" she asked on a laugh, but then she had another thought.

Maybe Madeline didn't wake up alone this morning.

"She said she had an unexpected fitting and she had

to drive to the bride's house," Rose told her. "But she'll be here later."

Or...was she shacked up with Adam Logan? But even as she conjured the image in her mind, she knew that couldn't have been what happened. Hopefully, Madeline wasn't hiding at home, heartbroken from a bad date.

"Here come Wingates," Grace announced, peering outside. "Mom, Dad, the rest of your family, Rose. Raina and Chloe, who brought Travis. Yep, this will fill the place up for sure."

But this was family. For once, she was happy there were so many Wingates, because the way things looked, there weren't going to be any customers today.

A SMATTERING WAS the best Sadie could call the attendance of the grand opening. The few customers who dropped in were lovely and complimentary, but by mid-afternoon, Sadie was beginning to worry that Amelia Island didn't need or want a new chocolate shop.

Madeline finally arrived and then the only thing Sadie wanted was a full and detailed report, so she pulled her sister back to the office on a pretense of showing her something. Inside, she closed the door and gave Madeline an expectant look.

"So?"

"So, nothing." Madeline looked around. "What did you want to show me?"

"How was last night?" Sadie asked.

Madeline just stared at her, a blank look in eyes that seemed troubled and maybe a little red. "It was...short."

"Oh, Madeline! You didn't do the salad, apology, and pretend to have a headache thing, did you?"

She shook her head. "I didn't bother with the salad or headache, but he delivered his apology."

"And?"

"And I left without eating or talking or...anything."

"What? Why?" Sadie dropped her head back with a grunt. "Why can't you give him a chance? You looked so—"

"Please. Don't." The note of sadness in the words made Sadie lower to one of the chairs, her heart hurting.

"It was that bad?" she asked.

"It was nothing."

"*Nothing* made you this blue?" Sadie reached for her and brought her down to the other chair. "Tell me what happened, Madeline. Seriously. Tell me everything."

"You need to be out there with your customers."

"All two of them who aren't related to me?" She let out a mirthless laugh. "This is more important, hon. Tell me what happened. What did he say? How did you feel? Why did you leave so fast?"

"Because we said what we needed to say. He was an undercover FBI agent who I guess had to find a way into my boss's office and—"

"You guess? He didn't tell you?"

She lifted a shoulder. "He didn't give me details. He was sorry he left without...a goodbye."

"That's it? Did he say he cared about you or was it all an act?"

"I guess he did, but..." She closed her eyes like something had punched her. "Look, Sadie, it was a bad idea to get together, and I think he knows that now. There's no future for us, no reason to talk again. We're merely two people who knew each other in their twenties. End of story. And if he ever tells you it was more than that, trust me, he's lying."

Sadie let out a noisy sigh. "I had such high hopes for you."

"Well, sorry to dash them, but please, I'm begging you, do not try to maneuver us together anymore, okay? I can't take it."

She moaned. "I'm so sorry, Madeline."

"Don't be. It's not important." She started to push up. "How's the grand opening? You seem a little down."

"It's a lackluster turnout," she admitted. "But my cookie competition brought me customized logo bags."

"That was nice."

"He's nice. Like...I thought Adam was." Sadie smiled, taking Madeline's hand again, aching to give her comfort. "I'm sorry to push you into something you didn't want or like."

"It's fine. The conversation needed to happen and now I can move on with my life with all that behind me."

Sadie searched her face, sensing that "all that" was much more than Madeline was willing to admit. What had happened between those two? Then...and last night?

"I mean it, Sadie." She pointed a finger in Sadie's

face. "I see your wild wheels turning. No manipulating things to get us in a room together. *Please*."

"I won't," she promised. "But I can't stop him from contacting you."

"He won't," she said, the words leaving no room for argument.

"Hey, you guys!" Rose tapped on the door. "Can I come in?"

Sadie popped up and opened the door. "We're coming out, Rose—"

"Now," she said. "I think something very wonderful is about to happen."

Madeline and Sadie exchanged looks, but even "very wonderful" couldn't get a smile from her sister.

"Come on," Sadie said, reaching for Madeline's hand. "We could use some wonderful."

While they headed through the kitchen, Sadie leaned closer to Rose. "Does wonderful mean I have two dozen new customers?"

"No, but you might be about to have a new brother."

"What?"

As they pushed the door open, Sadie saw the whole family gathered in a loosely-formed circle, which might have happened organically or it might be because Isaiah had somehow managed to get them that way.

He was in the center, holding Nikki Lou on his hip, her little head dropped on his big shoulder like she was in the one place she wanted to be in the whole world.

And not a complaint about no chocolate, that little angel. They might give all the credit to Nikki Lou's special education program, but Sadie suspected the management of her autism diagnosis had a lot to do with the calming peace that Isaiah exuded. Nikki still had her outbursts and breakdowns, but they were fewer and farther between.

When Sadie and her sisters walked in, Isaiah cleared his throat loud enough for Nikki Lou to lift her head.

"Are all the Wingates here?" he asked.

"And no one else," Sadie joked, getting a round of sympathetic and encouraging responses.

Her father gave her a knowing look as he and Mom came over to stand next to her. "All businesses start slow, Sadie. I have complete faith in you."

"Thanks, Dad. What's going on?"

"Isaiah wants to..." He gave her a squeeze and leaned into her to whisper in her ear, "Pop the question."

Oh! With a few chills of joy, she let Dad lead her into the circle, where an expectant hush fell over the room.

When all eyes were on Isaiah—and Grace, who looked a little too bright to be surprised by this—he lowered Nikki Lou to the floor and whispered, "Go stand by your mom, Nik."

She scampered to Grace, who wrapped her arms around her little girl, but kept her gaze on Isaiah. Yeah, she knew, Sadie thought, unable to wipe the smile from her face.

The shop forgotten, along with the nonexistent customers, Sadie let herself enjoy the moment of seeing her dear sister find love again after losing her husband so tragically in Afghanistan.

"Wingate fam," Isaiah started, taking a quick glance around. "Since we're all gathered on this beautiful Saturday afternoon, I have something to say."

While he talked, Sadie's gaze moved from sister to sister. She stopped to study Gabe, her dear brother-in-law, who had one arm around Rose and the other clasping both hands of his two youngest daughters, their older boys watching with wry smiles. So much love in that D'Angelo family.

Tori and Justin were next to them, with Tori's kids. They were not quite a family yet, but she had no doubt the good doctor was taking notes from Isaiah's speech.

Chloe and her boyfriend, Travis, exchanged a smile, nowhere near the proposal stage, but Sadie suspected her baby sister would be walking down the aisle again, and this time, she wouldn't run away.

Raina had taken a chair, one hand on her large stomach, rubbing the babies that would give her all the love she needed right then. Next to Sadie, her parents stood as close as two people married for forty years could be, pride and joy emanating from them.

That left Madeline, who was part of the circle, but somehow...separate. She had her arms crossed and a look of agony on her face, and once again, Sadie's heart broke. She should never have encouraged her sister to go on the date. It had hurt her too much.

"I think it comes as no surprise to anyone in this room," Isaiah continued in his booming baritone, "that I've fallen as hard for all y'all as I have for my sweet Gracie girl."

Isaiah's declaration and his Louisiana accent brought Sadie out of her reverie, smiling at the loud, "Aww," that rolled through the room like music.

"And with her, I've also fallen for Nikki Lou."

The little girl burrowed deeper into her mother's arms, a shy smile on her face when all eyes turned to her.

"So I have something to say," Isaiah continued. "Actually, something to ask." As the reaction bubbled around the room, he took a step closer to Grace and extended a hand to her, bringing both mother and daughter to the center of the circle with him.

Grace laughed, blinking back tears as she looked up at the big man who'd changed her life.

"God is mighty and good," he said. "He led me to you, used a ring and the greatest loss you've ever experienced, and brought us together as a family."

A tear rolled down Grace's cheek—and probably every other cheek in the room. But Sadie didn't look. She just let her own eyes fill and tears fall as she stayed riveted on the moment in front of her. The beautiful, enviable, perfect moment that...Sadie never got.

Isaiah lowered himself to one knee, his gaze locked on the woman he loved.

"I believe I am honoring Him by asking you, and Nikki Lou, a simple question."

No, Sadie never got the question or the knee drop or the ecstasy and certainty that lit her sister's face. Tristan had suggested eloping as a joke, a trick, and, she knew now, a way of stealing her secrets. He'd stolen her chance to have this, too.

Swallowing, she let her gaze move from Isaiah to Madeline, whose expression was a mix of misery and joy, kind of mirroring exactly what Sadie felt.

"Grace Margaret Wingate Jenkins, and you..." His dark gaze shifted down, meeting Nikki's wide blue eyes. "Miss Nicolette Louise Jenkins. Would you ladies together, and with the blessing of our Lord, do me the honor of becoming my wife...and daughter?"

He flipped open a black box that contained two rings nestled in two separate slots, one quite sparkly, one quite tiny.

For a few heartbeats, no one spoke. The dual proposal left them all speechless, most of all Grace, who might have been expecting this but was certainly not expecting *that*.

She took in a shuddering breath and said, "Yes, it's a thousand times yes for me. How about you, Nik?"

She looked a little confused, backing into Grace as she so frequently did, but the sparkle in the box beat out her shyness.

"Does this mean you're my daddy now?" she asked softly as she reached for it.

"I sure hope so," he said, a tear rolling down his cheek, too.

"Yes, Zayah." She nodded, her little face so sincere and serious. "Yes, please be my daddy."

The room exploded in a cheer as the rings went on and they all hugged and cried, loud enough that Nikki Lou cowered into Grace again. But Isaiah lifted her up, holding her with one powerful arm and the other around

Grace. With her head on his shoulder, Nikki held up her hand and admired her ring, calm even as the celebration grew around her. No one wanted this moment in family history to end.

But the front door opened and Sadie turned, her smile growing broader when at least six people came in, looking for chocolate.

The family dispersed into small groups as she scooted behind the counter to answer questions and happily ring up a few boxes. Before that sale was done, another couple came in, then two families, then a few women chatting in a group.

It got so crowded that the Wingates spread out, onto the street and the bench outside, with Rose and Tori and their kids offering to go back into the kitchen to help restock inventory.

"Did the beach cleanup end or the car show get boring?" Sadie asked a couple as she finished packing two boxes of truffles.

"No, we got the coupon from How the Cookie Crumbles," she said. "The owner's giving half off on boxes of a dozen cookies if we can show a receipt from here. Are you both run by the same company?"

"He's doing what?" Sadie choked the question, then looked in time to catch Rose's eye, who'd heard the exchange.

"Told you," Rose mouthed.

After ringing up the sale, Sadie stepped away from the register to get closer to her sister. "I need to go talk to him," she said. "Why would he do that?"

"So you'd go talk to him." She gave Sadie a nudge. "I'll cover for you."

Sadie slipped out the back, taking the side road that ran parallel to Centre Street until she reached the corner where the cookie shop was.

It wasn't terribly crowded in there, either, but then Scout had been sending all his business to her.

He was behind his own counter, boxing up some Dreamboats for waiting customers when he looked up and a slow smile formed.

"Don't be mad," he said, handing the box to one of his staff.

"Mad? I'm...not mad," she said. "Confused and grateful and feeling kind of...I don't know. Like you're too good to be true and the last time I thought that about someone, he was."

A soft flush warmed his cheeks. "Kitty came in here. She went by your store and said no one but your family was there and she didn't think you were going to last, that you're...'famous for flight,' I believe were her words."

"Well, I was. Once."

"She said she might rescind your place at the festival."

"What?" she choked. "Can she do that?"

"Queen Kitty can do anything she wants and I'm not about to let you get kicked out of that festival, Sadie."

"Why not?" she asked. "I mean, wouldn't that be better for you?"

"Define better," he replied with a laugh. "I want to win fair and square and I like competition," he replied.

"And..." He shifted from one foot to the other, glancing away, then looking right at her. "I like you."

"Oh." She inched back, the pureness and honesty of the words nearly knocking her over. They reminded her... of Isaiah.

"I know, not very artful, but did my evil plan work?"

She laughed, not sure if he meant he liked her or he *liked* her. For a second, she almost warned him off—he was too nice to let him think that she was available in any way, shape, or form.

So she just laughed and kept it light. "I doubt you're capable of an evil plan, Scout, but thank you."

"Trust me, you need to be crafty with Kitty. When those customers come back with their receipts, I can show them to Kitty."

Okay, he *was* just helping out another small business owner. Not...flirting with her. Or was he?

He liked her. She didn't know exactly what that meant, but right then, she kind of liked him, too.

Chapter Fourteen

Raina

P *asta. Opera. Chase.*

The thought of any or all of those kept Raina's foot on the accelerator as she drove down the beach highway toward her sanctuary. It had been a long and lovely day in town, surrounded by family, nibbling chocolate, celebrating love and life.

But now, all she wanted was...

Pasta. Opera. Chase.

Maybe not in that order, she thought with a smile as she drove past her parents' house, her mouth already watering for the first taste of eggplant and the *al dente* pasta made from scratch right on her kitchen counter. Part of her hoped it would be ready when she walked in, but part of her would love to recapture that night he taught her the art of pasta-making, cranking dough together, and laughing as the fettuccini slid out like magic from his hands.

Chase had moved into the guest suite downstairs a few days earlier, and so far, it had been easy, fun, and comfortable. He worked a lot at his boutique hotel, just twenty minutes down the beach, so he was often out of the house when she got up.

But he'd kept his cooking promise at dinnertime, and tonight, he'd guaranteed her a meal he knew she loved.

She hoped he'd play Italian opera through portable speakers, moved to tears by a wailing soprano. While she sat at the counter with bubbly Pellegrino he'd poured into a wine glass, they could talk. She couldn't wait to tell him about the day, to share Isaiah's insanely cute proposal, and relay the family joy that widowed Grace had found love again.

First, she'd change, she decided as she neared home. She'd put on a comfy top and pull her hair up—as she had every night. There were no pretenses with Chase, no need to look like she was closing a deal. She was closing a different kind of deal—days from giving birth—and having him there was nothing but the comfort and friendship he promised her it would be.

So her heart dropped a bit when she turned into her driveway and didn't see his convertible coup. He'd kept the car at Ocean Song while he was traveling, but she'd grown used to seeing it pulled to the side these past few days, always giving her the garage.

He wasn't here?

Surprised at the depth of her disappointment, she tapped the garage door button and realized she was actually holding her breath, hoping he'd forgotten to move his car and it would be parked inside.

No such luck.

On a noisy sigh, she parked, climbed out, and stepped

inside to a dim and empty kitchen. No sizzling *mirepoix* on the stove, no plaintive opera on the speaker, no wonderful man rolling dough at the island.

And no note. Not that she expected or deserved one. They weren't married, for heaven's sake. They weren't anything but friendly roommates and he was a busy man. He could be at work—although that was rare on a Saturday. Or out with friends—despite the fact that his closest acquaintances were mostly at Ocean Song. He could be on a date, for all she knew.

Even as she had the thought, she discarded it. She'd once assumed he was a player—rich, good-looking, charming. But she knew better now. Wherever Chase was, he had a reason to be there and he had no responsibility to be here for her, rolling dough and making her laugh.

But she was hungry, having limited her intake today with the expectation of a dinner tonight.

She poured some water and opened the pantry door, scanning the shelves for something filling, healthy, and not too heavy for her stomach. A handful of macadamia nuts did the trick, giving her enough energy to climb the stairs to her bedroom so she could change into something roomy and light.

Hitting a few light switches, she made her way to the hall, turning the corner and—

"Oh!" she gasped as a sharp pain cut her abdomen, making her reach for the wall to stay steady. "Whoa, whoa," she murmured, squeezing her eyes as it passed.

Maybe the macadamia nuts were a bad idea.

Taking a slow, deep breath, she straightened and waited to see if there would be another pain. There was...something. A tightening, like a band around her belly, the whole thing squeezing and literally changing shape in front of her eyes.

Holy cow. Was that a *contraction*? She had at least two more weeks!

It didn't hurt, exactly. Would they all be like that? Like an intense stretch and constriction of her whole stomach.

She gave it a few more minutes, then made her way upstairs, which was also dark and lonely with that dusky dimness that made her feel sad. It wasn't night, but the day was gone, and everything seemed to be painted in deep purple.

This time of day always felt in between and off-center. Like she felt right now. Not quite a mother, no longer someone's wife, and more of a vessel for growing babies than a woman with a vibrant life.

She'd read that the last weeks could be long and emotional, and these certainly were.

Perched on the side of the bed, she rubbed both hands over the Things, trying to rid herself of these sudden and unexpected blues.

"Hey, One and Two. Are you guys ready? 'Cause, kiddos, I am not."

Neither one moved. So, of course, Raina gave the lightest jab to the lower right section of her belly, where One was always good for a return kick, but not tonight.

"You asleep, One? Let's see if your twin is awake."

This time, she pressed on the top with the heel of her hand, hoping for that thrilling roll. She imagined it was a wee little backside, shifting into a new position. Thing Two was snoozing as well.

"Wake up, little munchkins," she whispered. "Tell me you love me and can't wait to turn my life upside down."

But they were quiet, so she stood, changed her clothes, and missed Chase some more, making her way back down to the kitchen where...she had another contraction.

At least, it sure felt like one. No real pain—not like she would define pain—but everything was so hard and stiff and tight.

"Is this the Braxton-Hicks I've been warned about?" she mused.

Maybe it was, and maybe it wasn't. But just in case, she decided to haul herself back upstairs to finally pack that bag they kept telling her she'd need. On the way up, she had another one, and now...she was worried.

Was it too soon? Would her water break? Was this...it?

She considered calling Tori or Rose, but instead, she moved through the process of packing a cosmetic bag with toothbrush and toothpaste, her favorite slippers, some clothes. What did she need to take, anyway? What was in this magical bag everyone seemed to have waiting at their door so their husband could forget it in the moment of water-breaking panic?

Her heart dropped at the thought, the word. Husband.

She'd never, ever planned to do this alone. It was supposed to be...Jack. Life was supposed to be with Jack, her partner and best friend.

As she zipped the bag, tears stung and the deepest, darkest sense of...of fear...overwhelmed her. Suddenly, she felt like she was drowning. Motherhood was daunting with one child and a husband.

But she was alone, having two of them!

"How did this happen?" she whispered, not surprised her voice cracked. Emotions swamped her, as real and overpowering as the last three contractions—she really couldn't call them anything else—making her let out a soft cry.

It didn't matter how it happened. She didn't want to be alone. She couldn't be alone. Jerking the suitcase she'd just packed, she rolled it down the hall and struggled to thunk it down the stairs. Alone. All by herself. With no husband, no help, no...one.

She fought tears—and lost—fully invested in the meltdown now. She'd fix this, because that's what she did, but right now, she wanted to feel sorry and scared and so very much alone.

Trying to decide where to go—Rose for hope or Tori for laughs or Suze and Dad so she could roll up and be the kid for one last time?

Sadie would welcome her into that cute apartment above the chocolate shop, and Madeline would tuck her in with love and tea. Chloe had a ton of space and sweet animals to distract her, and Grace would give up her own bed for Raina.

A Wingate was never alone, right?

But right now, with no idea if the next contraction was coming or not, or if it was even real, she didn't want to be alone.

She thudded the rolling suitcase over the threshold, into the garage, where she hit the button to raise the door, swiping at the tears pouring down her face. She rolled it behind the sedan and popped the trunk, suddenly blinded when headlights streamed light into the garage.

She blinked into the beam, unable to see the car, just bright halogen lights.

"Raina!"

She heard Chase's voice before she saw him, only able to make him out when he turned off his car and leaped out.

"Where are you going?" He rushed toward her, arms outstretched. "Are you okay? Oh, my God." He pressed his hands to her tear-streaked face. "What happened?"

She couldn't speak right away, only able to weather the next tidal wave of emotion that crashed over her with relentless power.

"Raina." He wrapped his arms around her and pulled her into his chest, which was strong and warm and the most wonderful thing she'd ever leaned against. Her round belly pressed into him, which normally would have made her back away, but it felt so, so good not to be alone. So good to be held by him, cared for and protected.

He eased away, searching her face. "Are you going to the hospital?"

She shook her head and swallowed the next sob. "I had some contractions, but they didn't hurt."

"How many? How far apart?"

"A few. I don't know. They weren't...it." She lifted a shoulder. "I could be wrong, but I think they were Braxton-Hicks. Those are—"

"Very common in the last month," he said, then made a face. "I've been reading."

The admission, so casual, so real, and so impossibly sweet nearly buckled her.

"Where are you going and how in God's name did you get that bag downstairs?"

She almost smiled. "I...did it myself. And I'm not sure where I was going to go. To one of many sisters, I guess." She managed a breath. "I didn't want to be alone and...and..."

"And I wasn't here," he said, sounding disgusted with himself. "We had an issue at Ocean Song and it took longer to deal with than I thought and, oh, Raina." He squeezed her again, stroking her hair. "I'm sorry."

"No, no." She willed herself not to cry, even though her whole body wanted to wail with relief at this moment. "I just got...overwhelmed."

"Of course you did. And you tried to handle everything yourself, Raina-style."

She laughed softly, so grateful he got it. And he could tease her without mocking her. It was a glorious trait that she loved.

"Do you want me to take you to one of your sisters' homes now?" he asked gently.

She looked up at him, still not quite trusting her voice, so she just shook her head.

"You want to stay home with me?"

So, so much. She nodded.

"And have a little something light to eat and maybe that foot rub I've promised you since forever?"

She nodded again, nearly folding in his arms.

"And if you have more contractions, you'll let me take you to the hospital?"

"I don't think I will," she whispered. "But, yes, I will let you."

He put his hands on her cheeks, looking into her eyes. "You are not alone, Raina."

"Oh." She might have melted a little.

He kissed the top of her head lightly. "Let's get you inside. How about I just put this bag near the door for the moment that we really need it?"

And she melted some more. Right into his arms, her head on his strong shoulder, her fight gone, her prayers answered.

"Yes," she whispered. "That would be perfect." Almost as perfect as he was.

SHE DIDN'T WANT pasta after all, but Chase made her scrambled eggs and tea, which was like heaven's meal. While he prepared dinner, she showered and put on comfy PJs and socks, and while they ate, she told him about the grand opening.

"I wanted to come, but a major delivery got messed up at the hotel, my main concierge was sick, and we have a huge event tonight."

"And you thought you could run Ocean Song without being here."

He eyed her as he stood and picked up both plates to clear the table. "I could, but...I like being here."

"I'll help you clean up," she offered.

"You'll do no such thing. Stretch out on the sofa, flip the electric fireplace to your favorite color, and prepare for the best foot rub you ever had."

She wasn't about to argue with that, taking her tea to the under-used living room at the front of the house and following his instructions. A few minutes later, all she could do was close her eyes and give in to his strong hands over her fuzzy socks.

He sat at the other end of the sofa, turned so he could easily rub her feet, somehow managing to make the contact close but not intimate. The electric fireplace that she'd once considered a crazy luxury in a beach house flickered with a soft blue light on the glass stones, giving the room a spa-like feel.

"I have dreamed of this for nine months," she admitted with a sigh. "I think of all the challenges of being a single pregnant woman, having no one to rub your feet is at the top of the list."

"What else is on that list?" he asked.

She considered the answer carefully. "I guess...what I went through tonight. That first contraction."

"Any more?" he asked, his fingers stilling.

"Not one," she assured him, rubbing her belly. "Just a few kicks. But up until that first one tonight, I haven't really felt alone. That's the beauty of being a Wingate."

"Did you go to birthing classes alone?"

She shook her head. "Are you kidding? With six sisters? They fought over who'd come with me and the last one? Both Rose *and* Tori came." She smiled at the memory and peeked at him through her lashes, taking in his strong, Italian profile, noticing that his eyes were closed as he concentrated on finding just the right spot to make her feel so good. "I didn't miss Jack," she said softly, even though what she was thinking was...

I don't miss Jack. Not now, not ever. Not with you.

He threw her a look. "Papers signed?"

"On New Year's Day," she said. "All in all, it was an easy divorce."

He snorted softly. "Is there such a thing?"

"From a legal and logistical standpoint, yes. I try not to think of the sixteen years of...all the other stuff." She sighed again as he finally let go of the first foot and started on the other. "I suppose I'll hit a few bumps in the road when the kids are born."

"You're a very good bump navigator," he said. "I have complete faith in you to be an absolutely stellar mother. Are you secretly hoping for two of the same gender or a mix?"

"I'm hoping they come out perfectly healthy and strong and not for a few more weeks." She patted her tummy. "I also feel like I have one of each. I could be wrong, and I don't want to know until that very moment, but I think of Thing One as a girl and Thing Two as a boy."

"Names?"

"Oh, here we go," she laughed and pressed her foot against his hand, rolling her eyes. "Charles."

He grinned at her. "What's your boy name, really?"

"Part of me wants to do a Reginald version to honor the long line—you know I'm Regina, don't you?"

"I do. You told me how..." His words faded.

"How my mother died in childbirth. My birth." She winced, and not because he'd hit a tender spot on the ball of her foot.

"Does that scare you?" he asked, easing his touch.

"It was forty-three years ago and another world, medically. My mother had no idea she was having twins and there's nothing hereditary about what happened to her and...yeah, it does scare me a little," she added on a whisper. "Anything I can't control scares me."

"Then kids are going to terrify you," he joked, but then he leaned closer to her. "You're going to be fine, you know."

"I know."

They were quiet for a moment, the whole house still and silent as he massaged and she got lost in the pure pleasure of it.

"I missed you in Italy," he whispered, so softly she barely heard the confession.

She didn't reply, but studied him through her half-closed lids again, wondering if he could feel her pulse increase through the socks.

"More than I...wanted to," he added. "More than I should have."

"You were grieving, Chase. Far away, missing Nonna, and—"

"Don't let me off the hook, Rain. I thought about you constantly." His fingers stopped moving as if waiting for a response.

But she had no idea what to say. She missed him, too? This was a bad idea?

Oh, by the way, did you notice this massive belly about to give birth to two *babies?*

"Chase."

"I know, I know. Dumb and awkward and compli-cated and..." He wrapped his whole hand around her foot, adding a slight bit of pressure. "All you have to do is say...no. Not interested. Too messy. Whatever you want to say. I will never broach the subject again and I promise you no discomfort whatsoever. Just say...you have no interest in...anything."

She swallowed. Took a deep breath. Formed the words in her brain. *No interest in anything. Not now, not ever, not yet, not...possible.*

But, defying all logic, she felt a slow smile pull as she opened her eyes and looked at him.

"I missed you, too," she breathed. "I...I don't know what that means, or what we could do with those feel-ings, but that's as far as I can go right now." She patted the top of her belly. "I'm too consumed with what's about to happen, Chase."

He didn't say a word, but held her gaze for a long, long time. They stared at each other, the mound of two unborn children, a few divorces, complicated pasts and a foggy future between them.

Then she gasped as her stomach tightened again, literally rising a bit, making his eyes widen as he saw it.

"Baby moving?"

"Another...contraction."

He leaned closer, holding his hand up. "May I?"

She nodded and watched as he very gingerly placed his hand on the top of her stomach. "Oh." He inched back. "I feel that tightening. Does it hurt?"

"Not in the sense of pain, just tension." She lifted her head up, bracing on her elbows. "I really think this is normal."

"It is," he said. "I looked it up when you came in and went upstairs before."

She laughed softly. "Thanks, Dr. Internet."

He studied her belly, which would have been slightly mortifying under any other circumstances, but the look on his face was sheer wonder and warmth, and his hand felt almost as good right there as it did on her swollen feet.

"Hey, Thing One and Thing Two," he whispered, fluttering his finger. "Uncle Chase checking in."

That made her laugh while the tautness subsided.

"He's the one who gives you the great food," Raina

joked. "And...oh, there's Two. Always moving his rump around."

As the side of her belly changed shape with the rolling action of the baby inside, Chase sucked in a breath. "Is that...is he..."

"Or she, yes, just getting more comfortable."

"Oh, wow." He scooted closer, mesmerized. "Raina! And down here, too," he said, placing his other hand lower on the other side of her abdomen.

"Those are my kids," she said, feeling the first jolt of maternal pride in her life.

He looked up at her, his eyes filled with wonder and, yes, tears. "Amazing."

"Isn't it?"

He wasn't the first to be in awe over her babies—she'd shared the feeling with her sisters, nieces, nephews, and parents. Even Dani and Blake had enjoyed moments of baby movement.

But no one had ever looked quite so...enthralled.

"You're so lucky," he said.

She almost made a joke, almost contradicted him, but right in that moment—seeing and feeling the miracle of her babies through his eyes—she knew she *was* lucky. After three miscarriages and one miserable divorce, she really had everything she wanted right there under Chase Madison's hands.

"I'm...happy," she admitted. "I always wanted children and regardless of the complicated circumstances, I now have two, and at forty-almost-four years old. I feel blessed."

"You are," he said, reluctantly lifting both hands. "And I'm honored to be on the sidelines watching you."

They smiled at each other, a quiet, comfortable peace between them.

Raina had no idea where this friendship was going—if anywhere—but she was very, very glad he was here right now.

"Okay, then, let's play with names," he said, lightening the mood. "Reginald? Really? And you're giving me grief about Charles?"

She laughed and relaxed and spent the next hour making up hilarious names while he finished the best darn foot rub a woman ever had.

Chapter Fifteen

Susannah

The day that the last guest checked out of Wingate House, Susannah arranged for the tree to come down. When she arrived at the inn that morning, she was surprised to be greeted by Grace at the front door.

She still wore a glow from her recent engagement, her sweet face beaming as she stood on the front porch.

"Hello, beautiful daughter," Susannah said when they hugged. "Is Nikki Lou in school today?"

"All day, so I hope you don't mind me hanging here. My manager is at the bookstore, and I feel like I should be here as we launch Wingate House Weddings!"

Susannah laughed. "And to think you weren't even at the secret meeting with your sisters."

"I'm glad you didn't spoil the surprise engagement, Mom, but I want to help in any way I can. After all, I'll be the inaugural bride." She took a deep breath and looked around the expansive grounds of the inn. "I can't think of a more beautiful place to get married."

Susannah followed her gaze, landing on the swing and the elm, that tree far enough from any structure not to cause problems. "And you're sure you don't want the ceremony in a church?" she asked.

"I thought Isaiah would, but he says God is wherever we are and during the months that Nikki and I lived upstairs after the fire, we spent so many hours under that tree on the swing. It's exactly where we want to get married." She thumbed over her shoulder toward the back of the inn. "Isaiah is with the tree cutter. It's going to be a huge job today."

"We can go talk to them in a bit, but I also wanted to do a complete inventory of all the rooms on every floor," Susannah said, reaching into her bag to slide out her tablet. "I brought my iPad to take pictures and notes, thinking we might want to change out some furniture and move some things."

Grace leaned back, giving her a thoughtful look. "So, it's working? You have something to fill your heart and day and you're able to let Dad breathe."

She flicked her hand. "He's breathing fine. And, yes, Grace. I love this idea, this future for Wingate House. It's just enough time to keep me occupied, but not a full-time job, which I do not want."

"Love it," she said. "And as the first bride, I have ideas."

"I'll need every one of them, honey. Thank you."

They walked in arm and arm, Susannah taking a look around the familiar inn.

"It's odd to think every room in the place is empty," she mused. Susannah *hoped* they were empty.

"Have you been through the inn lately?" Susannah asked. "Everything seem normal?"

"I guess. The last guests checked out last night, from the Coraline."

"Oh?" Susannah frowned. "Was everything okay with the suite?"

"Actually, it wasn't."

Susannah slowed her step, almost afraid to ask. "What was the problem?"

"Isaiah said they complained about the view, even though they got the best room in the place for the cost of the smallest on the first floor. And they just didn't seem happy, leaving in a rush before breakfast, saying something about the place feeling oddly empty."

"Yes, it is," Susannah said, thinking about her spilled purse. Did the guests have...an otherworldly incident they didn't want to mention?

"But the problem with the view will be fixed today," Grace said. "And when we rent to bridal parties, I was thinking the Coraline could be saved for the parents of the bride." She gave Susannah a squeeze. "Would you like that? Just you and Dad."

"The old haunted room?" Susannah asked, laughing so it didn't seem like she believed the family folklore.

Grace laughed, too, as they always did when they talked about that story that *no one believed*. Including Susannah, she reminded herself.

They strolled through the downstairs living area, talking about different ways to set up the rooms for receptions.

"The biggest cost will be tables and chairs," Susannah said. "But we can probably make a long-term deal with the local rental house."

"Please leave the piano in here," Grace said as they walked into the library. "Nikki Lou plays it all the time."

"It will stay, I promise."

Grace smiled, sighed, and turned. "I think we should have our first dance in here."

"I love that idea."

"It's where Isaiah asked to meet me for coffee the day we came here and found him in the kitchen. Do you remember?"

Susannah laughed at the memory. "I remember that you turned him down hard and fast because..."

"Because, one, I wasn't ready, and two, I didn't know he was just trying to return Nick's ring to me." She fondled the gold circle hanging from a chain around her neck.

"You're still wearing it?"

"We agreed I should never take it off," she said with a wistful smile. "It has so much meaning now. If Nick hadn't asked Isaiah, a complete stranger in the mess hall, to hold his wedding ring before patrol? We'd have never met. That one moment, that one snap decision changed my whole life. Saved it, in some ways."

Susannah reached for her. "Oh Grace, there is no better feeling for a mother than knowing her—"

A distant but piercing screech interrupted her, making both of them draw back in surprise.

"What was that?" Grace asked.

"It sounded like someone crying," Susannah whispered, quiet for a minute as they listened and heard it again. "From upstairs?"

Grace walked toward the steps, closing her eyes to listen. "Maybe the tree-cutting?" she suggested.

"I'd think that would be more like an electric saw, but let's go look."

They waited another beat and didn't hear anything, then headed along the corridor that led to the backyard.

There, they found Isaiah with two men and equipment, but no saws running. Isaiah came over to them, holding up a hand.

"Careful out here, ladies. They've started cutting some of the top branches and something could fall."

"Did you hear a weird noise?" Grace asked him. "Like someone screaming or crying?"

"Oh, I hear that a lot," Isaiah said on a chuckle.

"You do?" Susannah asked.

"It just started a few weeks ago," he said, pointing up. "That's what's causing it."

For a few seconds, Susannah thought he was pointing to heaven, but then realized he meant the tree.

"Those skinny branches against the old attic windows," he explained. "I think they just grew long enough to reach the glass and they make an awful screeching sound."

"Oh, that's what it is." Susannah pressed her hand to her chest, probably more relieved than she should be.

"What did you think it was?" he asked. "The ghost I've heard whispers about?"

She felt a flush of embarrassment. "Of course not, but it did sound..."

"Alive," Grace finished, not laughing as she had before. "It was really unnerving."

Instantly, he put an arm around her. "No worry, love. Nothing is alive in this inn now that the last guest checked out."

"When will the real sawing start?" Susannah asked, eyeing the men and machines.

"Today, they're just doing branches, which will get the tree clear and bare. Then they'll bring in a crew tomorrow to chop it all the way down in sections to be sure it's safe. I've got it covered, Miz Wingate."

"Thank you, Isaiah. We're going to do a room-by-room inventory and start the whole transformation inside."

With a little more chatting and a kiss exchanged between the couple, Susannah and Grace went back inside, heading straight up to start at the third-floor apartment, where Grace and Nikki Lou had lived while the bookstore was rebuilt after the fire.

"The apartment is perfect as is," Grace assured her as she opened the door. "It was such a sanctuary for us, Mom. I know you and Raina planned to rent it out for a high fee, but I can never thank you enough for giving us such a beautiful place to live after the fire."

"I'm just glad we had it ready, and that the bookstore could be repaired and rebuilt so quickly." Susannah took a look around the space, agreeing that very little needed to be done to make it bridal suite ready.

"I think we should transform the second bedroom into a dressing area, with a long mirrored vanity for bridal party hair and makeup," Susannah said. "The main bedroom can be for the bride the night before the wedding, and this living area for socializing. Can you just picture it?"

"Oh, yes!" Grace looked around, nodding. "You know, Mom, I don't think I'm going to do a major wedding party again. Nikki Lou, of course, but no one else. However, I would love if everyone got ready together up here."

"That's perfect," Susannah agreed. "And I can't wait for that."

They chatted a little bit more about the dressing area and then left.

"The Coraline next?" Grace asked. "I don't think it's been cleaned from the last guests, though."

"That's fine, I just want to do a quick walk-through." Susannah opened one of the double doors, instantly feeling colder in this room than the rest of the inn.

Ghosts would do that.

Once again, she forced the thought out of her brain and looked around. "Wow, you'd never know anyone had been in this room."

"Well, like I said, they left last night, so they never slept in the bed." Grace walked into the ensuite, but Susannah turned to the walk-in closet, where both doors were open.

She stepped inside, chilled again, peering into the darkness.

"Did you know—"

"Oh!" She jumped a foot at the sound of Grace's voice, nearly dropping her tablet.

"Oh, Mom, I didn't mean to scare you. I was going to ask if you ever closed up the connection between this room and the Madeline suite."

"Not yet," Susannah said. "Do you think we should, or maybe transform this into an official adjoining room?"

"Interesting thought. Might be fun for wedding guests who want that."

Susannah stepped deeper into the closet, feeling the bare wall. "There's a seam in the wall here," she said, putting her stuff on the floor to use both hands to find it. "Oh, here, if I push it—"

Just as she pushed, another high-pitched squeal cut through the air, making both of them shriek softly.

"Did you hear that?" Grace exclaimed, already backing out. "That was no branch."

Snagging her purse with shaky hands, Susannah was hot on her heels, back into the much brighter room. "What *is* that noise?"

"It's not branches," Grace said, looking out the window. "They've cut the ones that touched the attic. See? It must be the wind through the rafters."

Or not. All Susannah wanted to do was get out of that room, but she really didn't want to upset Grace or make her think the house—soon to be her wedding venue—was haunted.

"Must be," Susannah said, closing the closet door until it latched, anxious to get out of there. "Oh, I need some air, Grace. Let's finish this another day and get back out in the sunshine, shall we?"

IT WASN'T UNTIL EVENING, at home with Rex, that Susannah remembered her iPad. She'd left it in the closet of the Coraline and there, she was afraid, it might have to stay. She texted Isaiah, but he and Grace had gone off the island to run an errand and left Nikki with a sitter, so they wouldn't be back until very late.

She tried to put it out of her mind, but Rex was a little too observant. By the time they'd finished dinner, he'd been able to draw the whole truth out of her while they cleaned up together.

"Honey, you can't seriously think there's a ghost at the inn," he said, making light of it. "We played that up to get ghost-loving guests."

"I don't, but...I'm worried."

He shook his head, chuckling as he placed some condiments back in the fridge. "About what? The idea is wonderful. And that tree has to go, so don't think Coraline's mad about it."

She bit her lip as she pulled the lever to turn off the sink's faucet and look at him. "What if she doesn't want her house to be a wedding venue? She built the place to be a home, with your grandfather."

He started to laugh, then his smile faded. "You need to face her down, Suze."

"I thought you didn't believe in her."

"I don't, but you need to face your fears."

She sighed. "I guess, but..."

He walked over to her and put his hands on her shoulders. "Let's go over there right now, get your iPad, and have a good talking to with Coraline. She's my grandmother. I'm sure she'd love to hear from me."

She searched his face, fighting a smile but then she completely gave into it, and added a kiss. "You are so back, Rex Wingate."

"Back from...the stroke?"

She nodded. "My adventurous, action-oriented, fun, and wonderful husband. I love you so much and never want to live one day of my life without you."

He kissed her. "I'm only here because of you. C'mon. Get the keys. You can drive. I don't want to push my luck with you, boss."

Twenty minutes later, they pulled up to Wingate House, which was weirdly dark.

"Strange to have no guests," Rex said as he peered toward the building.

"I should have asked Isaiah to leave a light on somewhere," she said, driving around to the back lot usually reserved for guests, but it was as empty as the house.

"We will, after we confront Coraline."

She parked the car and threw him a look. "Be careful, Rex."

"You're kidding, right? No, never mind. You're not kidding." He reached over and took her hand. "I will be careful, I promise."

They entered through the back door, and turned on

the hall light, which took some of the odd gloom out of the house. They passed the downstairs guest rooms, rounded the corridor to the kitchen and main office, then took the back stairs to the second floor.

All the way, Susannah turned on every lamp and light switch she passed, which amused Rex even though she claimed it was so he didn't trip in the dark.

When they reached the top of the stairs, she sucked in a breath, staring at the doors to the Coraline suite at the end of the hall directly in front of them.

"I closed those doors, Rex."

"And maybe Isaiah opened them before he left to help with the air circulation. The AC's off and it's too warm for heat."

Accepting that logical explanation, she held her husband's hand and walked toward the suite, grateful there was a light switch for the chandelier right at the entrance to the room.

The yellow glow spilled over the room, brightening it, but making new shadows around the heavy Victorian antiques.

"Hello, Grandma Coraline," Rex said in a booming but playful voice.

"Don't aggravate her," Susannah whispered, only half kidding. "And why is that closet open again?"

"She's gone to meet my grandfather," he joked. "A little evening delight, if you catch my drift." He took her hand. "Come on, Suze. Let's see what the rendezvous was like."

"You're crazy." She laughed and walked with him. "But you go get my iPad, okay? It should be on the floor."

Still holding her hand, he took a few steps and peered into the closet. "Hello?" he bellowed, answered by nothing but silence. "Where's the light?"

"There isn't one in there," she said, hanging back, although she wasn't nearly as spooked as she'd been earlier. "Do you see my tablet? It should be on the floor."

"I think I do, but..." He disappeared inside. "What the heck is this?"

"What?" She peeked in, squinting into the darkness.

"It's like...lace or something." He emerged from the closet holding what looked like a yard or less of black lace, some of it intact, some of it looking like it had been hacked with a sharp knife.

"What?" Suze took it from his hands and tried to spread it out, certain she'd never seen anything like it. It was like a black lace tablecloth or... "Oh, my God," she whispered as her fingers found the edge of a small clip.

"What?"

"Is this a...black wedding veil?" she asked in an icy whisper.

Rex made a face. "That's creepy."

"Forget the tree, Rex. What if Coraline doesn't want people to get married in the home where she lived and died?"

"Susannah Wingate, stop. You do not believe in ghosts."

Right this minute? She wasn't sure. "This wasn't there today. Obviously, Isaiah hasn't been in here, because he would have brought my iPad out. So what is it if not...a message?"

"A message that the last housekeeper missed something a guest left behind in the closet or maybe—"

She gasped. "Did you hear that? The screech? The cry?" She backed away. "That sounded like a woman crying. Like...Coraline crying. Did you hear it?"

"I did," he acknowledged. "Faintly. I think it came from outside. The river, a boat passing, the wind, an animal in the backyard. Anything."

"Please, let's go. Please." She started to leave the room but stopped dead in her tracks as she stared at the pillows that she just realized looked completely different than when she'd been here today. Some were tumbled forward, some turned, one on the floor on the other side of the bed.

Rex put his arm around her and she jumped, making him laugh.

"Come on, I have your tablet. You should take your black wedding veil to Madeline tomorrow and see if she has an explanation."

She nodded, rushing out, anxious to leave and, sadly, not sure she could ever walk into Wingate House again.

Grace wanted Susannah and Rex to sleep in that room? Never. Not a chance.

Chapter Sixteen

Madeline

With her hands pressed to her lips, Madeline stared at the remnant of black lace spread on her work table, her mind whirring with possibilities.

"Is it a wedding veil?" Susannah asked, and not for the first time.

"It's..." She didn't even know where to begin. "Unbelievable, Suze. Where did you find it, again?"

"In the walk-in closet in the Coraline suite at Wingate House. Is it...valuable?"

Madeline let out a dry laugh. "I believe the word would be *priceless*."

"Really? Why?"

"I have never seen lace like this that wasn't in a museum," Madeline said. "It shouldn't even be handled with bare hands."

"Well, someone's bare hands have handled it and they had long, sharp nails. Someone angry and mean and scary."

She turned at the tone in Susannah's voice, a little

surprised by that. "You think it was a guest who brought this and took their bad mood out on it?"

"I think..." Susannah closed her eyes. "I don't want to tell you what I think. What kind of lace is it?"

She very gingerly picked up a corner that hadn't been destroyed, digging back in her mind to the History of Lace class she'd taken in college, the closest thing to art history one would study at the Fashion Institute.

"This is Alençon lace, sometimes called *point d'Alençon*, which is the region in France where it originated in the 1700s, I think. It was handmade and preserved by Carmelite nuns and, if my memory serves me, they only started adding this kind of detail"—she grazed her finger over tightly packed buttonhole stitches and a row of threaded brocade—"in the mid-1800s."

She let out a breath of admiration, studying the lace more closely. "It was reserved for the wealthiest women in the world, often called the Queen of Lace. Today, it goes for several thousand dollars a yard, or more. Not damaged, obviously, but intact? Costly."

"But...look at that clip. Doesn't that mean it could have been worn as a wedding veil?"

"Well, maybe," Madeline said, rooting for facts from that lace class. "Until the mid-1800s or so, most brides wore black dresses."

"Why?"

"For practicality, mostly. Dresses were expensive, so they wanted something that could be worn again, and dark colors hid dirt. However, they almost always wore white veils. Brides in all white didn't come into style until after Queen Victoria wore white in the mid-1800s."

"What would Coraline Wingate have worn?" Susannah asked.

Madeline looked up from the lace. "Dad's grand-mother who built Wingate House? How old was she when it was built a hundred years ago? Maybe in her thirties? Then, no, it's doubtful she wore black, and very doubtful this was a veil. I'd think that would be considered bad luck."

"Exactly." Susannah clucked. "Bad luck indeed."

"Do you have any records about Coraline's wedding? Was it here or in New York?"

"The museum might have something, or some knowledge," Susannah said. "I donated a lot of old photographs that I found in Wingate House when I renovated and I do think there was some history of that generation. But we're assuming the lace belongs to the inn and wasn't left there, which confuses me. Why wouldn't I have found it when I renovated?"

"I don't know, but a museum is exactly where this belongs, with people who know how to handle and treat it."

"Let me call Denise Robbins," Susannah said, already pulling out her phone. "She's an archivist at the museum and The Golden Age exhibit is her baby, all Victorian-era artifacts and images. She should have everything I gave her, and maybe more."

"She'll cry when she sees this," Madeline whispered,

touching the twisted stitches shaped into the form of flowers.

"Because it's so ruined?" Susannah asked.

"Because it's so extraordinary."

A little over an hour later, after wrapping the lace in tissue and placing it in a large, protective box Madeline used for her most expensive bridal veils, the two of them made the short walk to the Amelia Island Museum of History.

On the way, Madeline listened in stunned silence as Susannah confessed...that she believed in ghosts.

"Suze," Madeline whispered as they turned the corner on Third Street, waving to Sarah Beth when they passed her boutique. "You're joking, right?"

"I wish I were, Madeline. But if you could hear that scream. It's *haunting*. There's no other way to describe it."

"There has to be another explanation, one that isn't....supernatural."

Susannah threw a look at the large box Madeline carried. "It's not just a ghost, but if this is really a black wedding veil? Then maybe Coraline is sending a message about using Wingate House as a wedding venue."

"And that message would be...?" Madeline lifted a brow.

Susannah shrugged. "She doesn't like the idea."

"Well, she doesn't get a say," Madeline said as they reached the brick building that was once a county jail.

"But she built the place," Susannah said. "And when I did the renovation, I tried so hard to honor her original vision for Wingate House. It was never meant to be...a party house."

Inside, they were quickly ushered to meet with Denise, an older woman with long salt-and-pepper hair and a flowered maxi dress. She clearly adored Susannah, but wasted very little time before leading them to the Victorian exhibit.

"You know we have a small Wingate section," Denise said proudly. "All of the photos and artifacts from the original Wingate House that you shared are here. Is the lace you mentioned in the box?"

"Yes," Madeline replied as she stepped to the area reserved for The Golden Age of Amelia Island exhibit, and paused at the section dedicated to residents who named Wingate Way.

With no small sense of pride, she leaned in to look at the photo of Coraline and Reginald the First, a painted portrait, instantly seeing certain family resemblances.

Denise led them to a large table that had been cleared and covered with special preservation cloth, chatting about the lace while she snapped on gloves and offered some to Madeline for handling the treasure in her box.

As they pulled it out, Denise gasped and then moaned when she saw how mangled certain sections were.

"What a shame someone did that!" She tenderly lifted a torn section of lace. "It looks so...deliberate. Like someone whacked it with sharp scissors just to make a statement."

Madeline glanced at Susannah, who had paled at the words.

She didn't *really* think this was the act of a mad ghost, did she?

"It's a fresh tear, too," Denise added, fingering the edge. "See, Madeline? You can tell by how the threads are split but not frayed from time and air."

Examining it, Madeline nodded. "You're right. This damage is recent."

Susannah let out a soft whimper. "What a shame."

"It really is," Denise said. "Can I keep this for a while? I have a Victorian fashion and clothing expert down in Orlando I work with. I could probably get her up here to look at it and do some dating work in the next few weeks. I promise we'll take the best care of it."

"That's fine," Susannah said. "I'd rather it were here than at the inn."

Maybe the ghost would stay quiet, Madeline thought with a wry smile as she pulled out her phone.

"Let me take some close-up pictures of it," she said to Denise. "I want to do some digging of my own on this particular lace. It might give us an idea of the date and use."

After they'd finished, Madeline and Susannah walked back to Wingate Way together, kicking around ideas for where the lace could have come from, and how it got destroyed.

"Because it wasn't a ghost, Suze."

"I know, but..." Susannah gave her a look, and tipped

her head toward the baskets of flowers in front of Coming Up Roses. "Want to tell Rose? She might have thoughts."

"Oh, she'll have thoughts and they'll be the same as mine." Madeline checked her watch. "I'm going to be behind on a dress I hoped to finish this afternoon, so I'll pass. If I hear Rose howling in laughter, I'll know what she thinks about Coraline's ghost."

Susannah slid her a look. "She's not as pragmatic as you."

"Few are," Madeline joked, giving her a wave and taking the front door into the salon, where she knew there was a bridal party shopping right now.

She loved to chat with the brides, and sometimes give advice on their choices, even though Cathie, her floor manager, was an excellent stylist on her own. And despite today's delay, the dress she was working on was in good shape, she thought as she opened the door, so she could afford to—

She froze at the sight of a man in a velvet chair in the front of the salon. The place where fathers of the brides sometimes waited or, for the more unorthodox couples, a fiancé.

But the last person she expected to see sitting there just gave an easy smile that made her knees a little wobbly.

"What are you doing here?"

"Maddie." Adam stood slowly. "We have to talk."

～

SHE CHOSE to go back outside, and not just because the weather was perfect. Madeline didn't want Adam in her studio upstairs, and she certainly didn't want him in the salon.

Once she recovered from her shock, she agreed to a walk down Wingate Way, behind the Riverfront Café and down to the long stretch of the wharf.

To any outsider, they looked like a normal couple taking a sun-washed stroll to admire the many docked boats on the lovely Amelia River.

But there was nothing normal about the encounter, which is what kept Madeline tense as they started off.

"I haven't slept much," he confessed after a minute or two of walking in silence.

She glanced up at him, not sure if that was her fault, but she could see the vaguest shadows under his eyes, giving credence to his words.

"Have you?" he asked.

"Like a baby."

He smiled down at her. "Pun intended?"

It took her a second to realize what he meant. "So we're going right there, no preamble, no small-talk, no dancing around the elephant...on the wharf?"

Chuckling, he paused at a sprawling yacht docked on the riverside, looking up to examine the three decks, staring intently at what was visible of the expensive vessel. His gaze dropped to the stern, where the name *Captain's Table* was painted.

"She's a beauty," he mused. "I wonder who owns it."

"You should know, since you probably paid for a few

gallons of gas with that expensive wine you bought at Cassano's," she said, the comment getting him to look at her instead of the boat. "Nico and Ginny Cassano own that."

His eyes flicked up with interest. "Really."

"Yep. They upgraded from another one about a year ago and it's docked here whenever they're not cruising the Caribbean."

"Do you know them?"

"In passing," she said, crossing her arms and resisting the urge to tap her foot on the weathered planks in impatience. "Did we come out here to discuss the locals who have a lot of money or...your sleepless nights?"

He stared at her for a long moment, then angled his head in concession, taking one more look at the boat.

"Maddie, I had no idea you were pregnant back then."

"I know. I didn't tell you. I only realized it a few days before..."

"And I was so preoccupied with the job at hand, accumulating evidence, and arresting an embezzler."

She cringed, a thousand questions rising up like the river breeze fluttering some strands that had escaped her clip. But there was one thing she had to know, and if he brought her down here to talk, then she wanted an answer.

"Did you target me to get to Elana Mau?" she asked.

He blew out a breath. "Yes and no."

With a grunt, she dropped her head back. "Straight answers, *please*."

"That is a straight answer. I was given a list of three possible assets—targets to get into the Elana Mau operation—and a few weeks to trail them and decide on my approach."

She shivered at the thought of being an asset, or a target, who'd been trailed. All she'd been back then was a carefree up-and-coming young dress designer living her best big city life.

"There was an accountant in the Chanel operation who worked out at a local gym, and I considered befriending him," he continued. "And there was an older woman who Ms. Mau visited regularly and talked to, another Chinese lady."

"Mimi Wang," she said. "Elana's surrogate mother. How could you have gotten close to her?"

"By living in the apartment next door, and listening to their conversations."

Another shudder rocked her. "And you picked me, her apprentice, over the accountant and the sweet Chinese lady."

"I did," he said on a laugh, "and my boss ribbed me for the decision."

"I didn't know that's how undercover worked. I thought you..." She threw him a look. "I don't know what I thought. In the movies—"

"Nothing about them is real."

"But getting to pick your, uh, mark. That's kind of interesting," she conceded. "And, in some bizarre way, flattering. You must have thought I'd be easy."

"I thought you were beautiful and fascinating," he

said without hesitation. "And, to be honest, I suspected you were my best chance to get inside the actual office. And for what it's worth, another agent befriended the accountant, and he was probably more instrumental in closing the case than I was."

"Oh." She pressed her hand to her chest, closing her eyes as it all hit her again. "I was so clueless."

They paused at a bench at the end of the wharf, silently agreeing to sit there and look out at the water. The afternoon sun glistened, and highlighted the foliage in the small islands that broke up the river.

But all Madeline could see was the cavernous floor of Northeast Fabrics, and hear the hum of the looms, and the clip-clop of her clogs as she made her way down the center aisle.

"How did you trail me?" she asked. "Before you picked me, I mean."

"When you'd leave for lunch and go to that diner you liked, always ordering a Reuben and Coke."

She closed her eyes, a wave of nausea at war with bone-deep fascination. If she hadn't been the one targeted, the whole thing would have been so darn interesting to her. "And I never saw you?"

"You tell me."

"How would I miss you?" she countered. "You're over six feet tall, you're handsome as all get out, and you...are not someone I wouldn't notice."

He shrugged. "Part of the job of a good undercover cop is to not stand out," he said. "Even when I sat on the same bus as you after work."

"The same..." She looked skyward and laughed. "What an idiot. And then, how did you get the job at Northeast? Did the FBI force them to hire you? And you learned how to work a loom? Back then, before YouTube?"

"I got myself hired, and learned the loom fast. It was just my job. And I met you right away, when you went sailing down the floor, losing a shoe like Cinderella, and looking..." He gave her a side-eye, chuckling. "Pretty ridiculous and adorable."

She felt a soft flush, not sure she'd ever been ridiculous or adorable. "And an easy mark," she whispered.

He turned on the bench to face her. "Nothing was easy after that, Maddie. As much as I told myself I couldn't, shouldn't, or wouldn't, I fell hard for you. Everything about you just...suited me. Your spirit, your talent, your deep goodness. I was twenty-five and you were everything I wanted."

She stared at him, her chest rising and falling with labored breaths of disbelief.

"You had to know that," he insisted. "I didn't fake any of that. I didn't want it, either, because it only made what I had to do harder. But when we'd spend the weekend together..." He slid into a smile. "The Bronx Zoo? Remember the train and when we fed the penguins?"

She frowned, vaguely able to call up the memory, but then she shook her head. "I put everything that had to do with you and those days in a locked box," she told him. "I refused to let those images come out because it hurt too much. So you might have thought about the penguins a few times in the past twenty-five years, but after you were gone..."

"You buried me."

"Deep," she whispered. "Never to be unearthed."

"It changed you," he said softly.

"Ya think?" she scoffed.

"You value control now."

She lifted one brow. "More than you can imagine. After that, and after...the miscarriage...my whole world and value system shifted. I've never broken a promise, because you did. I'm never late, never out of order, never not in complete control of my world."

"And you never loved again? Not even close?"

She closed her eyes. "No. I don't think I've ever even gone on a date since."

He let out a soft grunt. "Maddie, Maddie. I'm so sorry. If I had known you were pregnant, I would have moved heaven and Earth not to leave you. I'd have quit my job. I'd have moved back to Florida. I'd have..." He shifted in his seat and took her hand. "I would have married you."

She studied their joined hands. His, strong and tanned and steady. And hers, much smaller and trembling with nerves.

"Not if I lost the baby, which I did."

"Because of me. Because I disappeared and left you."

She looked up at him. "We don't really know that for sure."

"Don't let me off the hook," he said, coming a millimeter closer. "You were wrecked with stress, broken from betrayal, and abandoned. You were right when you said it was my fault, and I take the blame. I can't change history or decisions I made then, but Maddie..." He lifted their hands, bringing her knuckles close to his lips. "If I could redo any of that, I swear to you, I would."

She sat very still, holding his hand. Nothing moved but the breeze, the only sound the splash of water on the wood pilings, a distant ding of a sailboat's rigging.

Right then, her heart, her broken heart...finally felt a tiny bit healed.

"I forgive you," she said softly, the words surprising her as they slipped out.

He squeezed her hand. "You do? You will?" His whole face lit with hope, and that touched her.

"If you swear you will never target me again." She eased her hand out of his.

He laughed. "I won't."

"I mean it, Adam. I can't believe I was used to destroy someone I cared about. I know she was a criminal, but it still bothers me."

"I promise you are not and never will be a target."

"And you will never, ever lie to me."

"Never."

She eyed him, believing the statement, but a whole new bunch of questions rose, none of them about their past, but so many about him.

"What about you?" she asked. "Did you ever marry? When did you get out of the undercover business? How did you end up at the chocolate company and what did you think when you met Sadie and realized she was my sister?"

He looked hard at her, his deep brown eyes moving over hers. "I was married briefly to another FBI agent, it was a disaster. We didn't have kids. I left law enforcement after twenty years, and went to Europe to blow off steam. While I was there, a friend introduced me to the Saint Pierres' company and I got a gig mostly to secure their computer systems. Gregoire liked me and used me for a lot of other things, including guarding him. As far as Sadie? You could have knocked me over with a feather when I realized the last names meant you were sisters."

"So it's truly a coincidence?" As she asked the question, she realized she didn't quite believe that.

He turned to her, took her hand again and squeezed it. "I swear on...whatever you swear on. It was purely a coincidence, unless you believe in fate trying to bring us back together."

She eyed him warily. "I don't believe in fate."

"Then it's strictly a wonderful coincidence."

"Wonderful?" She lifted a brow.

"If you've truly forgiven me." He tightened his grasp on her hand. "Have you?"

She considered the question, and all the ways she could answer it, all the caveats and

conditions she could set, and the parameters.

Then she sighed and nodded and answered the only way she knew how—honestly. "Yes, I have."

He lifted her hand to his lips and pressed a kiss on her knuckle, closing his eyes, his gratitude palpable.

"Then can we have that date again, Maddie? You pick the time and place, but please, can we just...catch up and talk and reconnect and all the other cliché things we haven't done in years?"

Once again, she sighed and nodded. "Give me some time but...yes."

Chapter Seventeen

Sadie

During a trip to the local farmers market the Saturday before the Fernandina Food Festival, Sadie met the man who would change her life. So much so, that on Monday, she got in her brand-new—used, but serviceable—Honda Accord and drove all the way down to St. Augustine to meet him again.

Vikram Patel had tasted her chocolate, understood her vision, and, best of all, owned The Spice Loft, where she could buy Kashmir lavender. The delicacy was the rarest, most expensive, and most delicious form of the flower that no one—including the Saint Pierre family—was using in chocolate.

Yes, Tristan knew lavender was her secret ingredient, but he didn't know that this treasured variety, grown exclusively in the Himalayas, brought a mind-blowing essence to every bite...including the one she hoped would be named Best Bite and be featured in *Amelia Life*.

She could have taken the interstate to St. Augustine for a shorter drive, but Sadie decided to head down the more meandering ocean highway to the historic city south of Jacksonville. That way, the water frequently appeared in sight to her left, and a warm breeze whipped through the open windows of her car.

The scent in the air reminded her of the south of France, which reminded her of Nice, which reminded her of the month she'd spent there with Tristan.

Which reminded her that her heart was broken.

But she must have a bit of Rose's optimistic streak in her blood, because she thought about him less frequently these days. Yes, she woke every morning with an ache in her chest that felt like the aftermath of a migraine in her head. Dull, distant, but definitely still sore from the pain she'd endured.

She was better every day, and there was no doubt she was on the mend, but the highs of life with Tristan had left a mark on her. Would she ever have that much fun with a man again? Could anyone make her laugh as much? Amaze or impress or delight her so much?

She sucked in some clean, salty air as she neared St. Augustine, and the punch of those nights in Nice hit hard one more time. Glorious nights, adventurous days, long conversations about chocolate and life and love and their future.

Had it all been...fake? All an effort to steal an ingredient? Surely he wasn't that...that awful. How could she have fallen in love with a man like that?

Letting out a whimper, she checked the GPS, found her turn, and caught sight of an appealing bakery called Crème de la Cocoa, which reminded her of...Scout.

Now *there* was a man who deserved her thoughts on

a sunny afternoon. A good man, a kind man, an honest man.

A...nice man? Was there anything wrong with that?

"Oh, Sadie Wingate, you fool," she chided herself. Why did she always seek adventure and...danger? Not that Tristan had been a dangerous man—only to her heart —but she loved the way he lived life on the edge of the next surprise.

Except sometimes, searching for the next thing could be tiresome and surprises could hurt.

Spotting a parking lot near her destination, she pulled in, paid the meter, and headed into the historic district. Walking through a warren of cobblestone streets lined with boutiques, restaurants, bars, and souvenir shops, she made her way through St. Augustine.

Like Amelia Island, this little beach town had a rich history, and oodles of tourists. Even on a weekday, the town was packed, but she threaded the crowds, and found her way to pedestrian-only St. George Street.

It didn't take long for her to find the two-story stone building that housed a walk-through mall, where, at the very end, she reached The Spice Loft.

She could have just followed the aroma and found it without a GPS.

There was only one customer facing a large display case, but the minute Sadie walked in, she spotted Vikram stocking a shelf next to the register.

He turned when she entered, his face lighting up. "Hello, there!" he said, his Indian accent lyrical and strong. "I remember you. The woman who wants Kashmir lavender."

"More than life itself," she said on a laugh. "It's my secret ingredient for chocolate world domination."

"And I have a pound of it ground for you in the back."

"Perfect," she said, glancing around. "And I'll need cardamom and cinnamon, since I'm guessing yours is better than anyone else's."

"You are right," he said as he disappeared into the back.

She wandered to a tasting table, ready to dive into his samples, when someone behind her cleared his throat.

"Um, Sadie?"

Whipping around, she gasped at the sight of the very man she'd just been thinking about, blinking in surprise because this was so far from where she'd expect to see him.

"Scout? What are you doing here?"

"Probably the same thing you are," Scout said, his face slightly flushed, as if he were as surprised as she was. "That was Mr. Patel's first appearance at our local farmers market and his ingredients were amazing. We should have carpooled."

She stood frozen for a moment, hearing only one word in that explanation: *ingredients.*

Had he heard her secret?

He took a step closer, a look in his eyes she couldn't quite decipher. Warm and friendly, of course, but also... astonished. Over seeing her or overhearing about the Kashmir lavender?

"Here we go." Vikram emerged from the back with a few containers in his hands, his dark eyes moving from Sadie to Scout. "And I have your cracked Malabar pepper aged in bourbon crates, sir."

She looked up at Scout, whose expression now looked...like he'd been caught.

"So it *was* bourbon," she said with a smile.

"And yours? Lavender?"

"Oh." She closed her eyes and dropped her head back. "What are the chances you'd be in this store and hear that?"

He chuckled. "It's fate."

"Serendipity," she agreed.

"Kismet," Vikram added, looking between them again. "Actually, you both came from the same farmers market and I invited you individually to visit the store. I assume you know each other?"

"Even better now," Scout said, walking to the counter. "Put these all on one, please, along with anything else my friend wants."

"Oh, no," Sadie said. "That lavender is expensive."

"All secrets are," he teased. "But I'd like it to be a gift, Sadie. How about lunch while we're down here and so far from home? Or do you need to get back to your shop?"

"My sister's manager is covering for me," she said, nodding. "I'd love a bite, as long as it's on me to thank you for the spices."

"Deal."

A few minutes later, carrying all their various spices, they stepped back onto St. George Street, pausing as the sunshine poured over them and tourists passed by like a steady stream of water.

"How well do you know St. Augustine?" Scout asked.

"Only from when I was a kid and we'd come down here as a family or on field trips. I did visit once a few years ago with some of my sisters at Christmastime for the Night of Lights and we ate in a place called..." She turned left and right, peering at the signs that hung out over the brick-covered avenue. "There it is. Prohibition Kitchen. Want to try it?"

"Sounds drinky," he joked.

"There's a bar, but the food was great, too. I seem to recall a massive soft pretzel and warm cheese sauce that was the best I ever had."

"Oh, now *that's* what should be prohibited in the Prohibition Kitchen," he said on a laugh. "Carbs."

"But where would your business be without them?"

"Gone, but so would my..." He patted his stomach, which really didn't deserve the self-deprecation he gave it.

"We'll share one," she said, urging him on.

They only waited a few minutes inside a cavernous restaurant, sitting near a raucous long bar while they admired the tin ceiling and the clever, historic vibe. Then, they were seated at a table for two on a balcony overlooking the whole restaurant. In no time, that pretzel was between them, with cheesy dipping sauce bubbling and ready to be enjoyed.

"This is a pleasant surprise," Scout said when they

toasted with their sodas. "We're seventy-five miles from home and our businesses are walking distance."

She smiled and broke off a piece of the pretzel. "You know what's a surprise? The fact that you know my secret ingredient."

"Pleasant or not?"

She shrugged. "It's a secret for a reason, but..."

"You can trust me, Sadie. I have secrets of my own."

"I know," she said. "Bourbon-flavored pepper. And now that I think about that Dreamboat brownie—and I'm not going to lie, I *have* thought about it—I realize I was sleeping on the pepper. It's there and so subtle." She pointed to him. "Well done, you. Was that your mom's recipe?"

"She used bourbon and pepper, but not the way I do. Any bourbon that my dad didn't drink, that is."

At the sadness in his voice, she frowned, instinctively knowing that wasn't a joke. "Oh, that's...tough."

He tried to wave it off, looking like he might have regretted the admission and didn't want to talk about it. And she totally understood that. "No more secrets have to be revealed today," she said, offering him an out.

With a grateful smile, he broke off a piece of pretzel and dipped it in the cheese. "So, what made you leave Europe for life on Amelia Island?"

She felt a little bit of blood drain from her face. "Ehh, let's file that under the secrets we're not revealing."

"Oh?" He lifted a brow. "Okay. Well, then. Cookies and candy it is. Safe subjects only."

"Not necessarily, but..." She turned away and looked

out over the restaurant, down to the crowded bar and the tables below. "I can't believe I just said my ingredient outright."

"Don't worry, your secret—any and all of them—is safe with me. Does anyone else in the world know?"

Oh, goodness, was every topic going to lead back to Tristan? She didn't want to lie, but she didn't want to evade yet another question.

"One person," she admitted. "But he's on the other side of the world, and I'm here, in St. Augustine, of all places."

He looked up from the cheese as if he'd just figured out that one person on the other side of the world must be the reason she was here.

"Yes, St. Augustine," he said, looking as if he weren't sure how to answer. "Home of the spice whisperer."

There. Safe subject. Good for him.

"Right?" She scooted closer. "I couldn't believe what Vikram sold. Well, obviously, he got us both down here and into his store, so props to him for using that farmers market to his advantage."

For a moment, he didn't say anything, but was definitely thinking, because she could practically see the wheels turning behind his blue-green eyes.

"You know what would be cool?" he asked. "I mean, now that we both know each other's secret ingredients? What if we combined our secret ingredients into one amazing thing that we both sold at each of our stores? Like a crossover product."

"Oh, I like that idea." She leaned back, letting that

sink in. "Bourbon and lavender in one cookie or a truffle?"

"Some combination of both. A cruffle or a trookie. Oh, I know!" He snapped his fingers and grinned. "A crownie!"

That made her belly-laugh. "Like a candy brownie?"

"Okay, forget the name, but I use a lot of chocolate in my recipes, and what if I used yours? I'd give you credit if I sold it."

"Aw, that's so sweet." And, of course, nice, because *nice* was this man's middle name. Maybe his full name. "I'd be happy to put a tray of crownies in my store," she told him.

"We could name it something funny like..." He leaned in to stage whisper, "The Scadie."

"The...oh, I get it. A couple name."

"A *trookie* name," he corrected, laughing with her.

"Actually, it's a great marketing hook," she said. "And I love me one of those."

He finished his last bite and wiped his mouth with a napkin, looking like he was ready to run out of there and make their dessert right that minute. "Let's put our secrets together and see what we create. Wouldn't that be fun, Sadie?"

She studied him, taking in his eyes, bright with mirth and hope and so much joy she could taste it like her last lick of creamy cheddar.

He was, for all intents and purposes, the polar opposite of Tristan Saint Pierre. Right then, he was exactly what she needed.

"You know what, Scout? I was just thinking all the fun was gone from my life and here you are—"

"Making it fun again," he joked. "One bourbon lavender Scadie at a time, which would probably break a lot of baking and candy-making rules. And I am not usually a rulebreaker by nature."

She winked. "Well, welcome to life with Sadie Wingate."

His eyes flashed like she'd just dangled a diamond, and that silent—and genuine—compliment touched her somewhere deep inside.

For the rest of the time, they brainstormed desserts, recipes, and more ridiculous combo names, laughing all the way back to Sadie's car.

"How about we test some recipes tonight?" he asked as she opened her door.

"Absolutely," she agreed. "My kitchen or yours?"

"Well, you have the chocolate-making equipment, and a great oven if we go the cookie or brownie route."

"Perfect. See you around eight?"

He nodded, holding the door for her as she climbed in. "Think about recipes and dessert ideas, Sadie."

She looked up at him, feeling her face muscles after all the smiles. "I won't think about anything else," she assured him as he closed the door for her.

And for the first time since she left Brussels, she didn't think about Tristan at all.

She just let her mind roam over crownies and trookies and how to make a chocolate-dipped shortbread cookie...

and the very nice man who literally made her face hurt from laughing.

"WE CAN DIP, stuff, cover, combine, drop, drizzle, or...*enrobe*." Sadie dragged out the last word, one of her favorites from her years of writing ad copy for chocolate, making Scout laugh as he leaned against the stainless prep table in her kitchen.

"Do you have a vision?" Scout asked as he scanned the cocoa butter, nibs, cream, sugar, and a few tools she'd laid out for refining whatever chocolate they made.

"Depends. Are we making a cookie or a candy?"

"Both," he replied without hesitation. "At least that's what I'd like to do. It could be a combination of the best of both our worlds." He crossed his arms and narrowed his eyes. "How about a cookie base—shortbread, I suppose—then a mountain of your creamy chocolate ganache, coated with chocolate and topped with a toasted crumble."

"Does that use your bourbon pepper?" she asked. "Because I love the idea of combining our secrets."

"So do I, and you're right, there's no bourbon pepper in the shortbread. That's in brownies. So..." He held up his finger and pointed it playfully. "How about this? A twist on the classic cookie sandwich. Brownie patties with a chocolate stuffing."

She thought about that, picturing the finished product in her head. "I like it, and we could try it, but that's a lot of ganache in something you hold for multiple bites. It could get messy."

"Good thinking about the bite," he said, tapping the stainless steel. "Very smart. Okay, okay. What about a cake-pop? Easy to hold, even for more than one bite, and it could be a great blend of our work. And I've been wanting to add one to my menu because they're popular, but not technically a cookie."

"Oh, that has potential." She clapped her hands, instantly getting a clear vision. "Maybe with your Dream-boat brownie in the middle encased in my *couverture*? Simple, playful, fun on a stick."

He laughed at that. "My mom would call it the Pogo Pop," he joked. "And please tell me I get to use that grinder machine. I don't know what you call it, but it looks like fun."

"A *melangeur*, and it's a blast," she assured him, grabbing two aprons for them. "Let's make chocolate."

This was her favorite part with Tristan, too, the combination of physicality and creativity.

No surprise to her, Scout jumped right in, and quickly absorbed and understood the process from start to finish.

She could tell his baker's heart was right at home here, and he had a deft, competent touch with the heat, working the crank to refine the cocoa with the finesse of an experienced chocolatier.

"Is it time for the big moment?" he asked, pointing to the lavender tin. "Or do I need to turn away and pretend I never saw it?"

She laughed. "Well, the secret's kind of out."

"I bet there's more to it than just this ingredient."

"You're right," she agreed. "However, you should know that the last time I gave this secret away? I got burned. Bad."

"I'm so sorry," he said. "I understand when trust is difficult. If it makes you feel any better, I'll completely pull back the curtain on the bourbon pepper and...any other secrets you want to share tonight."

She smiled at him, feeling a slight shift in her heart as their friendship seemed to deepen right in the time they were in this kitchen.

"That sounds like a deal, Scout." She picked up the lavender tin and held it to him. "It's potent, so a small pinch, then we'll taste."

He added some flakes and continued stirring the warm chocolate, waving his hand toward his nose to coax the fragrance in his direction. "It's amazing. Taste test?"

"You do it," she said.

"No, no. It's your secret ingredient. You taste first."

She snagged two small plastic spoons. "Together. It will be our dessert, not mine."

He nodded with agreement, then, at the same time, they dipped their spoons and took a taste.

"Oh." He closed his eyes and moaned. "Oh, Sadie."

She swallowed her taste, letting it roll on her tongue, picking up the essence of lavender and cinnamon and lovely, lovely cocoa. "Yes, it's good. Very, very good. Might be better."

"I don't know how."

"I do," she said, smiling up at him. "If it *enrobed* a bourbon pepper brownie..."

He laughed and kept stirring, the two of them working with a trust bond now as they completed the chocolate, created the brownie mix, formed the cake pops, and slid them into the heat, closing her oven with a satisfying thud.

"After they bake, we'll cool, shape, and move to the marble for the chocolate draping." She nodded to the shiny white workstation table that would be covered with a shallow pool of liquid chocolate for rolling the pops in a few minutes. "Want a cup of my favorite Belgian mint tea, or would you like something stronger? I don't have bourbon, but there's wine upstairs."

"Mint tea sounds great," he said. "I actually don't drink. I mentioned why at lunch."

She glanced at him as she walked to the electric tea kettle, thinking back to his throwaway but meaningful comment.

"Yes, you did. Your father." She gestured for him to get comfortable at one of the seats near the prep table.

The scrape of the stool legs barely covered his sigh. "My other big secret," he said. "Both of them, as it were, involving bourbon."

She gave him a sad smile as she turned on the kettle, quiet in case he wanted to elaborate. When he didn't, she said, "Well, that had to have been so difficult for you."

"You have no idea," he finally admitted. "But it was worse on my mom."

"They stuck it out, though, right? They were still married when he passed?"

"Oh, yeah. She was a 'till death do us part' kind of woman. But, honestly, I think she was relieved when he died. Ashamed she felt that way, but honest with me about it. That's why I did everything in my power to help her come down here and start her cookie shop. It's a darn shame she didn't get more years to just live her dream."

She turned from the counter as the steam bubbles started to hum to life, sensing the door was open to ask personal questions. "How did it affect you?"

"My dad's problems?" He thought about it, brushing back some of his brown hair, which, of course, made it endearingly tousled. "I guess it made me feel like my job was to be the man of the family, even from a distance. She was my responsibility and I accepted that."

"Is that why you're still single?" she ventured, making a face and adding, "Not that it's any of my business, but color me curious."

He smiled and tipped his head. "It's fine. I'm forty and single, so I get the curiosity. I, um, came close with a girl—sorry, a woman—"

She brushed off the correction, never sensitive about being called a girl.

"Up in Pittsburgh," he finished. "We were together for almost seven years, and when my mom died and I decided I wanted to move here, she...she..."

"Didn't want to leave her life in...the 'Burgh?" she guessed.

He smiled that she remembered his hometown nickname. "We really are unloading secrets tonight, aren't we?"

"I guess we're past ingredients. But don't tell me anything you're not comfortable talking about, Scout."

Giving him time, she opened the box of Belgian tea she'd stashed in her suitcase when she'd packed in a hurry to leave Brussels. Only four bags left, but she was happy to share them with this man.

Bringing the steaming cups and saucers to the prep table, she gave him one and took the other stool.

Nodding his thanks, he stayed quiet as he dragged the bag through the water, inhaling the scent. "That smells good."

She took a deep sniff, instantly transported back to late nights in Brussels.

"My mother's death was such a turning point in my life," he admitted softly, bringing her back to the present. "Not only did it force me to decide what I wanted to do with the rest of my life and where I wanted to live, but I knew it was time to, uh..." He gave a shy laugh. "Close the deal with Sharon."

"Ah, yes." She lifted her mug but kept her gaze on him. "The seven-year itch?"

He smiled. "And it might have been scratched if I'd been the right guy for her. But it was a turning point for her, too, and..." He bobbed the tea bag. "I gave an ultimatum and got turned down."

"What?" She drew back. "I wasn't expecting that. I thought it would be the other way around."

"Really?" He gave a dry laugh as he removed his tea

bag. "I would have said yes so fast I'd have left a contrail on the way to the altar."

"Aww. But who could turn you down, Scout?"

He almost choked on his first sip. "And now you sound like the late, great Gayla Jacobson, who believed I was the second Jewish guy to walk on water."

She laughed at that. "You are always putting yourself down. And while it's charming, it's not deserved. You're an awesome man."

He smiled at her over the rim of his teacup. "You're just saying that because you know my bourbon pepper and I know your Kashmir lavender."

She leaned closer and put a hand on his arm. "I'm saying it because it's true and I happen to speak from experience."

"With awesome guys?"

It was her turn to choke. "From the opposite of awesome."

"The one who broke your trust?" he asked. "Stole your secrets? Made you leave Europe and move home?"

With every guess, her brows lifted higher with disbelief. "I guess you know everything already."

"I know nothing," he said. "I'm just putting the puzzle pieces together and seeing a very beautiful, talented woman who has trust issues and secrets, and who gave up a pretty amazing job to live in a small town in north Florida. Well, of course, your family is here."

She made a face. "Which has always been a plus and a minus for me."

"Really? I can't imagine anything as great as having that crew around all the time."

She sighed, and lifted a shoulder. "I love them all, don't get me wrong. But sometimes, I feel squeezed in the middle, since I'm that weird position of being the oldest of the three girls that Susannah had, but right in the center of the seven of us. Sometimes, I feel suffocated and lost and even invisible, and when that happens, I take off."

He searched her face. "Are you going to take off again?"

She sighed. "I don't know. I've had a...rough time."

"If you want to tell me more..." He let the invitation hang in the air, as heavy as the rich scent of his brownies and her chocolate.

"I married him," she finally whispered. "The one who broke my trust," she added.

"You're...married?" he asked, his voice rough with disbelief.

"No, I'm not. It was...dissolved."

He frowned. "What does that mean?"

"It means I married a chocolatier who was the second son of the very wealthy family I worked for. We eloped in Copenhagen, and I strongly suspect the only reason he married me was to get a chocolate recipe that I invented and you just helped make."

"Are you serious, Sadie?"

She nodded, committed to the truth now, and ready for the lightness that would come from getting it off her shoulders.

"He got what he wanted, dumped me like yesterday's trash, and paid me off with the money I used to build out this store."

"Whoa." He shook his head in disbelief. "I'm so sorry you went through that."

She swallowed, gut-punched by how different he was from Tristan, how pure and real and incapable of deceit. Guileless, yes, but that didn't make him dumb. It made him kind of...lovable.

Lovable? Oh, boy. That was *not* what they were supposed to be cooking in this kitchen tonight.

"Well, I smell something wonderful," she said, pushing up and inhaling noisily. "Brownies always seem to tell you when they're done, don't they?"

As she walked to the oven to get things back on track, she glanced over her shoulder and caught him staring into his teacup, lost in thought.

He looked up as if he just realized where he was, giving her a sad smile, making her wish she knew the secret ingredient for life as well as chocolate.

Chapter Eighteen

Raina

The residents and retailers of Amelia Island loved nothing more than closing the main street to traffic, setting up booths, and showcasing all the talents and wares of the locals. The Fernandina Food Festival was jammed with people, vibrating with excitement, and bathed in a mix of sweet and savory aromas that made every mouth water for more.

Unless, of course, that mouth belonged to a woman who was thirty-nine weeks pregnant and wanted to be anywhere but walking down Wingate Way between food vendors.

"You look like hell on a stick." Sadie leaned over her sidewalk booth and got right in Raina's face, frowning despite the long line forming in front of Charmed by Chocolate. "Where's Chase? He brought you, right?"

"He had to talk to someone, so I thought I'd hang at this booth."

"Want a cake pop?" Sadie asked, opening up one of her acrylic displays. "It'll cure what ails you."

"Will it induce labor?" Raina asked dryly. "'Cause if it doesn't, that magic pop is no good to me."

"Taste it," she insisted, removing a chocolate-covered ball on a stick and forcing Raina to take it. "It's the result of my sweet pairing with Scout Jacobson."

Raina almost choked and hadn't even taken a bite. "Your...sweet...*what*?"

"Sorry," Sadie said. "It's the ad copy writer in me. We combined recipes. Try it."

Raina just took a sniff, wishing the dizzying aroma didn't make her, well, dizzy.

Sadie scooted to the side with a quick glance at Rose and Kenzie, who seemed to have the crowds handled. "Seriously, are you okay?"

"Meh." Raina rubbed her belly. "I've enjoyed root canals more than this festival, but it's fine."

"Raina! Go home!"

At the plea in Sadie's voice, Rose looked over, concerned. "Are you okay, Raindrop?"

"Yes, I'm fine, I swear."

Another customer walked up and Sadie had to work, so Raina slipped behind the table to stand behind Rose while she finished a truffle transaction.

The minute she did, her sister spun around, so close she smooshed the baby bump. "Whoa there, Thing One and Two." She patted Raina's belly. "Auntie Rose is here to tell you to kick some sense into your mother and get her to go home."

Raina laughed and patted them. "I will when Chase gets back. The babies are very calm, though. They must want me to eat more, but then I'd have heartburn at Defcon 1, another lovely side-effect of pregnancy."

"Oh, I remember that." She put a hand on Raina's shoulder. "I also remember that the last week was sheer misery, and Raina! You have twins in there."

As her voice grew serious and her smile faded, Raina followed her sister's train of thought.

Twins. Few people on Earth knew the power of that as well as the two of them.

Rose and Raina had shared a womb, although when Charlotte Wingate had been pregnant nearly forty-four years ago, she'd had no idea she was carrying twins. She was healthy and had a perfect pregnancy and, back then, sonograms were rare.

She also had no idea that she would suffer from an amniotic embolism an hour after her surprise second baby was born. Another girl for Rex, number four.

Moments later, the trouble started.

After Charlotte passed, poor Rex had been tasked with naming the baby they hadn't expected. Rose had been born first, and given the name they'd planned for a girl. At that moment, he believed there would never be another child, let alone the son he longed for. With his wife gone, there would never be Reginald Wingate...the Fourth.

So he'd named her Regina, called her Raina, and loved all his daughters twice as much as any other father. Were those the early seeds for Raina to grow into a fearless single mother? A tiny child who only knew a single father...at least until Suze came along three years later.

"Rain?" Rose's voice cut through her fog. "Honey, you're scaring me."

Raina blinked and focused on her sister's face, her twin in so many ways, her opposite in others. Rose had pale blond hair; Raina's was nearly black. Rose had brown eyes, Raina's were blue, exactly the reverse of what was expected.

Rose was optimistic and bright and made being a mother of four look effortless. Raina wrestled every problem to the ground, provided the strongest shoulder to lean on, and...had no idea how she was going to raise two children on her own.

Rose's fingers closed over her arm, digging into the skin. "Raina, you have to sit down. You're pale. You're quivering. And you look like you're about to burst into tears."

"I'm scared," she whispered, breathing the admission because she wasn't sure she could stand to hear the truth spoken out loud. "This is the scariest thing I've ever done, bar none."

"I know, baby." Rose drew her closer. "I know, I know. It's daunting and you must be petrified."

How could that be? Nothing scared Raina Wingate. She was the strong one, the one most like Rex, the one who swooped in and solved whatever problems they had.

Could she do that for two tiny babies, all alone?

She had to. She absolutely *had* to.

"I can do it," she said to herself as much as to her sister.

"Of course! You can do anything!" Rose proclaimed. "You're the most inspiring woman I know, Raina!"

She hugged Rose, but clung to the sentiment, too.

She could do this. She could have twins—and all three of them, babies and mother, would come out alive and well. She could raise two kids—she had six sisters to help and guide her. She could be a single mother without a strong and competent man by her side—even if *she really didn't want to.*

The truth of that nearly brought her to her knees.

But this was the hand she was dealt, and after three miscarriages? This was her one personal miracle and triumph that—

"Hey."

Raina turned at the single syllable, spoken softly and in a masculine voice she'd gotten entirely too used to hearing these past few weeks, looking up into Chase's brown eyes. They were the same color as Rose's, she realized with surprise. The color of that chocolate cake pop she'd yet to eat, and just as sweet.

"Hey, you," she said, yanking her whole being back to the present. "Where ya been?"

"Talking to the new chef at Goldfinch. Did you know he was a sous-chef at a Michelin-starred restaurant up in New England?" Chase looked from Raina to Rose. "I want to steal him for Ocean Song so I can..." His gaze dragged back to Raina, suddenly growing serious. "You need to get off your feet."

"I told you," Rose practically sang the words. "Oh,

look. Sadie is swamped. Chase, get her home, please. 'Scuze me, you two."

When Rose scooted away, Raina stood a little unsteadily next to Chase, foggy for no good reason. She leaned into him and slid her arm around his, holding up the cake pop she almost forgot she had.

"You want it?"

He looked like he wanted to say no, then took it from her, reaching to snag a paper napkin from a pile on the booth. "Thanks."

"Apparently, it's the result of a sweet pairing."

"Excuse me?" His brow lifted in question as he took a bite, then wiped any crumbs with his napkin.

"Sadie and Scout combined forces to take the world of desserts by storm."

"Really?" He finished chewing and swallowed, his eyes slipping shut for a moment. "Yeah. That was...wow. I need to serve those at the hotel."

She smiled. "I'll tell Sadie."

He eyed her as he finished the pop and took one final swipe with his napkin, then tossed it and the stick in the trash bin.

"So, Raina, do you need to make more rounds and see friends and fam, or can I take you to the car, get you home, and help you nest to your heart's desire?" He tapped her chin playfully. "I think there are a few more throw blankets you can rearrange on the sofa and a light-bulb you haven't dimmed in the nursery."

She chuckled, still feeling his fingertip on her skin. "Nesting is part of having a baby. Or two."

"I know, I know. I've read the books, remember?"

"You *have* read the books," she acknowledged. "And I'm still a little amazed by that."

He smiled down at her, quiet for a beat like he was sometimes. She wondered what he was thinking in those seconds, and always fell deeper into his eyes.

"Can we just slip out of here without a big goodbye?" he urged, tugging her to the street. "You don't look quite right, Raina."

"I don't feel quite right, either," she confessed, realizing she was swooning in the middle of town, falling into someone's *eyes*. What was wrong with her?

Slowly, she looked at the group gathered around the booth as evening neared and the place buzzed about the Best Bite contest. But all Raina could see were the many people she loved. Sister after sister, mother and father, in-laws, nieces, nephews, and—

"Oh!" she grunted with a stab of stomach pain.

"What?" Chase asked quickly.

"Noth..." No, she wasn't going to lie, because that was no Braxton-Hicks. It wasn't even a contraction. Whatever it was, it was *not* nothing.

What if her water broke? Right here in the middle of the street at the Fernandina Food Festival?

She gasped at the thought, knowing that she'd heard at least fifteen different descriptions of that moment— from the feeling that a champagne cork had popped to a gushy nightmare all down the legs. This wasn't like any of them.

"Let's go," she insisted. "No goodbyes, no announcements."

"Are you...do you think it's go time?" he asked, concern in his eyes.

"I'm not sure. I honestly don't know, but I want to leave."

"But if it is, Raina"—he tipped his head to the family behind them—"they have to know."

She glanced at the group again, hearing the laughter and chatter, feeling the anticipation and expectation, sensing nothing but love.

"Sadie needs them right now," she said. "This is her big night and after what she went through to get here? She should be surrounded by family. If I so much as breathe the word 'labor' to them, they will all feel they have to leave her. Then everyone might wait for what might be twelve or even twenty-four hours—or two more days if this is a false alarm—and ruin the whole event for Sadie."

"But if you go to the hospital—"

"Then we'll call and...Madeline will set up a split-shift session," she said on a laugh.

Wait. Where *was* Made—

Another pain twisted like a butcher's knife in her gut, making her suck in a noisy breath.

"We're out," Chase said in response, not giving it one more second's hesitation. As they walked, the muscles gripped and contracted, making her pace slow to a crawl, but she refused to fold.

Sensing that, Chase kept a strong and steady arm

around her, guiding her through the crowd, moving one block, then another, closer and closer to his car. With each step, the pain eased.

"Can you make it to the car?" he asked when they were about one more block from the lot. "It's not far, but I can find a first responder in seconds and we can have you in an ambulance before you can say...Charles Wingate."

"Do *not* make me laugh," she ground out, fighting a smile at their inside joke. "And don't get an ambulance, Chase. This could be a false alarm. It could be early hours. But it's definitely not hospital time. I can sense that much."

"All right," he said. "You know your body. Two more minutes on foot, then you'll be home sweet home."

With Chase sweet Chase.

She looked up at him, knowing the gratitude she felt must have been written all over her face. Gratitude and...affection.

His eyes flicked with surprise and a secret smile when he caught her gaze. Then he reached for her hands and pulled her closer, and she thought he was going to kiss her.

"We got this, Rain," he whispered as he pressed his lips on her hair, right above her forehead. A kiss, but one that was chaste and supportive. Like a brother. Was that how he felt about her?

Because right this minute, probably hours from having her whole body surrender to the birth of two children, she was not feeling like his sister.

And that was the scariest thing of all.

She let him guide her to the car and answered Rose's panicked, "Why did you leave without saying goodbye," text with a quick explanation that she wanted to get off her feet. In the passenger seat, she closed her eyes, realizing she was bracing for the next contraction.

It was a good fifteen minutes until it came, just as they pulled into the driveway. She weathered it in the car, then Chase set her up on the sofa with blankets, her timer app on, and a cup of tea.

"I need to think about something else," she whispered as he settled in with her, putting her feet in his lap. "I can't lay here and worry."

"A movie? A book?"

She shook her head and closed her eyes. "Tell me everything about your childhood."

"My childhood?"

"Everything you remember. Your parents, your grandparents, your friends, your life. Tell me your story, Charles Madison."

He chuckled and thumbed the ball of her foot. "Okay. It's not that interesting."

"I'll be the judge of that."

With another laugh and a deep breath, he shared his earliest memory—sitting on Nonna's lap while she read a book about kittens and mittens—and Raina drifted in and out of sleep, deeply comforted and not scared at all.

Chapter Nineteen

Madeline

They hadn't gone on a date...yet. Adam and Madeline had several more conversations in person and by text since the day they'd walked on the wharf. They'd met twice for coffee, and one afternoon, she'd given him a full tour of her shop.

Each time, the conversations had gotten lighter and the tension had eased. They exchanged more superficial details about their lives, laughed at a few old jokes, and shared some memories—all of which were surprisingly more vivid to Adam than Madeline.

None of that had significant romantic overtones, but their friendship had grown and become...not solid, exactly, but greatly improved.

However, Madeline couldn't call their plans to attend the Fernandina Food Festival together anything *but* an official date. Adam picked her up at home, spending a few minutes admiring the townhouse. They walked into town together, and when they crossed Centre Street with a few dozen tourists, he took her hand and didn't let it go.

So this, she knew, was a date. A date with...*the undercover cop who broke her heart.*

On one hand, the public nature of their first real date made the whole thing far less intimate and personal. But being this out in the open meant they were, well, out in the open for all to see. Friends, townsfolk, some customers, and, of course, the entire Wingate family that was out in full force to support Sadie.

No one in her family, except Sadie, knew of her history with Adam. If he'd landed on their radar at all, it was because he'd accompanied Tristan Saint Pierre that fateful night their short-lived brother-in-law had come to the ballroom at Ocean Song.

Now, all they knew was that Adam Logan, former computer security consultant with Chocolat de Saint Pierre, had come back to the States for personal reasons. As a favor and due to his technology skills, he'd been helping Sadie install and manage some software for her business.

If anyone asked how Madeline and Adam had met, the simple answer was through Sadie. Why not?

Theirs was ancient history that never needed to be unearthed. Her sisters and parents would only be interested in the fact that Madeline had a date. She couldn't blame them, given her utter lack of romance for as long as anyone could remember.

Since she didn't want Adam to be embarrassed or put on the spot, at least until the Best Bite contest started, she decided to avoid Wingate Way for a while.

Instead, she suggested they stick to exploring the far

more crowded Centre Street, which was always the true heart of any street festival in Fernandina Beach.

In addition to food booths run both by local restaurants and some home chefs who wanted to participate, there was an array of non-food-related displays and tables —crafts, gifts, souvenirs, and some businesses handing out free gifts and promotional materials.

They meandered down the middle of the pedestrian-only avenue, peeking at the wares, soaking up the street music, inhaling delicious aromas, and enjoying the energy that pulsed from one end of town to the other.

"You know, I grew up an hour from here and I don't think my family ever came to Amelia Island," he mused, threading Madeline's fingers with his as they strolled, probably oblivious to how that touch made her feel. "It's gotta be one of the cutest small towns in Florida."

"A well-kept secret," she agreed, thinking about the mention of his family and the fact that he had been born and raised in northeast Florida, about an hour south of here.

She knew his parents were gone, having passed away in their eighties, but he had a brother who still lived in Duval County, and his sister was down near Ponte Vedra Beach.

"So, did you pick Jacksonville as your home base because of your siblings?" she asked, realizing he never really elaborated on why he'd come here, of all places.

He slid her a look. "That was one of the draws."

The implication was clear, and she wasn't sure how

to take it. He'd come here for *her*? She found that hard to believe.

"And work, right?" she pressed.

He nodded, not elaborating but pulling her close to a spice booth. "Look. Free samples of pepper jelly. My weakness."

"Too hot for me, but knock yourself out."

He snatched a paper plate arranged for tasting. "You don't like ghost peppers, Maddie?" He grinned as he lifted a cracker covered with red jelly she knew would burn her mouth.

"Oh! Ghosts! I totally forgot!" She snapped her fingers and tapped her head in disbelief. She never forgot things like meeting someone at a time and place. She never forgot *anything*...until now.

"I'm supposed to catch up with Denise at the history museum booth for the ghost thing."

He took a bite and his eyes flashed with the impact of the peppers. "Whoa. Hot. Good. The ghost thing? Who's Denise? A ghosthunter?"

"Kind of," she said on a laugh, pointing at how his eyes watered. "Really hot, aren't they?"

"Off the charts. You sure you don't want some?" He lifted the second cracker from the plate, offering to feed it to her in a move that was intimate and playful and made her toes curl.

How could this man have such an effect on her? Twenty-five years later? How? It was frustrating...and exhilarating.

"Pass," she said, waving away the plate and wishing

she had the power to just pass on him, too.

But, clearly, where Adam Logan was concerned, Madeline was...powerless.

"Tell me about the ghosthunter," he said after he chewed the cracker himself and tossed the plate in the trash. "Or were you kidding?"

"I wish. The real hunter, I'm afraid, is my mother, Susannah."

"This is Suze, right? Technically your stepmother and closest friend?"

She smiled, appreciating that he listened and remembered. "Yes. Well, she's in the process of transforming Wingate House—"

"Where I couldn't get a room," he interjected, dipping his head close to hers. "I liked the name, so I called to make a reservation for this weekend, but alas, I was sent packing and ended up in the Ritz-Carlton."

"Not a bad second choice," she said. "But don't feel slighted—Wingate House is not technically an inn anymore."

As she talked, she guided him toward the intersection that would take them to the museum, tamping down the low-grade stress she felt because she was already a few minutes late for the arranged meeting.

"We're turning it into a small wedding venue," she explained. "In the process, Susannah, who is spearheading the effort, has decided my great-grandmother, Coraline Wingate, really does haunt the place, as folklore has claimed for years."

He looked interested. "A great-grandmother ghost, huh? What makes Suze think that?"

As they walked toward the museum, she told him the story of the black lace, the weird screams her mother heard, and a little about the history of Wingate House.

He seemed intrigued, asking questions that she tried to answer, but they reached the brick building and saw the row of tables in front of it. There, docents were ready with materials and offers to take guests inside for mini-tours.

But her gaze zeroed right in on Susannah...and Rex.

"Oh." She hadn't been expecting him.

Adam looked down at her, then into the crowd, and back at her. "You look like you saw this ghost you're telling me about."

"Only slightly scarier," she admitted. "My dad."

"The infamous Rex Wingate? I saw him that night with Tristan in the hotel ballroom, but I've never actually met him. Introduce me?"

She took a breath, considering that. "He can be..."

Adam started laughing. "I'm not scared of meeting your father, Maddie," he said. "I know the party line is that we met through my work with Sadie."

"You know that?"

"She told me the last time I worked on her inventory software. Your secret—*our* secret—is safe. But I do want to meet your father." He looked past her at the people near the museum table. "The white-haired guy with his arm around the blonde, I'm guessing?"

"That's one way to describe him," she said.

"He looks very healthy for a man who had a stroke... how long ago?"

"Last spring," she said. "And he—"

Just then, Dad turned and looked right at her, his whole face brightening when he spotted her.

"Maddie!" He raised his hand to beckon her closer, but as he did, he froze, his attention shifting to the man next to her.

"Oh, someone else who calls you Maddie," Adam noted as they started toward him.

"The only other someone," she said, almost regretting the admission when he reacted with surprise.

"Color me...honored."

"I'm about to color you...Rexed. Be good."

"You're nervous," he whispered on a laugh. "Should I be?"

She looked up at him. "I don't know. Are you hiding anything?"

For one flash of a millisecond, she saw something in his eyes...fear, guilt, a secret? Her heart dropped, but she was too close to Suze and Dad now. Whatever it was, she'd have to grill him later. For now, Dad could do those honors.

Adam gave her fingers a quick squeeze before letting go, making sure no one saw they'd been holding hands. Points for being a gentleman, she thought, sneaking one more quick look at the tall, dark, handsome...*undercover cop who broke her heart.*

She couldn't forget that.

"Oh, there you are!" Suze called as they came closer,

beaming at Madeline. Her smile wavered a bit, too, as she glanced at Adam. "Hello..."

Madeline took a breath and put a hand on Adam's shoulder. "Susannah and Rex Wingate," she said, oddly formal but not sure how else to handle the names. "This is Adam Logan. Adam, my parents."

As they shook hands and exchanged hellos, her father's eyes—as dark and sharp as Adam's—narrowed when he looked hard at Adam.

"I know you," Rex said.

"We've met, more or less," Adam said. "I was with Mr. Saint Pierre at the—"

"You stormed my anniversary party at Ocean Song." Rex drew back, scowling as if in the face of the enemy. "You work for them."

"Not anymore," he said quickly.

"I found it, Susannah!" Denise came rushing out of the museum toward the table, ending the exchange.

Susannah leaned in to them. "That's the archivist and a specialist in all things Victorian," she explained for Adam's benefit.

"I have a picture," the archivist announced. "Grainy and barely discernable, but we have found Coraline's mother, Greta Livingston Shand."

"My great-grandmother," Dad said. "Though I never met her."

"Well, I can tell you this," Denise held up a manila envelope. "Your great-grandmother had sway in New York City. I have a curator friend who specializes in antique wedding announcements in the *New York Times,* going back to when they launched the feature in 1851."

Madeline sneaked a look at Adam, expecting him to be bored, but he listened, riveted. When he noticed her attention, his dark gaze slid to her, a gleam in his eyes that she recognized from every inside joke they ever had.

"Ghosts," he mouthed with a tease in his eyes.

"Shh." Aware of him with every cell in her body, Madeline tried to concentrate and care about Greta, who was her great-great-grandmother.

"Here she is!" Denise exclaimed, pulling out a piece of paper from the envelope to show them a copy of an old newspaper page. "Look. White dress and veil, but she's carrying a train of black silk and the announcement says it was 'imported French lace' from *her* mother's wedding gown. This could be your lace!"

Or not. Madeline nearly moaned. It was such a stretch.

Susannah brought the picture close. "Is that the same lace?" she asked Madeline, who leaned over and squinted at the grainy image.

"I'd need to see a much better picture."

"Sadly, that's impossible," Denise said. "Unless you know someone very high up at the *New York Times* archives."

"I might be able to help you," Adam said, making them all turn to him. "I know some folks there and how to, um, get them to part with...things."

Oh, the undercover cop emerges, Madeline thought.

"That would be wonderful!" Susannah exclaimed as if Adam had offered up the actual Holy Grail.

As she and Denise cooed over this bit of news, Madeline turned to her father, who was standing a few feet away, watching the scene unfold.

No, correction—he was staring at Adam and she knew it.

"So, Maddie." With just the flick of his brow, he silently summoned her closer.

"Really, Dad?" she whispered when she was next to him. "You're going to have an opinion on this?"

He lifted a shoulder, as if to say he had an opinion on everything, then tipped his head in resignation. "How can I argue with tall, dark, and a little salt-and-pepper at the temples? And apparently he has magical skills with the *New York Times*."

She snorted softly. "Why would you *argue* with anything?" she asked.

"Because I'm not used to..."

She waited for him to finish, imagining all the things he wasn't used to. Her dating? A man on her arm? That flush in her cheeks she could feel every time she looked at Adam? Is that what he wasn't used to?

"Being replaced."

"Please," she scoffed. "We're at a festival together, Dad. No one is replacing anything."

Adam stepped away from the lace conversation to join this one, joking about the urgency of the lace. After a minute and some small-talk, he crossed his arms and pinned his gaze on Rex.

"Mr. Wingate," he started. "I know you are a man who knows who's who in this town. Can you do me a favor and give me some inside scoop on a few locals?"

"Sure, if you tell me why," Dad replied.

"I'm helping a friend broker a boat deal and I saw one called *Captain's Table*. I was wondering if you could facilitate a meeting with the owner or know someone who can."

He hadn't asked her to help with that, Madeline thought, but then she remembered the conversation on the dock. He actually *had* asked if she knew who owned the yacht, and if she knew them personally, but her response had been vague.

"I can help," Dad said, but took a step closer. "But I'd like an answer from you, too."

"Anything, sir."

"What the heck is wrong with those Saint Pierres, anyway?" her father demanded. "Why would that Tristan marry, then discard, my daughter?"

Madeline braced for Adam's response, having no idea if he'd defend his former employer or sidestep the question completely.

But Adam looked her father right in the eye and answered without hesitation. "Because they are corrupt, misguided, entitled thieves who have no integrity."

Madeline blinked at the bluntness.

"In my opinion, your daughter dodged a bullet," he finished.

"Yes, I agree," Rex said, a slow smile breaking as he gave Adam an approving nod. "I'll be happy to make a few calls about that yacht. I'm sure Nico Cassano would sell. The man would sell his grandmother for the right price."

Adam gave a soft laugh at that, and turned his full attention back to Madeline. "Did you need to spend more time with Susannah, or..." He gave her a look that she interpreted as, "Could we get on with this date?"

Yes, please, she silently replied.

Suze and Denise were hunched over the newspaper picture, deep in conversation.

"I think I've contributed what I could," she said, turning back to her father. "Dad, tell Suze I'll do all the black lace research she needs tomorrow. And we'll see you at the Best Bite contest."

With that and a quick goodbye, Adam whisked her away with a solid hand on her back.

"So, who's buying a yacht?" she asked.

"Just...someone I know." And there it was again. The vague answer. That flash of...something. Something that set off alarms, waved red flags, and reminded her he was...*an undercover cop who broke her heart.*

"You know someone who can afford a yacht who's not named Saint Pierre?"

"It's...business, Maddie." He added some pressure to his touch. "Let's go back to the food. I want more pepper jelly."

She started to walk with him, a slow brew of discontent deep in her belly. He'd lied to her once, used her before, made her his...mark. It would *not* happen again.

"Adam," she said, bringing them both to a halt. "We have to talk."

THEY MADE their way to the river wharf again, which was far enough from Wingate Way for her to feel secluded, but very much out in the open.

They sat on a different empty bench while Madeline inhaled a breath of briny air, getting remnant diesel fumes from a docked yacht...maybe even the one his "friend" wanted to buy.

"What are you hiding?" she demanded as she let that breath out.

"Maddie, I—"

"No." She pointed a finger at him. "Not again. Never again. You may not lie to me, or deceive me for your job or my own protection. You will tell me exactly what you are doing and if I—or anyone in my family—might be your *target*."

He stared at her, a glimmer of admiration in his eyes. "Wow. You knew?"

Her heart dropped. "Knew...what?"

"The minute I started to work."

She let out a soft groan as her shoulders dropped. "I *am* your stinking mark again."

"No. No, you are not." He reached for her hands and took one in each of his. "And I'm going to break all the rules and tell you absolutely everything right now."

She closed her eyes. "Why is there anything at all to

tell me? Why do you have to be undercover? Why can't you just be a normal software guy who doesn't have... targets or friends who buy yachts?"

"Because then I'd be dull and bored out of my mind."

Her eyes flashed open at the raw honesty in his voice.

"I can't stay out of the game," he said. "The adrenaline rush is too good. And the bottom line? I work for the good guys now. Like I did before. No more Saint Pierres."

She looked so deep into his eyes, she felt like she'd climbed into his soul. And all she saw was honesty.

Or the reflection of the most naïve forty-nine-year-old woman who'd ever lived.

"I did come to Jacksonville because of you," he said softly, making her suck in a silent breath. "And you can believe that, or not."

"It's...a stretch."

"Not at all," he countered. "After I saw you that night when we stormed the ballroom, I could not...I didn't want..." He huffed out a breath. "I wanted to give this a shot. This. You. Us."

Us? At the word, she couldn't breathe.

"And because I grew up down in Jax, I have contacts in the PD and the local FBI office. They hire contractors, and pay well, especially for investigations that require a certain..."

"Ability to blend in?" she finished for him.

He smiled. "You could do it, you know. You like being in the background, and absorbing what's going on around you, I've noticed."

"Kind of like a wallflower," she said dryly.

"Nothing like a wallflower," he volleyed.

She eyed him warily, wanting the truth and not compliments. "Who is buying the Cassanos' yacht and what are you really doing by acting as a broker?"

For a few beats, he said nothing, thinking and then nodding as if he'd just surrendered.

"Nico Cassano is on the radar of the FBI. They want someone up here trying to get to him and dig a little more into his business activities. I'm thinking about pretending to broker a boat deal to get on that vessel."

She inched back, eyes wide as she tried to process that.

"You got a better idea? I tried the restaurant hoping the owner might be there..." He cocked his head. "But someone left before we even had a sip of wine."

She shook her head, vaguely aware that her whole body was humming. "So, this whole time you've been... pursuing me, it's also been to get to the Cassano family?"

"And the whole time, you've been making wedding dresses. People work, Maddie. I'm an investigator, and this is my job. It doesn't negate me having a relationship."

She swallowed, holding his gaze.

He took her hand. "Didn't we learn that the hard way?"

Her heart shifted around as she let out a long, slow breath. How could she fight this? Why would she?

"Listen to me, Maddie. I'm fifty years old, and you're right behind me. Why should we be alone because I have to do a little poking around the locals? If I promise, if I swear an oath that I will never, ever lie to you again about anything, will you give me a chance?"

All she could do was stare at him and want to believe him with everything in her.

"Please." He closed his hands over one of hers. "We've lost decades, Maddie. Can't we have...something together?"

She finally exhaled and felt herself nod. "Only if you're honest. About every single thing."

He pressed their hands to his chest. "I promise, Maddie. I *promise*."

Oh, that word. Promise. Could he keep one? Could she bear it if he didn't?

He leaned in and she thought he might kiss her, but he put his arm around her. "Don't we need to go to that contest thing?"

"Oh, my gosh!" she exclaimed, looking at her watch with a gasp. "I'm never late! What is wrong with me?"

He just laughed as if he knew exactly who and what was wrong with her.

"Come on." He stood and reached for her hand, tucking her close to him as they started to walk. "Let's go try to explain me away to the rest of your family."

"I'm afraid," she said on a bittersweet sigh, "that there is no way to explain you."

He leaned close enough to whisper, "That's my secret weapon."

And it was quite effective, she thought as they made their way down Wingate Way, past familiar shops and storefronts.

"What's it like to have a street named after you?" he asked.

"Not me. One of those Wingates from long ago, the son of the woman who wore the dress in that picture." She looked up at him. "That was very kind of you to offer to help."

"My pleasure. Oh, look—there's a crowd at Sadie's."

A crowd of people she knew and loved, who were all about to meet...her date.

Well, that hadn't been on her bingo card for New Year's surprises, she thought as her gaze scanned each face, some close, some in clusters, some way behind the booth. Like...that man.

That man walking toward Sadie who...didn't belong. The man with the platinum blond hair. The tall, handsome, boyish—

"Tristan." She stared as a cold and clammy fear gripped her heart and the sense that already, in five minutes, Adam's promise was broken.

Chapter Twenty

Sadie

"The Scadie has been my most popular item," Scout said, beaming at the remaining display case at Sadie's booth. This one housed the last of her truffles since the cake pops were sold out.

Everything else had been taken into the store as they prepared to go hear the final judging and award ceremony.

"Same!" she agreed. "The cake pop concept was a winner, but Scout, you cannot call it a Scadie! It sounds like a disease."

He cracked up. "I think it sounds like a wonderful collaboration. And, by the way, I've heard nothing but rave reviews for your chocolate. It's going to be a fight to the finish when the Best Bite awards are announced. I hope you'll sit with me so I can congratulate you."

Gazing up at him, she just couldn't wipe the smile off her face. "I have to say, Scout, as competitors go? You're—"

"Sadie!"

She startled at the name, barked from behind, in a voice that made her stomach clench.

Whipping around, she gasped at the sight of Tristan bounding toward her, his jaw set in a determined line that contradicted his outstretched arms.

"Tristan! What are you—"

"Look at you!" He engulfed her in an embrace before she could finish, crushing her with a hug. "God, I've missed you." He inched back, searched her face for a second, and then pressed his lips hard against hers, getting the briefest kiss before she shoved him away.

"What are you doing here, Tristan?"

"I just told you. I missed you and I can't live without you."

Around her, she sensed rather than saw family members slowing their movements, taking a few steps closer, circling the exchange, waiting for her cue. Gabe and Isaiah, Travis and Justin, but her quick glance landed on Scout, who looked utterly dismayed.

"You need to leave," she ground out, pushing Tristan farther away. "Before every man in my family and a few that aren't let you have it."

"I'm not afraid of your family, and you're not afraid of mine," he said, clutching her. "Sadie, we belong together."

Before she could answer, Adam plowed toward them out of nowhere and got right in Tristan's face.

"What the hell are you doing here?" he demanded.

Tristan flicked him a look. "Drop dead, Logan. You're not invited to this conversation."

"She doesn't want you mauling her," he said. "And nobody wants to see your face."

"I think Sadie can decide that for herself." He squeezed her. "I have a proposal for you, my love. Let's go inside and let me do this properly."

She shuttered her eyes. "Will you leave if I do?"

"I'll leave if you say no, but I don't think you will." He drew her closer and brought his lips to her ear. "I have a plan, Sadie. For us. Forever. Please."

She started to argue, but he pressed his fingers to her lips. "Five minutes alone, then I'll leave."

"Tristan, I—"

"You were my wife," he said in that low and sultry accent. "You owe me five minutes."

"She doesn't owe you—"

"Get lost, Adam," he spat back. "This is between us. Am I right, Sadie?"

She sensed Adam's whole body tense and the vibration of discontent from the entire crowd. The last thing she needed was a public fight. Kitty would blackball her from everything, and for good reason.

Backing away, she held up both hands.

"Everybody calm down," she said. "Let me talk to Tristan while you go get seats for the judging."

She needed to get Tristan out of here, now. And she knew that hearing him out was the only way.

"Please," she added, giving everyone a look, including Scout, who'd stepped back but continued to watch warily. "I got this," she told them. "I'll meet you all at the contest."

"Don't go inside with him," Adam warned.

She shot him a look that said she wouldn't dream of it.

Very slowly, the small group dispersed, following as the festivalgoers headed to the small outdoor seating area and stage near the marina.

When they had privacy, she turned to Tristan, arms crossed. "Listen to me, you can't—"

"Do anything without you," he finished, his eyes full of warmth and sincerity. "I mean it, Sadie. All the light is gone, the power is out, and I can't make anything work. Can we go inside?" He tugged her toward the store. "I want to see what you've done and tell you my plans. Big plans. World domination plans. With you."

A few cells in her body that hadn't gotten the message that they hated this guy stood up, shook off, and got a little excited. But common sense prevailed.

"I'm not taking you in there. I'm not listening to your plans. I'm not falling for you again. I'm not doing anything but asking you to leave."

"Sadie." He stepped toward her, but she backed away. He nodded, like he understood the brush off, instead looking at the display case with her last few truffles. "So what have we here? Looks like someone had a good teacher."

She shook her head. "Don't, Tristan."

But he reached into the case and grabbed a truffle, tossing the whole thing in his mouth. "Oh. Yes. Incredible."

"I know, and it's about to win the Best Bite contest

in..." She looked over her shoulder at the crowd gathered in front of the stage, listening to a local band play. "A few minutes. And I want to be there."

He finished the truffle. "Gotta love that *lavender*."

She gave a tight smile.

"Except it didn't work that well for me," he said, swallowing the last bit. "I need you to show me exactly what you did." He pointed to the store. "Now?"

"No. I've given you enough."

Seething, he reached in and snapped his fingers around another truffle, so hard he squeezed it. Swearing under his breath, he shook off the chunks of chocolate and wiped the remnant on his jeans. That's when she noticed that his hands were trembling.

"Are you okay?"

"No!" he snapped. "I'm not okay, Sadie. I'm..." He inhaled deeply, his nostrils quivering. "I need you."

"I'm not—"

"I need your help," he growled, looking at her with abject fear in his eyes.

Was this a trick or was he in trouble? Did it matter to her? No, no, no. Nothing about him mattered to her and she had to remember that.

"Tristan, we're done. Finished. Now and forever. Whatever help you need, go get it from your family. You picked them over me and now I'm picking mine over you." She pointed toward the street. "Leave me alone and let me get on with my life."

He lifted a playful brow. "I have a much better idea, my love. Let's you and me build a brand. *The* brand. The best chocolate in the world, sold in the finest retailers, unlike any other. We can do it, Sadie. Me and you. We're unstoppable."

"You stopped us cold," she said, glaring at him. "You ended our marriage, let me get sent away, and broke my heart."

"And I'm sorry," he said, reaching for her. "It was the single most idiotic thing I've ever done. I'm begging you, Sadie. Please. Let me stay here with you, off the radar, and—"

"Off what radar?"

"It's just an expression," he said quickly.

An American expression he didn't use.

"I want to be here with you." He closed the space between them and put his chocolate-stained hands toward her. "We'll hide up in that little apartment. We'll make it a lovers'—"

She swatted his hands away before he touched her. "No, Tristan. I'm not interested. This is my life now and you're not in it."

"This?" he scoffed, gesturing wildly at her shop. "*This* is your life now, Sadie? This dumpy neighborhood shop with a slum-style flat upstairs? You're too sophisticated for this, too continental for this measly town with one street and your tacky oversized family that—"

She whacked his cheek so hard it stung the palm of her hand. "You don't deserve to say my family's name," she said through gritted teeth.

"The family that smothers you? You love them now?"

"You bet I do," she said, and the truth of that rocked

her. "My family is wonderful and loving and not a single one would stab the other. They've lifted me, loved me, and helped me create something that's all mine. I don't need you, and I won't help you, Tristan. So get out. *Now*."

The loudspeaker crackled and she turned to glance at the stage where an emcee was bringing things to order for the awards. "I'm not going to miss this! We're done!"

She started to run, but he grabbed her arm. "Sadie, I'm desperate. I need a place to hide. Can I just go in there without you?"

She stared at him, sensing that something was really, really wrong, but she simply couldn't help him. He wasn't a good man. She knew a good man—knew plenty of them—and he wasn't one of them.

"Climb under the table in my booth. Eat the rest of the truffles. Take your desperation to someone who cares." She wrested her arm free, brushing off the chocolate remnants, and tore down Wingate Way. Free. She was finally free of him as the wind sang in her ears. She reached the back row of seats with a heaving chest.

"Are you okay?" Scout suddenly appeared next to her, instantly putting a tender arm around her. "Was that your ex? Is he gone?"

She caught her breath, trying to speak, looking into his eyes. Now, *this* was a good man.

"Yes. Yes to all," she managed. "Have they announced anything yet?"

"George is just getting started," he said, nodding to

Kitty's husband at the microphone. "And you're sure you're all right?"

"Never been better." Without giving it too much thought, she dropped her head to the side and let it briefly rest on his shoulder.

While George babbled on about the three categories —Local Restaurant, Home Chef, and Dessert—Sadie tried to forget the past ten minutes.

Instead, she concentrated on the three long tables, each filled with five judges and four tasting trays in front of them. Through it all, she kept looking over her shoulder, half expecting Tristan to storm this event, too.

The third time she looked, she saw Adam rushing toward her, with Madeline next to him. He held his phone to his ear, muttering something into it.

"Where did he go?" Adam shouted as he got closer.

"I have no idea. I sent him off but he could be anywhere. Why?"

"We have to find him," Madeline said. "There's a warrant for his arrest."

"What?"

Adam spoke into the phone, his voice low so she didn't quite hear what he was saying, then he tucked it under his chin.

"I'm on with the FBI in Jacksonville," he told her. "Tristan hacked the company computer system and transferred a lot of money to an account in the Cayman Islands, then got the heck out of Brussels. His father contacted the *Federale Politie*."

Sadie swayed at the news, immediately recognizing

the name of federal Dutch law enforcement. "No wonder he wanted to be off the radar," she murmured, her stomach turning at the thought of what a liar he was. "But I have no idea where he is now."

"I do," Scout said quietly. "Look."

They all turned to follow his gesture to the side of the stage, where Tristan stood in conversation with Kitty Worthington.

Sadie choked in shock. "What the—"

"I got him," Adam announced into the phone. "Keep me tracked using this phone, and send backup."

He stuffed the phone in his pocket and turned to Madeline, grabbing her shoulders. "You don't move. Any of you. The police will handle this." He pulled Madeline closer. "Believe me now?"

"Yes," she whispered.

He shocked them all by giving her a swift kiss on the lips, then took off, disappearing around the side of the makeshift stage and blending into the crowd.

They watched Tristan walk off the stage, turn, and head toward the water, and then they couldn't see either one of the men anymore.

"Where did he go?" Sadie moaned, frustrated and scared.

"Adam will get him," Madeline whispered, looking dazed from the kiss. "He's one of the good guys."

She smiled and slid a glance to Scout, who was still peering in the crowd after Tristan.

"One of a few," Sadie added, sliding an arm around

her sister just as Kitty Worthington marched up to the microphone.

"Excuse me, ladies and gentlemen and judges, I have a quick announcement." She cleared her throat and adjusted her gold-rimmed glasses, her silver shellacked hair glistening under the stage lights. "We have a change in the Dessert category."

Sadie tensed, vaguely aware that Scout took her free hand and gave it a squeeze.

"One of the entries has been disqualified," Kitty announced. "Our judges are asked to remove the chocolate truffle from Charmed by Chocolate from their tasting plates, as it is no longer under consideration." She looked over her glasses toward the back of the crowd, directly at Sadie. "It has been revealed that the recipe is not original and was, in fact, stolen from a world-famous Belgian chocolatier."

Sadie's blood turned to ice. "What? Are you *kidding* me?" She turned to Scout, whose whole face was dark with fury. "How could he—"

"Hold on!" Scout tore into the crowd, following the same route Adam had gone, meeting Kitty as she stepped off the stage, ready to fight for Sadie like the hero he truly was.

"Disqualified?" Madeline choked.

By now, the rest of the family had found her, slowly building a Wingate Wall of protection around her, announcing their displeasure and rumbling about the bad decision, then shocked by the news about Tristan.

With each new arrival, she felt more loved, more protected, more...enrobed.

Not once was she smothered, and it was about time she realized that. But what was happening on that stage hurt a lot, no matter how much her family surrounded her.

"I can't watch," she muttered, dropping her head into her hands. "I can't accept this. I can't believe what's happening."

Madeline put both arms around her and held her close. "Adam told us to stay here," she said.

"What's going on?" Rose demanded as she nestled next to them, and then Tori came up on the other side. From behind, Susannah and Rex got closer, everyone asking for answers Sadie didn't have.

They'd finished the Home Chef category when Scout ran back to the group, taking her attention from the gathering of judges almost completely blocked by Kitty now.

"Lost cause?" she guessed at the disappointment in his eyes.

"Maybe." He put a hand on his chest to catch his breath. "I tried. I'm afraid she fell for the sexy accent."

"Yeah, the guy with the international alert out for his arrest." Sadie rolled her eyes. "Did you see anything?"

"I don't know where they went," he said. "But I wanted to be here with you."

She smiled up at him, her heart squeezing with affection. "Thanks, Scout."

He smiled down at her. "Fingers crossed."

"For you?" she asked.

"For us."

For...*us*?

"One of my best customers was up there in the front and they had a box of—"

"And we have a winner for the Best Dessert Bite on Amelia Island," George Worthington announced, waving a card he held in his hand. "A late entry, too. Congratulations to How the Cookie Crumbles—"

"You won!"

"—*and* Charmed by Chocolate for a co-created cake pop treat called...the Scadie?" He screwed up his face amidst a smattering of laughter. "Whatever you call it, the judges were unanimous! Please come up and accept your award."

Sadie choked. "We didn't enter that!"

"You heard the man," Scout said, a smile forming. "Late entry, courtesy of that customer who not only parted with a box, but now qualifies for free brownies for life."

"Scout!" She grabbed him by the shoulders. "Are you serious?"

"As a heart attack, which"—he put his hand on his chest again—"I better not have right now. Go ahead, Sadie. You accept this one and be sure to give Kitty the hairy eyeball."

She laughed at his clichés, grabbing his hand. "Not without you, I won't."

All around them, the Wingates cheered noisily while

Sadie and Scout held hands and walked side by side up the middle aisle to the stage.

Kitty lifted the giant trophy with two hands, stepping toward Scout, but he guided Sadie closer, making sure it was given to her. While she took it, he leaned into the microphone and cleared his throat.

"Thank you," he said, sounding a little nervous. Then he glanced at Sadie and added, "And thank you for supporting local businesses like the newest one, Charmed by Chocolate. We won because of this woman right here, who is a master chocolatier and a hometown girl and has never stolen anything in her life. 'Cept maybe a few hearts," he added with a laugh, and got a louder one in response.

He reached to bring Sadie forward to speak, but before she could say a word, everything was drowned out by the scream of sirens and flashing lights as three, no, four police cars zoomed down Wingate Way toward the wharf.

Still holding the trophy, she darted off the stage with Scout—along with half the audience and all her family. Everyone rushed toward the water, around the tall stone wall that blocked the wind for the people who waited for ferries to Cumberland Island.

There, Adam held Tristan pinned to the wall, hands locked over his head, Adam's knee firmly in his gut.

Tristan writhed and kicked, but he was no match for the former FBI agent, who didn't even look winded, despite the cut oozing a trickle of blood down his cheek.

Catching sight of Sadie, Tristan narrowed his eyes

and glowered at her just as a team of cops moved in, using megaphones to order the crowd back as they swooped in to take over the arrest from Adam.

Once free, Adam walked toward them, his hair tousled, his gaze searching the crowd...for Madeline, Sadie realized. She was much farther back in the crowd, so he gestured for Scout and Sadie to come with him.

"He's finished," he said gruffly. "He's scum like the rest of his family, and he's going to be extradited back to Belgium and headed to jail."

"Speaking of family," Scout said, pointing at the group of Wingates. "They're trying to get your attention."

Sadie held up the trophy and jogged toward them, only then realizing they were all shouting about something else entirely.

Rose grabbed her arm and dug her nails in. "Raina's in labor!" she cried out. "She just got to the hospital and we're all on our way there!"

Of course, every last Wingate and the people they loved marched to cars and trucks en masse, ready to pour out their love on one of their own.

Sadie just smiled at them, knowing she'd never have it any other way.

Chapter Twenty-one

Raina

"Breathe, Raina. *Breathe.*"

She didn't *want* to breathe! She didn't want to move or sweat or endure this unendurable barbaric torture for one more second. She opened her mouth to scream, but nothing came out as she reached the peak of pain, the worst, searing, body-ripping agony...and then it eased. Little by little, second by second, she tumbled down the other side of Mount Misery and the contraction came to an end.

"Good job, Raina."

She opened her eyes and blinked through tears and sweat, panting as she made out the shape of a man's head, dark hair, brown eyes, that sweet smile that showed up at the end of every contraction.

"Oh, it's you," she murmured.

Chase's lips flicked with humor. "You were expecting someone else?"

She almost smiled, but that would be ridiculous. Nothing could make her smile. Not Chase, not a nurse, not an ice chip, not a single thing but having these babies arrive and put her out of her misery.

"Did you text the 7 *Sis* group chat on my phone?" she asked, panting.

"I did, and your family is on the way," he told her. "I was told your timing was perfect. Sadie won the contest—sort of. They'll explain it to you. And some...other stuff happened." His voice trailed off. "You don't care, do you?"

She shook her head violently. "Not one bit."

He placed the lightest hand on her shoulder, the careful way one might touch a feral dog momentarily lying on its back.

"Don't talk, Raina," he said softly. "Rest. There's another one coming in about two minutes."

With a groan, she reached her hand out helplessly. "Ice."

He grabbed the ice cup and spoon, moving with military precision on an action he'd done a dozen times since they'd arrived...a while ago. She had no idea how long they'd been here, in this room with pale blue walls. Maybe an hour. Maybe a lifetime.

All she knew was that every two minutes she had to crawl over broken glass, endure the twisting, burning, impossibly powerful band of torment that squeezed the lower half of her massive belly, and get to the excruciating peak. Then breathe until it was over.

She also knew that she could never have done this without Chase.

With the little bit of strength she had in her hand, she closed her fingers around his strong wrist as he held the spoon to her lips.

"Are you okay?" he asked when she gave him a squeeze.

All she had the strength to do was look into his eyes, aching to tell him how much he meant to her, but she just couldn't. It was too much. Too hard. And, oh, *man*. The band of agony was tightening around her body again.

"Another one?" he asked, dropping the spoon and ice on the plastic utility table and taking both her hands. "Squeeze my hands, Raina. Squeeze hard. And breathe!"

She puffed and puffed, suffering with every inhale, certain her belly would simply tear from top to bottom at any moment.

"Oh. *Ohhh!*" She let go of him and clutched the bed rails as the searing pain lifted her higher. "I can't. I can't. Chase, no. *I can't do this!*"

"Yes, you can, Raina. You can do anything. Breathe. Just breathe." He knew better than to touch her, since the last time he did that mid-contraction, she practically bit off his hand.

Deep in the back of her mind, she knew they would laugh about this someday. They would always remember how they'd timed the contractions on the sofa, and called the doctor together, and grabbed that bag he'd put by the door, then made the short drive to the medical center where lovely Dr. Millwood was already waiting for them.

Someday, they'd laugh and sigh and remember it fondly. But today was not that day.

"Soon?" she asked Chase. "Can I please get them out soon?"

"The nurse said it's going to be a while," he reminded her gently. "You're not quite there yet."

She groaned and turned her head from side to side just as the door opened a sliver.

"Knock, knock," Tori called.

"The cavalry is here," Chase said on a sigh that could only be interpreted as relieved.

"Oh, Chase." Raina seized his hand, panicked. "I'll miss you."

He laughed softly. "You say that now. Wait until your next contraction. Come on in," he called, standing up and reluctantly letting go of her hand. "You have about forty seconds until all hell breaks loose."

Rose, Tori, and Susannah came fluttering into the room, instantly surrounding the bed, replacing Chase.

"We thought we'd start with us three so we don't overwhelm you," Suze said, brushing hair off Raina's sweaty forehead.

"Yeah, there's a line down the hall," Tori said. "Send them home or keep them here?"

"How are you, Raindrop?" Rose was at her other side, oozing comfort and positive smiles.

As they cooed and oohed, touched and kissed, Raina accepted the love, but her eyes followed Chase.

He stepped back, arms crossed, a glimmer of amusement in his eyes.

Had he looked that good all night? While she writhed and sweated and cried and...yeah. He had. He looked gorgeous in his dark T-shirt, but he'd let her ball that cotton into a fist during the worst of a contraction. And that was what she loved about him.

Loved. Oh, boy. She was *delirious*.

Susannah stroked her forehead, and Rose took her hand, and Tori peppered her with questions, but Raina lay very still and locked gazes with Chase, hoping he knew what he meant to her.

"I'm going to let these experts take over," he said, smiling at her. "It's been a pleasure," he added with a laugh. "Not for you, though."

As the other women turned to shower him with compliments and praise, Raina managed a smile. "Thank you," she mouthed.

He touched his lips and blew her a light kiss. "You got this, Rain. Next time I see you, I'll meet Charles and his friend."

She gave a slight laugh, but the second he left, the pressure of the next contraction wrenched across her abdomen and nothing was funny.

Tori leaned over her. "Probably not a good time to comment on how hot he looked or the fact that the nurse told us 'the father' was in here with you."

"Not if you want to live..." Raina grunted from somewhere deep in her soul and started up the mountain one more time. "Hang on, girls. This one's gonna be rough."

They swooped in, taking her hands, holding her head, and offering loving words of comfort and encouragement.

Hours drifted by, in and out of anguish, peppered by

momentary relief, plenty of ice, the rare smile, a lot of love, and after what felt like the longest night of her life, she was ready.

Well, as ready as a person could be to give birth to, and then raise, two children.

～

THING ONE WAS BORN at 3:08 a.m., a healthy six pounds, nineteen inches, and bald as the proverbial cue ball. Thing Two arrived four minutes later, a bit smaller at five and a half pounds, but sporting some flaxen peach fuzz.

Susannah had sent all the men and kids home at midnight, so the babies were born surrounded by six aunts and their grandmother, all of whom pronounced them the two most beautiful newborn girls they'd ever seen.

Girls.

Raina had two perfect, healthy, glorious daughters.

With a sigh, she let her eyes flutter open and take in the dimly lit hospital room. She judged it to be about six in the morning from the sliver of light sneaking in through the blinds.

Next to her, in two tiny bassinets labeled Wingate One and Wingate Two, lay her tightly wrapped babies, wearing pastel hospital caps, eyes closed, cheeks pink, wee chests rising and falling with sleep.

Emotion swamped her, a tsunami of love unlike

anything she'd ever felt. Was it humanly possible to love this much? It felt physical, shockingly powerful, and somehow different from carrying them inside her.

These were her girls! Her baby angels and part of her life for the rest of her days. Was this even real?

She pushed up—*that* hurt a little more than expected —and gazed at their tiny faces, button noses, impossibly small mouths to feed.

"Good morning, little Things," she whispered. "I love you. I love you so much, it hurts. I'm sorry you don't have your names on your little beds yet, but you two wore your mother out and I couldn't tell anyone anything but good-bye. But I have named you."

One smacked her rosebud lips and let out a shuddering sigh; the other twitched her nose and fluttered her eyelids. They looked the same...but different already. Like Rose and Raina.

Her arms ached to hold one or both of them and tell them their names, but did she...pick them up? Alone? Without a nurse?

A jolt of panic kicked her as she realized she would have to figure that out and learn how to pick up her babies and feed them and love them and bathe them and raise them and teach them how to be—

The door latch clicked and she practically moaned with relief. Nurses came in and out of here constantly, so she shouldn't have worried. She'd just ask—

"Are you awake?" The male voice was barely a whisper, but enough to send chills over her body.

"Chase." She breathed his name.

The door opened slowly, revealing two massive pink balloons and a bouquet of Ocean Song roses carried by the dearest man who'd ever walked the Earth.

"I'm sorry it's so early, but I wanted to beat the rush. Rose texted me a few hours ago and even filled my flower order," he added.

"Oh, thank you. Please. Come in."

He took a few steps, moving the balloons and flowers to the side, his gaze on her, then slowly to the bassinets. He started to say something, but it seemed his words got trapped in his throat, and all he could do was stare.

"Come meet the newest Wingate women," she said.

"Oh, yes. There are never enough of those in the world." He put the vase and balloons on the counter, and went right to her side. "Excellent work, Mom."

"I couldn't have..." She reached for his hand, as choked up as she'd been a moment ago looking at the babies. "Thank you seems inadequate. I should probably add I'm sorry for anything mean I said or for attempting to break your fingers."

"It's fine," he laughed, giving his free hand a clench in and out. "I recovered."

"Do you want to meet them?"

"Yes." He glanced over her at the babies. "But first, how are you?"

"I'm good. Sore and tired, but insanely happy."

That made him smile. "I knew you would be," he said. "And you deserve to be."

"Come around." She waved him to the other side of the bed. "I was just thinking I wanted to pick them up but..." She bit her lip and chuckled. "I don't really know how."

He laughed softly. "I'll help. Let me just wash my hands."

After he did, and dried with paper towels, he rounded the bed to stand next to the babies. "You know, you're going to have to crack and give them actual names, not numbers."

"I have named them both but I haven't made it official. You can be the first to know."

He looked at her, a flash in his eyes. "Me?"

"You earned the honor last night. And the weeks before. And just in general by being..." Her voice cracked. "Sorry, I'm a hormonal emotional mess."

"No apologies." He leaned over, looking from one to the other, sheer awe on his face. "Raina, they're perfect. Good heavens, they're *exquisite!*"

"They're pretty, aren't they?"

"Are you sure we should lift one?" he asked. "Shouldn't we let sleeping babies lie?"

The *we* touched her. "I think that's dogs, Chase. And I want to hold one. In fact, I want to hold both. Can you help?"

"Absolutely. Let's get the bed back higher." He picked up the remote and touched a button, earning a surprised look. "Oh, I learned that last night. Don't you remember?"

"I don't remember much," she admitted. "So one more sweeping apology again for anything I said or did."

"What you did..." He turned to the babies. "Is nothing less than a miracle."

She smiled at the pure reverence in his voice. "And it'll be another miracle if we can pick them up, hold them, and not drop either one."

"Hush. We've got this." He leaned over the closest baby and reached his large hands around her tiny body. "Hold her head, right?" He slid his palm under her little head and very carefully lifted her, cradling her against his chest for a moment. "Hello, sweet angel. Are you Thing One?"

"Yes, but now she's Lillian," Raina said. "After my grandmother."

"Lillian." He breathed the name like it was a prayer.

"We'll call her Lily because..." She beamed at the baby. "Every girl's life is better with a twin named after a flower."

"Aw, Rose will love that. Would you like her?"

"Right here," she said, forming a crook with her arm as he carefully rested the baby against her.

"Here you go, Lily," he whispered.

The infant replied with a barely audible whimper and a smack of her lips. They took a moment to admire her, silent and maybe a little overwhelmed.

"One at a time or..." He tipped his head to the other baby.

"I'll take both, just for a bit."

He repeated the steps with the second baby, who sighed as he lifted her.

"Hold her for a second," Raina said, looking at him. "But hold her tight."

"I promise," he assured her. "Nothing will ever happen to..." He traced her cheek with his finger, then gave Raina a questioning look.

"Charlotte," she said. "And we'll call her..."

"Charlie," he finished, his voice breaking with emotion. He stared at the newborn for a second, then at Raina, who wasn't surprised to see tears in his eyes that matched the ones in hers.

"Well," he managed to say. "I know someone who's dancing in heaven today."

She laughed. "I admit I've loved Charlie Wingate for a girl from the moment Rose suggested it. I didn't want to get you too excited in case I changed my mind, Charles Madison."

His eyes glinted with pride and joy. "I know she's named for your mother, Raina, but...I do think my nonna is happy with Charlie."

"I'm glad. Aren't they perfect names? Charlie and Lily."

He touched Charlie's nose again, a tear rolling down his cheek. "Everything about both of them is perfect... including..." He eased the baby into Raina's other arm. "Their mother."

He wiped that tear and perched on the edge of the bed, smiling at Raina and her two precious bundles.

"I'd take a picture," he said, "but there's no way I'll

ever forget what you look like right now. Absolutely radiant and beautiful."

On a long, happy sigh, she dropped her head back, lost in the moment of pre-dawn peace and love, her babies in her arms, a good man at her side, and so many high hopes for the future.

Chapter Twenty-two

Susannah

Madeline and Susannah sat at the kitchen counter with their heads close together as they compared the black lace remnant with the much clearer image from the *New York Times* that Adam had pulled impressive strings to get for them.

"In my professional opinion," Madeline said, angling the picture and shifting her gaze from one to the other, "this lace that Greta is carrying is the same as this lace." She gestured toward the corner of lace peeking out from the white cotton muslin that protected it. "See the buttonhole stitch and the pattern motif?"

Susannah made a face. "Kind of."

"I can see it," Madeline assured her. "See that bilateral scalloped edge on the floral pattern on one side, and a singular scallop on the other? Very distinctive and rare, and so difficult to make. It's on both the lace and the image. The *Times* article said Greta carried a piece of lace from her mother's wedding gown."

"Mary Sturgis Livingston, who certainly never

visited Amelia Island. Why would that lace be in Wingate House?"

"My guess is Greta gave it to her daughter, Coraline, who kept it." Madeline frowned. "Let me get this straight. Coraline is my great-grandmother, Greta is my great-great-grandmother, and Mary is my great-great-*great*-grandmother? So cool. Grace should carry this in her wedding on Saturday!"

Susannah drew back and shook her head. "But the screaming—"

"Was a tree hitting the attic, or the wind or an animal, Suze. Have you heard it since?"

"No," she admitted. "Not once. I've been there plenty these past few weeks doing the final transformation into a wedding venue."

"This was probably stuck in that closet access place for years. Or, maybe Coraline carried it, too, and it was her secret sign to her husband that, you know, tonight's the night." Madeline tipped her head. "Something they started on their wedding night and continued all the years they were married." She gave a wistful smile. "That's sweet, don't you think?"

"If it was sweet, then why did someone claw this lace and ruin it? That isn't natural wear and tear, so..."

"So it got ripped at some point over the years," Madeline said. "We have two choices with that lace. We can preserve it as-is at the museum, or you can let me take a pass at cutting and sewing an edge on it, turning it into a handkerchief, and letting future Wingate brides carry it as their something old."

"I guess I like that idea," Susannah said on a sigh.

Would cutting the lace make the ghost mad? She didn't dare give voice to that ridiculous thought.

She didn't have to. Madeline leaned in and gave her a wary look. "You're not still scared of a sound you heard once over a month ago, are you? The tree is gone, the view is beautiful, and we're all staying there tomorrow night after the rehearsal, right?"

Right. Susannah nodded, hating the low-grade fear that bubbled up in her chest.

"You and Dad in the Coraline suite?" Madeline pressed. "Where you can put this nonsense to bed once and for all?"

Of course, practical Madeline would never consider the possibility that the ghost was real.

"Yes, we are," Susannah said brightly, knowing full well she'd chicken out before then. "Can you stay for dinner, Madeline? Rex is at the office and we were going to eat on the later side, but you're welcome to stay."

"Honestly, I have something else I'd like to do."

Susannah looked up at the vague, somewhat mysterious tone in Madeline's voice. "A date with Adam?" she guessed.

Madeline's eyes flashed, then she laughed. "No. Why would you say that?"

"You sound...cagey."

She rolled her eyes. "I meant I'd like to take this lace and make a handkerchief and bring it to the surprise shower we're having after the rehearsal dinner. Not cagey at all."

"Oh." If she sounded disappointed, it was because, well, she was. "I like him and..."

"I like him, too, Suze," she said gently. "I know the entire family is walking on eggshells around me on the subject of Adam Logan."

"Well, we're all curious," Susannah acknowledged. "You've seen him a few times these last weeks since the festival and Raina's babies were born."

"A few," she conceded. "And he's coming to Grace's wedding with me."

"Ohhh." Susannah dragged the word out, fighting a smile.

"As a friend," Madeline said. "If and when that changes, you'll be one of the first to know." She added a kiss on Susannah's cheek. "Now, off I go to make the perfect vintage accent for my sister's Victorian-themed wedding."

When Madeline left, Susannah stared at the picture and tried to tamp down the growing and inexplicable fear in her heart. It wasn't that she was afraid of ghosts...she was afraid this one was telling her something.

Was transforming Wingate House into a wedding venue a bad idea? Would the marriages that took place there somehow be...cursed?

Her phone buzzed with a text from Rex telling her he and Blake were going to a new listing together and he'd be even later than he thought.

She responded, then looked hard at the picture of the lace overlay one more time, wishing she could rid herself of this fear.

There was only one way. One simple way. Exactly what Rex had told her to do, and she never really had.

She had to face down the ghost of Coraline and find out the truth. If she didn't want weddings at Wingate House, then Susannah would return the whole place to an inn and run it herself.

But she had to find out, and she had to do it before Grace got married there.

Grabbing her bag, a light jacket, and the picture from the paper, she headed out to do a little ghost hunting.

Dusk had fallen by the time Susannah reached Wingate House. In the waning light, the Victorian mansion looked dark, empty, and eerie. Susannah refused to let that stop her as she parked in the back and used the code to enter the hallway to the downstairs guest rooms.

This part of the inn remained the same—they'd done nothing but a light refresh. But as she turned the corner and stepped deeper into the common areas, the change in the place was evident, at least to someone who'd spent a lot of time in the century-old structure.

She stood in the main hallway, next to the massive oak stairs, looking into the rooms at the front of the house. Everything was still and silent. Moving past the glass doors that led into the wine-tasting room that would serve as a bar for weddings, she tapped on a few more lights.

Walking toward the front, she paused, resting her hand on the ornate newel that stood sentry at the bottom of the stairs. She looked left to the large living room and right to the drawing room with its cheery fireplace.

That led to the library and dining area, which was already set up with tables for the guests to eat dinner after the wedding. While certainly not an "open concept" as in today's homes, they'd done a wonderful job of furnishing the rooms for a function. They'd made sure that one space naturally led to another, and that there was plenty of seating and room for dancing.

The house was ideal for small weddings like Grace's, which would be all things elegant, simple, and intimate.

Unless...something, or someone, screamed.

Swallowing hard, she started up the stairs, which creaked with her weight, a sound she'd always loved but now made her jittery.

"Calm down, Suze," she said softly, stopping at the top of the steps.

It was very dark up here, so she walked straight to a table lamp tucked between wing-backed chairs in a sitting area, spilling light from the gleaming hardwood to the brown tin ceiling.

The place smelled clean and fresh, ready for the Wingates to sleep here after the rehearsal dinner. After the men and kids retired for the night, the sisters planned to hold a small surprise bridal shower for Grace up in the third-floor apartment—now the bridal suite.

Susannah considered going up there where she felt...safer.

But that was ridiculous.

"There is no ghost," she said, purposely not whispering the thought.

This place was empty, and she was going in that suite, in that closet, and shake this once and for all.

She turned left down the back hall, straight to the double doors that led to the Coraline suite. Taking a deep breath, she walked in and flipped on the light to bathe the room in a soft glow.

All was still. Beautiful, in fact. The deep green and gold quilt was smooth on the bed, the pillows in place. The drapes were open, offering a now-unobstructed view to the water, where some boats floated, and the lights of the wharf glinted in the waning light.

The room felt clean and safe and...empty.

She headed to the closet and opened the doors, peering into the darkness. She'd asked Isaiah to install a light, so she was able to touch a switch and see into every corner, all the way back to the other door, which led to the Madeline suite.

She walked back there slowly, making it almost to the other door when something on the floor caught her eye.

Was that...a piece of newspaper? Old, yellowed newsprint that was...soaking wet?

She dropped to her knees to look closer, but that just gave her a whiff of something awful. Like rotten eggs. Worse.

She stood and looked around the completely empty closet, seeing nothing. Not on the floor, the walls, the ceiling...*wait*.

She peered directly overhead to a small recessed

square she'd never noticed before, covered with a plank of wood painted the same color as the walls and ceiling.

There was attic access from this closet?

Yes, of course, the attic space would run along the eaves and over this closet. She squinted at the wood, realizing that it didn't fully cover the opening. There was a narrow gap between—

She gasped when the wood board rocked, tapping on the ceiling like...like...

Someone had walked over it.

She backed away in horror, her heart hammering so hard she couldn't believe that whoever or whatever was up there didn't hear it.

"Who are you?" she demanded, though her voice sounded reed thin. "Hello? Coraline?"

The wood rocked again and then she heard the shriek—the long, high-pitched, ear-splitting scream of a...

No, not a woman. That wasn't human. That wasn't a person, it was a—

Suddenly, the wood slid to the side and something small fell to the ground—no, it *leaped*. A rat? She shrieked and ran out, her hands covering her mouth as she slammed the closet door behind her.

She heard a scratch, and the softest, sweetest *meow* ever let out.

Wait...what? Was that...

Very slowly, as if she expected to face certain death on the other side, she inched open the door and looked down to meet the green-eyed gaze of a tiny striped kitten who looked at her like Susannah was the queen he'd been waiting to worship his whole life.

"Excuse me?" she choked on a laugh as adrenaline and relief swamped her body so hard she got dizzy. "A kitten?"

He purred and took a few tentative steps closer, then reached her leg and rubbed her ankle, all the while looking up with a plea for love—and probably food—in his beautiful eyes.

"Baby!" She dropped down and lifted him in her hands, tinier even than the newborns she'd held so frequently in the last two weeks.

All this over a kitten?

And if there was one, were there more? And a mama?

Cooing and stroking the tiny creature in one hand, she used the other to fish her phone from her bag. Isaiah was staying at a hotel with some of his family who'd come for the wedding, but she knew he was the man for this job.

Susannah wasn't climbing into that attic, but her son-in-law-to-be certainly would.

After apologizing for the interruption, she told him the problem and he promised he'd be there as soon as he could.

While she waited, she took her little buddy downstairs to the kitchen and found a saucer of cream meant for coffee, which might not be the right thing to feed him but it was that or...eggs and canned peaches.

"We'll go with cream," she told him, tucking him deep into her chest. "So, did you cause all the commotion, kitty? You aren't big enough to knock my purse off the bed or push cushions. I'm thinking it was your mother, huh? Isaiah will find out."

While he hungrily lapped the cream, Madeline texted a picture of a black handkerchief she'd made from the lace. Smiling, Susannah texted her back with a simple request that she come to the inn *now* for a surprise.

Much closer than Isaiah, Madeline arrived in a few minutes, calling out for Susannah as she walked in the back door.

"Look who caused all this trouble!" She held up her furry little bundle, laughing with deep joy and relief.

"Oh, my goodness!" Madeline's whole face brightened. "A kitten! Now that, I believe in."

"There was no ghost," she scoffed, mostly at herself. "Just a cat, probably a pregnant one, judging by the size of this tiny thing. I bet she got into the attic by way of that tree and then, when it was cut down, was stuck up there."

"Maybe there's some old material in the rafters, and the cat found the lace," Madeline said. "That would explain the way it was clawed."

"Miz Wingate?" Isaiah's voice boomed through the hall along with his footsteps. "You okay, ma'am? I'm here with a ladder."

They met him outside the kitchen, with Susannah cradling the kitten.

"I'm just here with my new friend," she said.

"Are you kidding me?" He engulfed the miniature head in his huge hand. "I did poke into that attic when I cleared the last of the items, but I didn't see this little guy. He and his mom and any other kittens could have been way on the other side over the closet. I never went there."

"I think you will now," she said. "Can you go up through the closet?"

"Absolutely."

She shared her theory about the tree as they all walked upstairs together, behind Isaiah and the ladder dangling from his muscular arm like it was a toy. The kitty mewed the whole time Susannah admitted that she'd been here to find out once and for all if the place was haunted.

Isaiah didn't laugh, which she appreciated, but gave her a warm look at the top. "You were brave to go in the closet at all, Miz Wingate. You could have called."

"She wanted to face her fears," Madeline said, putting a hand on Susannah's shoulder. "And I'm proud of you for that."

Isaiah nodded as he slowed his step outside the suite. "Or you could just say a prayer, ma'am. The Lord erases fears."

She tipped her head in acknowledgement. "You're probably right, Isaiah. I forget about that."

He headed into the room and then the closet while she and Madeline stood in the doorway with the kitty, who showed no interest in leaving Susannah's arms.

With a flashlight on, he climbed up, moved the small wooden board, and disappeared into the attic. She could hear his heavy footsteps as he walked about, then his muffled voice talking to...a cat, she supposed.

"I found them!" he called. "Mama and two more babies coming down."

After he brought them all down, they carried the squirmy little angels and one very scared mother into the kitchen for food and love. Isaiah took cleaning supplies back to the attic to clean up and check for any open windows, while all the kitties ate and bathed and explored the office, which could be closed off and was safer than the kitchen.

While Madeline played with the cats, Susannah called Chloe with the news that she had a few new residents for Rocky's Rescues, her youngest daughter's animal shelter.

"You're not putting them all up for adoption, are you?" Madeline asked, cradling one that had beautiful black and white coloring. "'Cause...this guy?"

Susannah laughed. "You think I'd give up..." She stroked the gray-striped baby. "This one is going to be either Cora or Cory, depending on gender, and will be living at the beach house. First, Chloe will have them checked out, treated, and healthy enough to separate from mom in time."

"I found some things we didn't know were up there," Isaiah announced as he came in, setting the cleaning supplies down and bending over to pick up a pearly gray kitten. "I've put them in the hall in the back for you to examine." He clucked at the kitten. "I know a little girl who'd love you pretty good," he joked. "Wonder if you get along with dachshunds."

Madeline and Susannah laughed, both knowing

these cats were all going to be in Wingate homes soon enough.

"Chloe's coming with crates and supplies," Susannah told him, standing up. "But what kind of things did you find?"

"Wedding things," he said, grinning.

"Excuse me?"

"The kittens used a box of old papers for their litter box, which I took to the dumpster because, trust me, you didn't want to see or smell it. But the other one? I think you both want to look at that."

Madeline and Susannah relinquished the kittens to Isaiah and hurried toward the back hall.

There, he'd placed a massive box that had a weird blue plastic covering that had been ripped to shreds.

"What could that be?" Susannah asked.

"I know exactly what it is," Madeline said. "That's an old-school wedding gown preservation box, and the blue coloring means someone used formaldehyde to protect the fabric."

"Will it smell?" Susannah asked.

"Not to us, but it's probably why the cats rejected it once they took the plastic off."

They both kneeled and gingerly lifted the lid, gasping at the sight of yards and yards of white tulle and lace, with heavy black satin at the bottom.

"Oh, my goodness!" Madeline cooed as she gently moved the folds. "These are wedding gowns, Suze! Three of them, I think. Probably worn by Coraline, and her mother and...maybe even her mother." Madeline put her hand over her mouth. "What a treasure trove! Veils and combs and, oh, look at this black dress worn in the 1800s! We have to get this to the museum but I may want to put one on display at my salon."

As she moved the black dress, they spied a large picture frame, face down in the bottom of the box.

"What's that?" Susannah asked, reaching to ease it out.

As she turned it around, they both gasped at the blue house in the middle of a handmade needlepoint sampler.

"It's Wingate House!" Susannah exclaimed, taking in the three-story Victorian mansion that had been lovingly stitched in the middle, surrounded by trees and ivy, flowers and hearts, and bluebirds in every corner.

Along the bottom under the house, black-stitched script anchored the design, and Susannah squinted to read every word.

> *"Come live with me, and be my love*
> *And we will some new pleasures prove*
> *Of golden sands and crystal brooks*
> *With silken lines and silver hooks."*
> Coraline Wingate 1905

"Oh, Madeline," Susannah breathed. "It's perfect. 'Come live with me and be my love.' Isn't that from a famous poem?"

"It is. John Donne, if memory serves me. And Coraline stitched it," Madeline added. "Those samplers were signed by the artist, often with a quote or poem, then the name of the needlepointer and the year it was made. Was this place even built in 1905?"

"No, but you know what I think?" Susannah grazed the stitches with her finger. "I bet she used this as the inspiration when they designed Wingate House."

Madeline sighed. "What a find."

Susannah blinked back tears, the words blurring before her eyes. "I'm going to hang this downstairs so it's the first thing you see when you enter a house built to start lives together."

Isaiah hung it for her in the entryway, where it fit perfectly. She stared at the ancient work of art for a long time, taking it as Coraline's message from the grave, and her blessing over all the weddings that would take place at Wingate House.

Chapter Twenty-three

Madeline

While Nikki Lou drummed out the melody of a song called "I Choose You" on the piano in the library, Grace and Isaiah shared their first dance, surrounded by joyful friends and family.

The little girl—a truly gifted pianist already—made it through the first two verses, then the real pianist slipped onto the bench to finish and sing the lyrics, an exchange they'd practiced over and over during last night's rehearsal.

Finally finished with her role in the spotlight, Nikki scampered to her mother and tried to climb into the folds of the beaded slip gown Madeline had lovingly made for her sister.

Yes, Madeline admired the way the silk moved, the perfection of the portrait collar, and how the beaded fringe gave the dress an antique feel with a contemporary fit. Her smile pulled even more as she got lost in the romance of the couple's first dance, and she laughed when Isaiah scooped up Nikki Lou and invited her into their arms.

"You look happy," Adam said softly, making her aware that he was looking at her and not the newly-married couple.

"I am," she said, smiling up at him. "My sister is on a cloud, so how could I not be?"

"They do seem perfect for each other," he agreed as the song ended and everyone applauded.

Then, Grace and Isaiah invited Suze and Rex to dance, which they did, with everyone marveling at how smooth and healed their patriarch was.

After a few moments, Rex gestured for others to come to the dance floor.

Chloe and Travis, Rose and Gabe, and Justin and Tori joined in right away. Sadie was over by the chocolate fountain in the dining room, chatting with Scout, who'd made the cake.

Raina had returned to the drawing room where the babies were, and that left Madeline who...normally didn't dance. Or have a date.

"Come on," Adam said, putting a hand on her back. "Let's have our first dance, too."

She let him lead her to the small dance floor, turning and looking up as he took her right hand and slid an arm around her waist.

"Is it our first?" she asked. "I seem to recall we danced...at a club in New York once. A dark and divey club that I hated."

He chuckled at the memory. "You're right. The place was called Invasion. It was on 14th Street, and we danced to..." He screwed up his face. "'Believe' by Cher, I'm sorry to say. It was packed, you weren't happy, and we left and went to a diner for—"

"Apple pie," she finished, wistful at the crystal-clear memory. Many of those old moments had come back to her as she and Adam spent time together. With his help, the images from the past were finally released from the lockboxes where she'd buried them long ago.

"We ate pie and talked until two in the morning." Adam gazed down at her, making her remember sitting across from him at midnight in a diner, staring into the same brown eyes. Oh, she'd been in love.

"Now I finally know why the aroma of coffee and apple pie makes me feel...bittersweet."

He winced. "I'm sorry, Maddie. I—"

"No more apologies." She put her fingers on his lips and enjoyed the zing of electricity that caused. "Your sins are forgiven," she added. "And forgotten."

He gave her a doubtful look. "Forgotten? I doubt you can wipe away those bad memories, but Madeline, if you let me, we can make new ones."

She added some pressure to the hand resting on his shoulder, lost in the way their bodies moved together to the music.

"I'd like that," she said softly. "As long as there is—"

"Complete transparency," he said, dipping his face a little closer. "I promise full disclosure and nothing but honesty, no matter what I'm working on. You have my word."

She let the promise settle over her heart, thinking about what it meant.

"So...you're staying around? Still trying to get to"— she raised her eyebrows—"that family you mentioned to me?"

"I am, but..." He made a face. "I kind of failed on my last attempt."

"What happened? Did Dad call him about the yacht sale?"

He glanced around and she did, too, suddenly realizing that not only were they in the middle of the dance floor, surrounded by family, but lots of eyes were on them.

Curious, amused, hopeful, and, yes, loving looks, but there was certainly no privacy at a Wingate wedding.

"Would you like to take a walk and I can tell you about it?" he suggested.

"Oh, so much." And she meant that, getting a genuine thrill that he would confide in her about his business and let her get a better understanding of exactly what he did.

They finished the dance and slipped out the front door of Wingate House, stepping into the golden glow of the late afternoon. A few guests peppered the porch and lawn, but a lace- and flower-draped arch and thirty or so chairs were still set up on a grassy rise, all empty now.

They walked there together, admiring the breathtaking vista of the sun setting over the Amelia River. The water and sky were painted in peach and blue, the light silhouetting the boats and trees that lined the riverfront.

Adam turned two of the chairs in the back row toward the view, gesturing for them to sit.

They were quiet for a few minutes, their hands joined on her lap, taking in the moment with palpable contentment.

"We've come a long way," she said softly.

"Thanks to you giving me a chance," he replied. "I'm so grateful, Maddie. And I'll make that promise again and again—only truth, all the time."

"Good. So, what's the story with the Cassano case?"

He grunted. "Crash and burn, I'm afraid."

She frowned, searching his face. "What do you mean, precisely?"

"It's just..." He flicked his hand like he could make the subject disappear.

"Adam," she warned.

"I know, I know. I'm just not used to full transparency," he said on a laugh. "I'm not sure how much you want to know."

"Honestly? Everything. I want you to trust me completely," she said. "And that might mean explaining some terminology. You've mentioned trailing, infiltrating...and undercover. Is that all the same thing? And how do you do it?"

He regarded her with a wry smile. "You really want to know?"

"Yes! What you do is so interesting. I'm fascinated by it, and don't want vague answers."

"All right," he said, nodding. "Well, those terms are very different. Trailing is like tracing someone's movements, then reporting it to a team of investigators. I might or might not know the whole background of the case or what's significant to the investigation, and all I'm getting paid to do is tell them the whereabouts of an individual."

"So, you follow people?"

"Basically, yes. I might take pictures, or I might watch who they talk to, and maybe I'll see something that looks like a red flag. I report it all to whoever hired me for the assignment."

"Is it always the FBI?" she asked.

"Right now, yes. I'm good friends with SAC—Special Agent in Charge—of the Jacksonville office and Daryl's throwing me some jobs."

"I can't imagine there are many people to follow on Amelia Island."

"Just that one case now. They'd happily put me to work down there, too, but..." He leaned into her. "I like spending my time up here."

"And what's infiltrating?" she asked, too invested in the lesson to get sidetracked by flirting. "I guess what it sounds like, right?"

"Yep. That involves developing a relationship with the target, and finding a reason to spend time with them. Sometimes a lot, sometimes just once."

"Like selling a boat to get to know the owner," she said, remembering how he'd said that was one way to "infiltrate" a local family. "But it didn't work?"

"Rex told me his assistant shut him down cold, and said the boat is categorically not for sale. So I won't be infiltrating by way of a yacht sale."

"Okay, I have to know. *Why* are you infiltrating the local restaurant owner?" she asked.

He hesitated a second and when she opened her mouth to complain, he held up a hand. "Yes, yes. I'll tell you. I'll trust you. But not anyone else. You can't—"

"I will *not* tell my family," she said. "I promise and, Adam Logan, when I make a promise, I do not break it."

"I know." He turned to her, holding her gaze, thinking for a minute. "Nico Cassano isn't just a local restaurant owner. You think he got a yacht and a Ferrari by selling chicken parm in a restaurant that hasn't been updated in decades?"

"I don't know," she said. "There's a lot of old money up here and people inherit, so..." She leaned in, mesmerized. "What does he do?"

"What *doesn't* he do is a better question," Adam said. "Nico is a major, major player in syndicated crime in Jacksonville, Tampa, and Miami. He's probably running a gambling operation—they are wildly lucrative in towns with NFL teams—and probably deals in drugs, runs prostitution, and commits tax fraud. Throw in a little loan-sharking, extortion, and racketeering and you have a much better picture of how Nico and his tidy little team got very wealthy."

Her jaw dropped. "But he lives here, in a nice house. He's owned Cassano's forever and his wife walks around and talks to customers and shows off her..." She curled her lip. "Diamonds, which are likely ill-gotten gains, huh?"

He laughed at the expression. "Extremely ill-gotten."

"So the restaurant's a cover?" she asked.

"The restaurant's primary purpose is most likely to

launder money," he told her. "All these syndicates need a high cash volume businesses to, uh, *structure finances*. He wants to be up here because this island is off the beaten path, and he can set up a very legitimate and safe life. But Nico's a criminal, no doubt about it, and the Feds are itching to get something concrete on him."

She dropped back on the chair, stunned. "I can't believe it. *La Cosa Nostra* in our sweet small town."

He gave her a hard look. "It's no joke, Maddie. This isn't *Sopranos on The Beach*. It's serious business."

"I know it is, and you have to catch him and get him out of here, Adam. We can't have money-laundering on Amelia Island!"

"Easier said than done," he admitted. "I need to find a way to worm into his business or life. I wouldn't go undercover—the other way of doing this job. That requires a whole new identity, and I've been out and about and talking to too many people for that. But I do need to think of something that could get me in front of the family. Did you say you know his wife, Ginny? Does she have any interests?"

"Spending money," she said on a snort. "In fact, their daughter..." Suddenly, a million chills blossomed over her arms. "Oh, my gosh, Adam."

"What about their daughter? Bella, right?"

"She just got engaged!"

"Oh, I know. And I think that's an arranged marriage, because her fiancé is part of an old Russian family, and up to his eyeballs in securities fraud. She's Nico's only kid, so my guess is that they're merging the family fortunes."

"But did you hear me? She just *got engaged*," Madeline repeated, giving him a "don't you get it?" look.

"I know. I track the family and..." He drew back. "What are you saying?"

"That she'll need a dress and if I know her—and her mother—she'll want custom. Oh, she probably wants to go to New York or Paris for a Vera Wang, but what if I could convince her to let me make her a Madeline Wingate exclusive design? Huh?" She gave his arm a jab. "How's that for *infiltrating*?"

He stared at her as if she'd just spoken Latin instead of handing him a brilliant solution to his problem. "Maddie—"

"Right? Genius! If you'd have trusted me and been honest and told me Elana was embezzling, I would have helped you find the evidence you needed then, too. I'm a do-right kind of woman."

He looked like he didn't know whether to laugh or not. "I'd never put you in that kind of danger," he said simply.

"Elana wasn't dangerous."

"You *never* know."

"But if all I'm doing is making a dress for Bella Cassano? They'd never know! I would go to her house, and her mother would be there. Lots of meetings, and fittings. And let me tell you, when I'm on my knees pinning a hem, people forget I'm there. I hear everything

—what the wedding costs, how awful the mother-in-law is, if the groom is—"

"No."

She blinked at the barked word. "Hear me out, Adam. Sometimes I have to spend hours with these people—every single piece of lace and bead and bow is done by *my hands*—and I can hear things. That's all you want? Just a report of what they're talking about? I could do that."

"You could *not* do that," he insisted. "Don't even think about it."

"And you know what else?" she continued, undeterred. "It is not unusual for me to be invited to the wedding so I can literally dress the bride. Sometimes the rehearsal dinner, too, if I make that dress as well." She lifted a brow. "Then they let me stay and bring a date, not that I ever have, but..." She pointed at him. "We could tag team."

"Madeline Wingate." He ground out her full name with a warning look in his eyes.

"I'm sorry. We *cannot* have a crime syndicate on Amelia Island. It's unthinkable."

He stared at her, a million emotions in his expression but she couldn't read a single one, except that he didn't like the idea.

"Couldn't I just try and pitch her business?" she pleaded. "It would not be the least bit out of place for me to give her a call or drop by the restaurant to chat with Ginny about Bella's dress plans."

He searched her face, thinking. "It wouldn't?"

"Adam, I'm an internationally recognized wedding dress designer, and this bride-to-be lives here in my town. Honestly, it would be weird if I *didn't* talk to her or her mother about the possibility. I frequently contact the brides after their announcements go out, especially the ones from the upscale families. Those girls pay huge money for a custom-designed dress."

He stared at her for a long time, the initial refusal in his eyes starting to fade. Of course, because the idea made perfect sense.

"I'm not going to get caught or do anything stupid," she said. "It's a perfectly natural way for me to hear things and even see things in their home. I'll have my camera out taking pictures during fittings and I'll befriend her—or more likely her mother—and see if she lets anything slip."

"You could...*no*," he caught himself. "No. I cannot let you put yourself in harm's way. I won't allow it."

She lifted a shoulder, undaunted. "Well, I'm contacting her anyway to get her dress business."

"You want that tainted money?" he challenged.

"I want to help you, and if there's that kind of crime in Amelia Island? I want it gone."

He shook his head. "I wouldn't have told you if I thought you'd step in and even think about doing this."

"Adam, maybe I can get information that could help. Or together, if I have access, get you that introduction into the family that you want. Then I'll make her dress, charge a fortune, and we all win. I'm not dumb, Adam. Let me help you by being your eyes and ears."

He sighed. "I'll think about it."

But all Madeline heard was...*yes*. "Adam, please. Give me a chance. I want to do this. I want to help you."

"I don't know, Maddie. I can't ever risk—"

She shut him up with a kiss, the longest, deepest, most soulful one she'd enjoyed in many, many years.

When they parted, his eyes were still closed, but there was a smile on his face.

"You kind of love this idea, don't you?" she whispered.

"I kind of love..." He breathed into the next kiss. "That you are on fire for the cause."

She kissed him again, on fire for more than the cause.

"So, yeah," he murmured against her lips. "We can think about it."

He kissed her again, and then she forgot about everything except her second chance with Adam.

Only this time, she'd be in on the game.

Don't miss the next book in the Seven Sisters series, *The Dressmaker on Amelia Island*. Madeline's well-structured life gets torn at the seams when she infiltrates a crime family and is swept up in the adventure of a lifetime.

Raina sinks into a new normal as a single mother to

newborn twins only to have everything threatened by the arrival of someone she should be able to trust...but can't.

And when Tori and Justin firmly disagree on an issue that affects the whole family, their love faces a test that could end their romance forever.

Once again, the winds of change are blowing over Amelia Island but the Wingate women face every crisis as a family with humor, heart, and hope. Come back to Amelia Island for the next book in the series!

The Seven Sister Series

Love Hope Holloway's books? If you haven't read her first two series, you're in for a treat! Chock full of family feels and beachy Florida settings, these sagas are for lovers of riveting and inspirational sagas about sisters, secrets, romance, mothers, and daughters...and the moments that make life worth living.

These series are complete, and available in e-book (also in Kindle Unlimited), paperback, and audio.

The Coconut Keys Series

Set in the heart of the Florida Keys, these seven delightful novels will make you laugh out loud, wipe a happy tear, and believe in all the hope and happiness of a second chance at life.

A Secret in the Keys – Book 1
A Reunion in the Keys – Book 2
A Season in the Keys – Book 3
A Haven in the Keys – Book 4
A Return to the Keys – Book 5
A Wedding in the Keys – Book 6
A Promise in the Keys – Book 7

The Shellseeker Beach Series

Come to Shellseeker Beach and fall in love with a "found family" of unforgettable characters who face life's challenges with humor, heart, and hope.

About the Author

Hope Holloway is the author of charming, heartwarming women's fiction featuring unforgettable families and friends, and the emotional challenges they conquer. After more than twenty years in marketing, she launched a new career as an author of beach reads and feel-good fiction. A mother of two adult children, Hope and her husband of thirty years live in Florida. When not writing, she can be found walking the beach with her two rescue dogs, who beg her to include animals in every book. Visit her site at www.hopeholloway.com.

Printed in the USA
CPSIA information can be obtained
at www.ICGtesting.com
LVHW050913150324
774367LV00001B/85